DEVIL'S DISSONANCE

Angela M Herrick

Purple Dragon Press

To Jay, thank you for the epic love story,
and
to Danny, thank you for the epic soundtrack.

CHAPTER 1

"Will you burden him?" asked the head priestess as she looked up solemnly at the young, statuesque bride.

Her cheeks reddened. She smiled at her groom. "Probably."

"Will you intend to?" the priestess asked.

"No," she said softly.

The priestess turned to the groom. "And what about you? Will you burden her?"

"I'm sure I will," he said, answering his love's smile with his own, eliciting laughter from their guests, which echoed off the large oak trees and the beautiful purple Creole cottage.

"Will you intend to?"

"Of course not," he said.

"There will be burdens on your path, some external, some internal. Together you will share these burdens. Together, you will overcome them," the priestess said.

Tom reached into his coat pocket and pulled out a stunning silver and onyx ring. "I always thought I would live my life alone, ensconced in darkness. Occasionally, well-meaning people would try to pull me into the light. They sought to change me, and when they couldn't, they'd reject me. But, in you, Lenora, I've found a kindred spirit. Someone who loves me as I am. Content to sit with me in the darkness for all eternity," Tom said, slipping the ring on his bride's finger.

Beck had never seen Tom Price smile so much. The small filmmaker with the frizzy black hair and his raven-haired bride brought to mind Gomez and Morticia Adams. The touching scene reminded Beck of her own beloved. She reached for her husband's hand as the drummers began to play softly. Meanwhile, the voodoo priestess shook a sacred rattle made from a gourd and covered with beads around the couple, "To welcome the ancestors, past, present, and future," she explained.

Not finding Jack's hand where she expected, Beck glanced at his lap. He was playing his own imaginary drum. The musician was hitting his hands on his lap in time to the rhythm, then slightly altering the beat, his eyes tightly shut.

"Jack," she whispered.

Jack stopped drumming for a split second as he held his hand up to shush her and resumed his lap drumming.

"Jack," she whispered more urgently, miffed that he was ignoring their friends' ceremony and being rude to her.

As Tom and Lenora were pronounced husband and wife, the head priestess took her place in between two younger priestesses. Each wore a white flowing gown and a feathered headdress. The head priestess wore the most elaborate one adorned with a small skull in the center. She stood tall and commanded, "Now we shall commence with the blessing of the spirits." All three women began to chant along with the drums.

Suddenly, Jack stood up, walked through the courtyard, and snuck around the front of the old cottage. *Not again.* Beck sighed and fanned herself with her program.

The drumming ceased, and the head priestess said, "Tom and Lenora, it is with joy that I send you out into the world to spread the beautiful light and darkness that you share with those around you. By the power vested in me, I now, for the first time, pronounce you married. Now kiss and go celebrate!"

The ceremony was over; it was time to walk across the street to Congo Square for the reception. As Beck stood up, she spotted Thomas and Elizabeth Platt. As the crowd moved along the side of the house, making their way down Rampart Street, she hurried over to greet them.

"I'm so glad you two made it," Beck said.

"We've always wanted to visit New Orleans. This seemed like the perfect excuse. I just didn't realize it would still be so steamy in October," Elizabeth said as she tucked a damp lock of her thick brown hair behind her ear.

Beck nodded, "It doesn't cool down until the end of November, but I can't imagine Tom having a Thanksgiving wedding." The friends chuckled.

"We just wrapped principal photography on Tom's first Figment Film. It was pretty much down to the wire. Reminded me of your wedding," Thomas said.

"Well, ours was more gothic than voodoo. So, it's not like he ripped us off. If anything, I imitated his style," Beck said.

Thomas shook his head. "That's not what I meant. I was referring to cramming your wedding into the same month as a movie premiere and Ah Ooga's farewell concert,"

"Don't forget how busy she was," Elizabeth added, "planning a wedding while we worked on post-production for Lovers In A Dangerous Time. Poor thing! Did you ever have your honeymoon?"

"No." Beck fiddled with her wedding ring and waited at the edge of the road for a break in the traffic. Carefully, she studied the crowd keeping an eye out for her husband. She turned and looked back at the front of the cottage. Jack was leaning against a pillar on the wraparound porch humming into his voice recorder. His eyes were closed, and he had his hand over his left ear.

"Your anniversary is this week. Are you going to stay and play awhile?" Elizabeth asked with a smile.

Beck shook her head and looked away. "It isn't a good time. We're both swamped. Besides, I don't think it's really a honeymoon two years after the fact," She stared at her husband, who was now listening to his recording, oblivious to the crowd in the front yard. She started to cross the street.

"Wait," Thomas said," Aren't you forgetting something?"

Beck and the Platts looked back at Jack, who smiled and waved them on.

"Never mind. I guess the honeymoon *is* over," Thomas murmured.

"Thomas! I'm sorry, Beck. Don't listen to him," Elizabeth said, taking Beck's arm as they crossed Rampart Street and approached Congo Square.

"It's fine. I'm used to it. When inspiration strikes, the Maestro has to capture it. That's just the way he is." Beck shrugged.

"Even in the middle of his best friend's wedding?" Thomas asked.

Beck fanned herself and looked back at her husband with a small frown.

Elizabeth took her arm and said, "Hey, you two will work it out. Happily, ever after is a journey, not a destination. You have to put in the time. There's no way around it."

Thomas smiled and said, "Elizabeth always says, 'Love is Journey.'"

Elizabeth rolled her eyes and chuckled. "I made one typo, and he'll never let it go."

"I'll never let *you* go," Thomas pulled his wife into an embrace. As they kissed, the band began to play. As the Platts started to sway to the music, Beck glanced around uncomfortably and headed to the bar.

The sunset streaked the sky with bold pinks, purples, and oranges. It looked aflame from the porch of the cottage where Tom and Lenora had become Mr. and Mrs. Price. Jack watched the guests cross the street. Then, he listened attentively to his recording once more. Finally satisfied with this new piece inspired by the ceremony, he made his way down the stairs.

Tom's wedding reminded him so much of his own. His bride had worn a deep purple gown, and her eyes shone like the darkest jade in the candlelight. His hand had shaken as he read his vows. Beck had reached out and gently placed her hand over his, calming him. He couldn't believe she was his.

Anxious to be with her again, Jack made his way in the darkness over to Congo Square. He hadn't spent much time in New Orleans, but he only needed to follow the drum beats and the sounds of merriment to locate the party. Peering through large oaks, he watched the crowd writhing in time to the music as circus performers entertained those who were seated on the sidelines.

As he walked the perimeter of the party searching for Beck, he tripped over a large tree root. Dusting himself off he noticed a collection of random items at the foot of a massive tree. Before he could investigate any further he heard Tom's distinct laugh.

In the center of the dance floor, Tom and Lenora danced with a snake wrapped around their shoulders. The crowd cheering them on. Jack watched the merriment for a moment, then scanned the crowd once more attempting to spot his wife's red curls, but she was nowhere to be found. He decided it would be best to stay put. She'd find him eventually, and if he was going to stay in one place, what better place than at the bar.

The bartender was busy chatting up a lady in a large top hat decorated with bones and skulls. He was showcasing different shots he could make.

"Since you like Mardi Gras so much, this is a King Cake shot. Tastes just like it."

As the woman reached for her shot, Jack cleared his throat, catching the bartender's attention. "Whiskey neat, please," Jack said to the bartender.

She whipped around to look at him. It was Beck. "There you are. I've been looking all over for you. The hat threw me off."

"It's Remi's. Isn't it cool?" Beck asked.

"Who's Remi?"

"At your service," the bartender said, handing Jack his drink.

"Oh. Well, I guess it's cool if you like wearing chicken feathers and bones on your head."

"They're not real," Beck scoffed.

"Of course they are," Remi said.

Beck took the hat off, careful not to touch any of the chicken parts, and handed it back to Remi. He popped the hat back on his head and waved his hand over her glass. "Don't drink that yet."

"Why not?" Beck asked.

The bartender grabbed a can of whipped cream and swirled the topping onto the shot. "It needed a little lagniappe," he explained.

"A lagniappe?" Jack asked.

"It means a little something extra," Beck said then downed the shot. "Wow, that does taste like King Cake."

Jack reached out and gently traced her upper lip with his thumb wiping off a thin line of whipped cream, then licking his finger. He grinned at Beck and said, "Lagniappe."

"You almost made me forget that I'm pissed at you," Beck said.

Jack took a big sip of his whiskey and sighed.

Beck leaned in closer. "You walked out on Tom's wedding. The man you claim is like a brother to you. That's rude."

"I was inspired, Tom would understand. Besides, I'm sure he didn't even notice," Jack said staring deeply into his glass while his wife's eyes burned into the side of his head.

"Well, I noticed. Thomas and Elizabeth noticed," she said.

"I'm sorry. How can I make it up to you?" Jack followed Beck's gaze to the dance floor. Her friends from Figment Films were gliding across the dance floor lost in one another's eyes. "You know we can't dance."

"That's never stopped us before," she said as she tried to pull Jack up from the barstool.

He refused to budge. "Let me finish my drink."

They sat in silence as Jack nursed the last of his whiskey. Suddenly, a cheer went up across the square. The bride and groom were making their way to a horse-drawn carriage. Jack and Beck hurried over to say goodbye.

As the carriage pulled out of sight, Elizabeth and Thomas approached.

"Where to now?" Thomas asked.

Beck looked at Jack expectantly, Jack felt the whiskey overtake his tired muscles. He hated to disappoint his wife, but they had to be at the airport dark and early

"Darlin', we have to leave in five hours."

Thomas clapped him on the back. "You can spare an hour to have a nightcap. Come on, we've been wanting to try Absinthe."

"You can sleep on the plane," Elizabeth added.

"If we go out drinking, we'll miss our plane," Jack said a little more forcefully than intended.

The Platts shifted their gaze to Beck who said, "You two have fun. We'll meet for dinner once we're all back in LA."

The couple exchanged hugs with Beck and nodded to Jack as they turned and crossed Rampart Street. He tried to catch Beck's eye, but she turned and walked back toward the bar in Congo Square.

Jack caught up to her, and put his hand on her shoulder. Without looking at him she grabbed her purse from the hook under the bar. "I forgot my purse." she mumbled. Then headed to the giant oak with all the objects gathered at its base. She opened her purse and pulled out a penny, placing it among the other items.

"What's that for?" he asked

Beck started back toward the street and said over her shoulder, "Lenora said an offering would bring good juju."

Jack narrowed his eyes at her. "You don't believe in juju."

Beck shrugged and kept walking. She didn't speak the entire trip back to the Olivier House. Upstairs in their room, she stood on the balcony her arms folded as she took in the sights below. He hated saying no to her, but he was running up against a deadline on a score. Unable to tolerate the silence any longer, Jack came up behind his bride and put his arms around her. "I'm sorry, Dollface. I like it here too. Let's plan on coming back when we can spend more time."

CHAPTER 2

Beck sat in her office gazing at the marine layer as it battled against the sunshine for dominance. She was rooting for the daylight, these foggy mornings made it hard to get going. Beck rubbed her eyes and reached for the mug of tea Jack had brought her before he went down to his studio. It had cooled long ago.

She stood and stretched, ready for a break. Even though she'd barely accomplished anything. The rewrites for her new comedy screenplay were due before shooting began on Friday. But Beck didn't feel like being funny. Ever since she'd returned from New Orleans, she couldn't shake this restless feeling.

In the basement, Jack was putting the finishing touches on a score for a thriller which was, at times, distracting.

I should shut the door and get back to work.

However, as she approached the door at the top of the stairs, Jack started to sing. No words, just "Bum, bum, bumpa, bumpa, bum, pa bum." repeatedly. His rich baritone voice filled the stairwell, drawing her to it. Oh, how she'd missed the sound of him singing.

She tiptoed down the stairs, but as she reached the second to last stair, it gave out a tired creak betraying her presence.

Jack stopped and spun around in his chair. "Do you need something?" he asked.

Beck didn't think he would let her stay and listen. "I just need to take a break. I've been staring at that screen all morning." It wasn't a complete lie.

"I can't stop right now, Beck."

"I didn't ask you to, I needed to move around, so I thought I would dust a little."

"Down here?" Jack asked.

"You won't let the housekeepers down here when you're working, and it's getting pretty thick."

Beck found a dust rag in the studio's half bath and started dusting the various artifacts.

Jack returned to work, and Beck delighted in his voice as she tidied up. Everything was soon clean, except Jack's creepy doll collection near the bottom of the stairs. Some of them were a little disturbing.

The ventriloquist dummy in the center of the menagerie terrified her. He looked exactly like the murderous dummy from the Twilight Zone episode she'd watched as a child. Jack had affectionately named him Bucky. Beck avoided him at all costs.

But Beck didn't want to miss out on a chance to hear her husband sing. Who knew when he'd do that again. So, Beck threw back her shoulders and marched over to the dolls.

I just won't touch him, she promised herself, gingerly picking up every doll around him to dust. She worked from the outside in, until only the dolls on either side of the dummy were left. She grabbed the naked doll with a missing eye on Bucky's right and dusted her, carefully polishing her one remaining blue eye.

As Beck went to return the one eyed doll, she let it drop the last few inches to avoid touching Bucky. Unfortunately, the naked doll knocked into him, sending his body into the doll on his left. The little brunette, who had her face in the corner for as long as Beck had known Jack, suddenly fell over, face up, causing several other dolls to fall onto the floor.

Jack sighed. "Beck, please be careful."

"Sorry, I'll fix it," she said, taking the doll and using its legs to push Bucky back into place. She stopped and looked at the doll for the first time. She had brown hair in loose curls and sparkling green eyes that matched her emerald dress and hair ribbons. Unlike the other dolls, she was pristine. Incredibly well preserved. Beck suddenly realized she had met this one before.

Beck gasped and said, "Hannalore?"

Jack paused the music. "What?"

"This is my doll," she said, cradling it gently.

"I've had that doll for years. I found her in an antique store during Ah Ooga's first tour."

"Where? In Louisiana?" she asked hopefully.

He scrunched his face as though he were deep in thought. "I don't remember. Somewhere in the south. We went from California to Florida. Eight men in an ancient Winnebago. The AC was busted. It was hell. Any time I had off, I'd walk to thrift stores and antique malls," Jack explained.

"One day, I was knocking around a store filled with china, crystal, you know, housewares, and jewelry. I was about to leave when I felt someone tug at my sleeve. So, I turned around, but no one was there. There was a flash of green light, and it was coming from her eyes. Must have been the sun hitting them. She's not my usual taste, too well-kept, but she had this energy about her. A strong juju from her previous owners. I couldn't leave her there."

"Why?" Beck asked as she stared at the doll.

"She felt like she had unfinished business."

"My mom gave her away. We moved houses, and she wasn't with my things."

"Why would she get rid of your doll?"

"She never liked Hannalore. That's her name," Beck said, gesturing to the doll cradled in her arms. "My grandmother had passed her down to my mom, and she said the doll gave her the creeps. She insisted that Oma put the doll away. When I came along, Oma gave Hannalore to me. As you can imagine, my mom was less than pleased."

"Oma?"

"My grandmother is German, a World War II bride," Beck explained.

"I thought you were Irish," Jack said.

"Mostly. Anyway, I loved Hannalore, so my mom was stuck with her until the move. That's when she took advantage of the chaos of the situation to get rid of Hannalore. She claimed the doll was giving me nightmares."

"Really?" Jack asked.

Beck shrugged. "I was having lots of nightmares, but there was a lot of crappy stuff going on. I assumed it had more to do with that than some haunted toy."

They both studied the doll. Jack said, "You know, Darlin', Germany is known for its doll-making. I'm sure there were tons of dolls made just like Hannalore."

Beck frowned and looked at the floor, "You're probably right," she said softly.

"I've got to get back to work. Do you need help putting the dolls back?"

"I can do it." Beck placed Hannalore gently between the corner and Bucky. A flash of green streaked from the doll's eyes, reflecting on the opposite wall.

"Can you please have her face the corner? It's really distracting when the sun hits her eyes," Jack said.

Beck did as Jack asked and returned to her desk. After she finally nailed the joke in the scene she was finishing, she recalled how her Hannalore's eyes seemed to glow at times, too, even at night. *How could that be? And how could Jack's doll reflect the sunshine in the basement, which only had a small window in the exterior door?*

CHAPTER 3

The following day, Beck was back at it, typing away while still in her nightgown. One more scene to revise before she could finally submit the script to Warner Bros. For an hour the work progressed smoothly. She was focused, playing a mixtape she'd made. Beck felt that the songs matched the tone of her screenplay, prompting her to type along to the beat of the music. As side one of her cassette tape finished, she took a break and checked her email.

She was amused to find that her mom, Rosalie, and her mother-in-law, Miriam had both sent her messages. Miriam wanted to confirm they were still on for lunch at her house on Saturday. They were writing a book of ghost stories together based on local history. Beck sent a quick reply saying she was looking forward to it.

Her mom's email was short and to the point. Rosalie explained that she had gotten home late from a meeting and found Beck's message about Hannalore. It had been too late to call, so she'd emailed instead.

Rosalie explained that Hannalore was a one-of-a-kind doll that Oma had gotten from one of her neighbors as a child. *That's a story for another day,* Rosalie had written. Attached to the email was a photo of Beck and Hannalore from when she was seven. Rosalie added that she'd be interested to hear if Jack's doll was the same. She reminded Beck that the doll had the artist's initials SJB on her bottom.

Beck studied the photo, like the doll downstairs, Hannalore wore an emerald velvet dress with matching ribbons in her brown curls. That was her doll. She was sure of it. Beck mused how romantic it would be if Jack had had something of hers all these years. She printed out the photo, which took forever, but it was essential to have it in color.

Jack heard the printer fire up in Beck's office. Just as he'd heard the screeching modem as she logged on and the faint yet annoying beat of her mixed tape. He was on edge. A final meeting was scheduled with Max Hall, the director of the thriller he'd been working on in an hour. He needed silence. He desperately needed to be left alone.

The printer finally stopped, and he was relieved to be able to work in peace. However, it was short-lived, as he heard Beck's footsteps coming down the stairs.

Beck said breathlessly, "I need to show you something."

"After my meeting," Jack said, not looking up.

"It'll only take a second."

"I don't have a second, " he said. "Don't you have work you're supposed to be doing, too?"

Beck crossed over to the dolls "I just want to see something, my doll had initials on her bottom." She quickly pulled the doll in the green dress away from the corner, catching one of the other doll's curls with Hannalore's feet which caused another domino effect. Beck tried to stop the chain reaction but overcorrected, disturbing a particularly delicate porcelain doll inside a bell jar, sending both to the floor and smashing the container and its contents into pieces.

Jack surveyed the destruction. Pieces of porcelain and glass littered the floor. Beck stood next to the mess holding the damned doll she was obsessed with. Her mouth hung open. For a moment, neither of them moved. *Does she realize what she's done?*

Nellie was over a hundred years old. He could feel his skin get hot as his pulse quickened.

Finally, Beck said, "Sorry. I'll clean it up."

"Get out," he grumbled.

"I'll be back with a broom," she said as she avoided his gaze and moved toward the stairs.

Jack needed space. The mess would keep. *Why won't she leave?* "I said get out!" he shouted before he could help himself.

Beck headed up the stairs, not looking back. She took a few deep breaths at the top of the stairs, determined not to cry. Then, remembering her own unfinished work, she sat back down at her computer and tried desperately to be funny.

But, the state of her marriage clouded her brain. How could she live in the same house with someone and feel so alone? Why had Jack asked her to marry him if he didn't want a life with her? He'd been so in love and attentive at first. Was that over now?

She decided music would help her regain her focus on the task at hand. She flipped her cassette tape over to the next side, and "Don't You Go" by Ah Ooga played through the speakers. As hurt as she was, Beck reached over to fast forward the song. However, hearing Jack's voice singing that particular song reminded her of when she was injured in Harlem, and he had cared for her so tenderly. The louder, the better. She turned up the volume and placed her hands back on the keyboard.

Jack came stomping up the stairs. "Did you not hear me?"

"What?" Beck asked loudly in an attempt to be heard over the music.

"It's too damn loud! Turn it down or turn it off."

"No! I'm working too. This is what I need to do *my* job," Beck yelled.

"At least wear your fucking headphones." He picked up her headphones from the desk, knocking Beck's keyboard to the ground in the process, and threw them across the room. Beck gasped.

"Oh Beck, geez, I'm so-" Jack stammered. Before he could finish, the downstairs doorbell rang. "Beck?" he said, one more time, but she refused to look at him. Instead, she crossed the room to retrieve her headphones. Tears covered her cheeks as she returned to her desk, plugging her headphones in and replacing her keyboard. The bell rang again, and Jack rushed downstairs to open the door for Max.

Beck sat down and wiped her eyes. Trying to ignore the tension headache pounding at her temples and the tightness in her chest. The stress and anxiety were painful, but she refused to let them stop her from making her deadline. As she finished her last sentence, the song ended. Yet, another Ah Ooga song followed it.

She lifted her fingers once more to fast forward to someone else's song, but as angry as she was at the man downstairs, hearing this younger version of her husband helped her remember happier times when their relationship was in its early days. She read carefully over her final changes and submitted the screenplay via email.

A film cue of Jack's, Beck's favorite, played next. She made no move this time to stop it. Instead, she melted into her chair, rubbing her temples, praying the ache would stop. She wanted to figure out her marriage and mend what was broken. Yet, she wanted the agony to end. Another piece of her, one she kept hidden even from herself, wanted to run away.

The seed of a buried secret watered too many nights by tears had at last burst to the surface, and she could no longer ignore it. As the orchestra played sweetly in her ears, she rubbed her aching head. "I wish I was anywhere but here," she whispered.

CHAPTER 4

Jack hurried across the studio. He could see the director waiting at the door. "Max, come on in."

"You seem winded. Are you all right?" Max said. As he stepped into the studio, his eyes immediately fell on the mess of shattered glass and porcelain that lay in front of the doll collection. "What happened?"

"Sometimes they try to escape," Jack said. "Ready to hear your music?"

Max sat down at the recording bay. "Are you kidding? I've been looking forward to this since you signed onto the project."

Jack loved working with Max. Years before, he had done a couple of excellent zombie films. When Jack discovered Max's follow-up film was underfunded, he offered to do the score for a silver dollar. Silver-dollar scores were something Jack would do when he believed in a film, but the picture lacked the funds to pay his typical fee. This time around, however, Max had the backing of a major studio for a thriller with big names attached.

In only two hours, all the music cues were selected and ready to record. They booked the orchestra for the week before Thanksgiving. In three weeks Jack would hear his music played by an orchestra, his favorite part of the process. There would inevitably be little tweaks here and there once they listened to the music live, but the hard part was over. Jack could rest easy for a couple of weeks before going into the session.

After Max left, Jack cleaned up the mess in the basement while he pondered how to clean up the mess upstairs. He needed to apologize to Beck. That was a given. Sure, he had a temper, but he couldn't remember the last time he'd thrown something.

Since Max was pleased with Jack's score, and Beck would be finished with her screenplay today, they would finally have some downtime. Maybe he could steal her away for their overdue honeymoon. Their and anniversary and Halloween were coming up later in the week. They could have true a vacation instead of traveling had to promote their work. *What's the point in making money if we never get to spend a little?*

Excited by his idea, Jack started to kick around possible destinations. The Caribbean was beautiful in late October. Beck had never been. They could go to Europe, but last year they went to a premiere in London, and she had been frozen the whole time. That trip would be better for a warmer time of year.

He made his way upstairs to the kitchen to feed Rufus. The old dog was snoring on his bed as he did most days. Only moving for two reasons: breakfast and dinner. Jack purposefully made as much noise as possible to wake him. The dog lumbered into the kitchen and ate his kibble while Jack tidied up.

Jack caught a glimpse of Tom and Lenora's elaborate Voodoo wedding invitation on the fridge. That was such a quick trip. Maybe Beck would like to go back.

Nah, we were just there last week. She'll want to go somewhere different.

Leading Rufus to the back door, Jack passed his Dia de las Muertos collection. He remembered how Beck had admired his dog and the sugar skulls the first time she came over. *Maybe we should go to Mexico.*

While Rufus did his business, Jack noticed the sunset. He checked his watch. After losing his Casio, his mom had gotten him a new one.

It was later than he'd realized. Why hadn't Beck fed Rufus? Was she still working on her screenplay?

He had avoided going to check on her, knowing she would still be angry. It was crucial to go in with an apology and a peace offering. He decided he would take her wherever she wanted to go.

As Jack and Rufus entered the house, Jack realized that he hadn't seen or heard from Beck since the confrontation. He peeked into her office, but there was no sign of her. The computer was still on and connected to the internet. The screen showed an email she'd sent to Warner Bros with her rewrites attached.

She's probably relaxing after work, he concluded. But as he bent over to turn off the computer, he noticed her headphones were on the floor under her chair. *That's odd.* He remembered seeing her pick them up earlier. Beck wasn't the kind of person to leave her things scattered around. He gently picked up the headphones up from the floor, examined them to make sure that he hadn't damaged them, and then placed them next to her keyboard.

He made his way to their bedroom, trying to walk softly in case she was asleep. But, as he entered the room, he could see that not only was the bed empty, it was made up without so much as a wrinkle in the comforter, every pillow still in place.

The bathroom door was open. Jack could see that she wasn't soaking in the tub or unwinding in a steamy shower. He thought through the places in the house where she could be. He had just been in the kitchen, living room, the backyard, her office, and their bedroom. *Did she go looking for me?* Jack hurried down to his studio, calling her name. The basement was empty.

He was sure he'd have heard the garage door if she'd left. But he and Max were pretty focused on the music. Jack walked into the mudroom, Beck's purse was on the hook, and both cars were in the garage. His stomach began to ache.

She might have gone for a walk, but they lived in Topanga Canyon. Beck knew better than to hike alone at dusk. The hills were home to snakes, coyotes, and wild cats. Besides, she was afraid of the dark, and her sneakers were sitting right there next to his on the mudroom shoe rack.

He imagined that she might have left without him knowing it. Going into her closet, he was relieved to find that all her clothes were still there. Her toothbrush and makeup were in the bathroom. She wouldn't have left without her things. Especially not her purse or her car. This was ridiculous. Why couldn't he find her?

Jack thought of the one place he hadn't looked: his jazz room. It was a long shot. Beck had only been there a few times to listen to records with him, but never by herself. He opened the door, and just as he suspected, the room was empty.

Rufus, who had been following behind him the entire time, pushed past Jack and unceremoniously plopped down on the rug in the center of the room. "Excellent idea, old boy. I'm sure there's a logical explanation for why we can't find your mommy. I'll grab a whiskey and join you," Jack said to Rufus, whose ears perked up when he heard "Mommy."

There was a knock at the door which startled Jack. They lived on a winding road in a gated community, and the homes were separated by acreage. An unexpected guest was rare. It wasn't like anyone would pop over from the next property to borrow a cup of sugar. So who the hell could it be?

CHAPTER 5

The light shining on Beck's face was much too bright. Her head was still throbbing. Someone with a large, strong hand grabbed her shoulder and shook her body, "Miss, wake up. You can't sleep in here, Miss. Wake up. This the telegraph office in here," a black man with a newsboy cap shouted as Beck squinted in the light.

As she stood, she felt her breasts sag slightly due to the lack of a bra. She looked down and saw she was still in her white cotton nightgown. Her face grew hot with embarrassment as she crossed her arms over her chest and exited the office. She looked around and realized she was in a large train station with arched entryways and carefully painted art deco features on the walls. A sign on the largest of the arches read: "Welcome to New Orleans."

The large clock read ten-thirty. It was dark, and not many people were around. The few she spotted were maids and porters, all dark-skinned. The men wore hats and suspenders. A couple of white ladies emerged from the restroom wearing elegant suits with shoulder pads. One of the ladies sported a dark brown pompadour, and her younger companion wore her blond locks in victory rolls. They passed by Beck, and the older woman uttered under her breath, "Floozy," as she noted Beck's attire and steered the younger lady out of the station.

Beck's head was spinning. It had happened again, she'd time traveled. In theory, she and Jack knew there was a possibility it could happen again. But the first time had been three years ago. They'd gone to Harlem in 1938. That's where the couple had met and fell in love.

But this was different, Beck was alone in New Orleans, sometime in the 1940s. She knew the period well from the old movies she loved to watch. The hair and fashion from the decade were among her favorites. Clothes, that's what she needed, to somehow to make herself presentable. Then she could go and search for Jack.

She looked at the shop windows in the station. There was dress shop was in the far left corner of the main hall. Beck made her way over and gasped at the gorgeous clothes. She'd only seen dresses like these when working on plays and movies; those were only costumes, not vintage.

I guess these aren't vintage, yet. She reasoned.

There was a "Closed" sign on the door and all the lights were off. She checked the door, which to her surprise, was unlocked. Beck stopped short of going in. She'd traveled without anything but her nightgown and her wedding ring. The only thing of value on her person. She wasn't sure she could bear to part with it. Though the thought of stealing a dress made her ill, she stepped in and quietly shut the door behind her.

While she took in her surroundings, she fiddled with her ring moving it from her left ring finger to her right. She wondered once more if Jack was here somewhere, not knowing if that would be a comfort to her or a complication.

She crept through the store into the back, locating the discounted dresses, hoping that stealing a dress was somehow less terrible if it wasn't full price. Even if it was still a sin, she reasoned it would at least be less conspicuous than stealing one of the fancy dresses that adorned the shop's window display.

The dresses on the clearance rack were primarily utility dresses that would have fallen out of favor after the war. With the full skirts on display out front and the utility dresses in the back,

Beck guessed she was somewhere between 1946 and 1949.

Beck needed to land somewhere between the outdated and fashion-forward for her attire. While mulling it over, she grabbed a pair of girdle panties off the shelf and slid them on, feeling more secure. She then located a bra in her size. Next, she scanned the middle of the store, her eyes drawn to a rack of trousers. Pants? That's totally wicked! She preferred pants, but if she went full Katherine Hepburn, she'd definitely stand out.

Her eyes finally landed on a rack of classics. One of the most flattering dresses of the century. It came in many colors, but Beck chose the dark teal. It had a full, sweeping skirt and shaped bodice that emphasized the hips, waist, and bust. Beck slipped it on, enjoying the splendid feel of the cotton and silk blend as it brushed against her calves just below her knees. The swinging sweep of the skirt demanded to be twirled. She tied the sash around her waist, highlighting her hourglass shape. The V-neck bodice had darts at the bust and waist, finished off with a notched collar. Just when she thought she couldn't love it more than she already did, she found the dress had pockets.

I could live here for the clothes alone.

Stockings and shoes were needed to finish the look. Beck was thrilled to discover that there were now some pairs without seams. She chose some black leather pumps strapped at the ankles because they had a thick Cuban heel to keep her upright. She placed the tags in her pocket, determined to somehow repay what she had taken. In her other pocket, she hid her wedding ring, afraid it would attract thieves.

Beck picked up her nightgown, knowing she'd need it. The white cotton gown had peasant sleeves and looked reasonable for the times, but it would look strange carrying it around.

In fact, while her costume was correct, her untamed curly locks and lack of makeup made her look out of place. Beck located the makeup at the sales counter, opened a Victory Red lipstick, and put some on, then opened a tube of mascara. She placed a drop on the brush and applied it to her lashes. Next, she powdered her face, smoothed her eyebrows into arches with her fingers, and brushed her cheeks with a light pink blush.

Good thing I have pockets, so I can steal more stuff. Beck sighed with shame as she slipped the stolen cosmetics into her pocket. Finally, she grabbed a snood to wrangle her crazy curls into.

It was midnight now, and mercifully not a soul was stirring around the station. Unlike Harlem, Beck was familiar with the Crescnt City. She had visited New Orleams a handful of times while growing up in Louisiana, and most recently for Tom and Lenora's wedding. But, she wasn't sure how the city beyond the train station would compare to 1995.

Like a player waiting in the wings, Beck struggled with twinges of stage fright as she prepared to enter the city. The fear of the unknown and the anxiety of all that had happened exhausted her. But sleep would have to wait while she searched for a safe place to close her eyes.

Come on, Beck, you can do this. She told herself. As she walked out into the dark city she thought about her earlier acting experiences. The countless hours of Improv exercises had helped her fit into 1930s Harlem. Surely they would help her now.

For twenty minutes, she zigged zagged off and on South Rampart Street, the street that separated the French Quarter from Treme', the African American neighborhood. To avoid menacing characters doing a deal in a back alley, Beck crossed into what looked like an African American nightclub district. Jazz music poured out onto the streets. In doorways, women beckoned to the few men who passed by this time of night. Their outfits reminded Beck of the costumes worn by the Cotton Club dancers in Harlem. However, due to the womens' repeated offer for "dates", she began to suspect that she was in the red-light district.

After crossing Canal Street's streetcar line, she returned to the French Quarter and moved south one block to Dauphine Street. The road was lined with large homes hidden behind courtyards intermingled with small wooden cottages and a general store.

The lack of people made her nervous, so she turned onto Bienville Street after a couple of blocks, following the sound of a jazz quartet toward Bourbon Street. Finding the block just as empty as Dauphine, she quickened her pace.

Suddenly, a petite woman with a blonde pageboy haircut wearing a pink cocktail dress crossed Bourbon at a similar speed. Several feet behind her was a tall man in pursuit.

"Hey, Baby, I bought you a drink. You owe me a dance," the man said, speeding up to cross Bourbon. He had to stop for a car at the corner, putting some distance between him and the frightened young woman.

As she closed in on Beck, she mouthed, "Help me."

Beck reached out and grabbed the woman pulling her into a bear hug, "It's alright, just play along," she whispered urgently.

"Where have you been? You had us so worried," Beck said in her native Southern drawl. As she ended the hug she kept her arm around the blonde's shoulders.

"Who is this?" the man asked as he approached the women.

"Why I'm her sister. The whole family's been out searching all night," Beck said.

"Is that so?" The man put his hand on his hip and smirked.

"Yes. Me and all four of our *big* brothers," Beck said.

"Uh oh, not Big Jimmy?" the blonde asked, playing along.

"Yes, ma'am, Big Jimmy is fit to be tied. He said it ain't fittin' for you to be out til the wee hours unaccompanied and that any man who'd keep you out that late has terrible intentions and oughta be castrated."

At this, the man fig leafed his hands over his crotch and gulped.

"While I'm glad to see that my sister was escorted by a gentleman who surely meant her no harm, I'm afraid I'm gonna have to ask you to say goodnight right here," Beck added.

"Goodnight, Miss Virginia," he said as his eyes fell on Beck's nightgown draped across her arm. "Wait, what's the gown for?"

Beck glanced at her gown and then met the stranger's gaze, "Papa said that if Virginia snuck out one more time, he'd send her off to the convent. I'm gonna put her in the nightgown and tell 'em I found her on the back sleeping porch," Beck said.

As she turned to walk away, she linked arms with Virginia steering her back up Bienville. For good measure, she added loudly over her shoulder, "Hurry along now, Sis. Papa said that if you weren't found soon. He'd come scouring the quarter with his shotgun."

She was relieved to hear the man's footsteps heading in the opposite direction.

"Jeepers! I thought I was done for. How did you know how to do all that?" Virginia asked.

"Stand up to bullies?"

"No, make all that stuff up about us being kin."

"Improv class," Beck said absently as she tried to figure out where to go.

Virginia scrunched up her face. "What's Improv?"

Beck could have kicked herself for the slip-up, "Uh, it's the art of thinking on your feet."

"Oh. My name's Virginia Broussard, but you can call me Ginny. All my friends do."

"Then, I'd be honored to. My name is Rebecca."

"Just Rebecca?"

Beck wasn't sure how to answer that. She had previously needed Beck as an alias, so she was reluctant to share her nickname. Post World War II, Louisiana wasn't a good place to have a German-sounding last name, so she said, "Taylor, it's Rebecca Taylor."

She swallowed hard, feeling like she had betrayed Jack. However, explaining that her last name was Jewish when she wasn't or that the name was her married name when there was no husband in sight seemed far too complicated.

"Pleased to meet you, Rebecca Taylor. You don't sound like you're from here," Ginny said.

"I'm from Shreveport," Beck said, knowing everyone had heard of Shreveport, and almost no one knew of her hometown of Bossier City. However, the two cities were just across the Red River, so she figured it was close enough.

"You're a long way from home without any luggage," Ginny said, looking concerned.

This time Beck was prepared to explain, "I came in on the last train tonight, and a man stole my bag. My nightgown was sticking out, and when I tried to grab my bag by the fabric, the gown slipped out. I'm afraid this and a pocket full of cosmetics is all I've got to my name."

Ginny's eyes were full of compassion, making Beck feel like a jerk for lying. "You poor, Darling. That's just too much. Come on. You're staying with me tonight. Thank God you weren't interfered with. I mean, stuff is stuff, and it can be replaced.

Honor's much harder to get back," Ginny said, taking a quick look over her shoulder, "Well, we've both been through it, and I know Mama and Daddy won't mind the company."

"If you're sure, it's alright," Beck said, relieved she'd have a safe place to sleep, at least for the night. Then, it was Ginny's turn to lead, as the ladies returned to Dauphine and walked a couple of blocks over to St. Louis Street. They stopped in front of one of the larger courtyard homes with butter yellow stucco and Ginny took a key from her handbag and unlocked the door to the courtyard.

As they stepped inside, Beck looked at the most elegant home she'd ever seen.

The home was in an L-shape on the property with an enclosed red brick paved courtyard. It was three stories tall with dark green wrought iron balconies on the upper two levels. Gas lanterns burned, illuminating the courtyard with a warm, welcoming glow. The home oozed with Southern charm, making Beck feel right at home before she even reached the front door.

Once inside, Ginny showed her to a room with a gorgeous four-poster bed on the third floor. "If you need anything, I'm right next door. In the morning, I'll come to get you so I can introduce you to my family."

As Beck closed the door, the loneliness set in. The rush of adrenaline as she dealt with her arrival had given her a slight reprieve. But Ginny's departure brought the feeling of isolation back to mind.

She emptied her pockets into the dresser and hung up her dress. Then, as she slipped on her nightgown, she caught a whiff of Jack's scent. A mixture of pine trees and ocean air. She'd always teased him that his soap made him smell like Big Sur.

"You're the one who buys it for me, so you must like how Big Sur smells," Jack often teased back.

Though a part of her was still upset about their fight, his scent reminded her that they were likely decades apart. She closed her eyes and tried to pictured happier times. Then, Beck retrieved her ring from the dresser and slid it onto her finger one more time before placing it in the pocket of her dress for safekeeping. She laid down on the bed, exhausted, but unable to fall asleep. Finally, she turned one of the pillows sideways and laid her head on it, pretending it was Jack's chest. It was a poor substitute. The pillow was cold and lacked Jack's heartbeat.

She rolled away from it and wrapped her arms around herself, smelling him on her nightgown again as she squeezed herself into a hug. It wasn't the same. Beck had a powerful imagination, but try as she might, she couldn't make Jack Herman appear. Still, she closed her eyes, breathing him in as the tears leaked from the corners of her eyes.

CHAPTER 6

"Rise and shine," Ginny said, patting Rebecca's shoulders.

Beck gasped and sat up suddenly, causing Ginny to jump back. Rubbing her eyes, Beck looked around, seeing the lavishly decorated room in the daylight for the first time. Her new friend had been busy. The drapes were drawn back, and the closet's door was open, revealing several outfits.

"I'm sorry. I forgot when- I mean where I was," Beck said, clearing her throat.

"I know yesterday was an ordeal for both of us. When I told Mama and Daddy, they were plumb grateful you happened along when you did. That makes you good people in our book. So, you can stay here until you get settled. That is if you want to stick around."

"That's so sweet of you and your family. I was planning to rent a room, but after yesterday…"

"Hot dog! I've always wanted a sister. I'm the only girl," Ginny said.

"Me too. I have two younger brothers."

"I'm in the middle of four brothers." Ginny stopped, and her eyes misted over. Her voice cracked as she added softly, "I mean, I was. We're a Gold Star family. My older brother, Jimmy died in Normandy."

"Oh Ginny, I'm sorry," Beck said as she squeezed Ginny's hand.

Ginny sat with her grief for a moment. Then, smiled at Beck and said, "Well, anyway, Mama and I went through our things and found some outfits and toiletries to help you."

"You shouldn't have."

"It was nothing. We have plenty of room and things we weren't using. Now, let's get you dolled up for breakfast. After that, I'm going to show you the town. What do you want to see?" Ginny asked as she held out two lovely dresses for Beck to choose from.

"Everything, but mostly I'd love to hear some bands play."

Like their daughter, the Broussards, who insisted Beck call them Claude and Evelyn, were charming hosts. They had an elaborate breakfast in their main dining room. After, Beck received a tour of the entire house.

Then the ladies stepped out for some window shopping and took in the sights around the river, walking off their heavy breakfast. Finally, when the cathedral bells chimed three o'clock, the sunshine gave over to a chilly rain. The trio decided it was time to rest their feet.

"Let's get something to warm us up at Cafe Du Monde," Ginny suggested.

The women grabbed beignets and hot cocoa. The perfect snack for the sudden change in the weather. As they finished, Ginny alerted Beck to wipe some powdered sugar off the corner of her mouth.

Beck thought back to the last time she visited Cafe Du Monde.

"It must have been good because you have half the sugar right here," Jack had said with a chuckle as he wiped the corner of her mouth and licked his finger.

"Hey, I was saving that," Beck teased back.

"Well, come on over here and take it back," he had said with a devilish grin.

She had laughed and leaned over the small black iron table to kiss him. Then, as they stood to leave, she realized she'd wiped nearly all of the powdered sugar from the table onto her black T-shirt.

Jack just smiled and shook his head, "I can't take you anywhere."

That evening as she prepared to visit Bourbon Street with her new friend, her husband was never far from her thoughts.

Tonight, she chose a royal blue, rayon evening dress, knowing it was his favorite color. But, as she pulled the sides of her hair up into Victory rolls, she wished he would come up and kiss that sensitive spot on the back of her neck.

But, if Beck was honest, that was the last time she thought about Jack Herman that evening. Ginny took her to the Old Absinthe House for dinner and drinks while they watched a fantastic dueling piano show. Next, they were off to the 500 Club, where they kicked up their heels to a lively band playing Dixieland jazz tunes.

As the night grew later, the ladies stopped by some of the smaller clubs with trios and quartets that played rhythm and blues and a different style of jazz called Bebop. However, they found these styles of music too complicated to dance to and returned to the 500 Club and danced until closing time.

The Crescent City was electric. There was excitement and music around every corner. Beck had forgotten just how much she loved the cuisine. For the first time in a long time, she felt like a participant in life instead of merely an observer.

Back at the house, she fell onto the bed. The music still buzzing in her brain while her feet tingled and her muscles ached from dancing. It was joyful exhaustion. *I could get used to this*, she admitted as she dozed.

However, a barely conscious Beck rolled over and reached for her absent husband, in the cold light of day.

CHAPTER 7

It took forever for Jack to reach the front door. The worry over his wife's disappearance had caused him to move in slow motion. He hoped against hope that she'd somehow be on the other side of the door or that they'd meet in the hallway on the way to answer it.

Instead, Marvin Ringgold, Ah Ooga's former saxophone player, was waiting patiently for Jack to open the door. He held a gold mailing envelope in his hand. When he caught sight of Jack as he opened the door, Marvin smiled gratefully.

"Marvin, come on in. I can't remember the last time I saw you," Jack said as he opened the door wider.

"The Farewell concert. Just over two years ago. One of my favorite memories," Marvin said as he and Jack sat in the living room.

"One of mine, too. May I offer you a drink?"

"I'll take some water, please. Yeah, I still can't believe you released a movie, married Beck, and performed that concert all in the same week. So much happiness and crazy all at once. It's enough to drive a man insane. "

Jack went into the kitchen to grab a glass. He called over his shoulder, "Yeah, well, it would be a short trip for me." As Jack returned with Marvin's water, he asked, "So, what brings you all this way?"

Marvin looked at the envelope for a moment and said, "Well, I'm afraid it's gonna be your turn to think I'm insane."

"Oh, I doubt that. What's going on?" Jack asked.

"I don't think I ever told you much about my family. We hailed from New Orleans. My people were Gens de couleur libres - free people of color. My great grandparents met at The French Opera House. He was a pianist and she was a soprano. When my grandfather was born in 1917, she retired," Marvin took a sip of water before he continued.

"A few years later, my great-grandfather died, leaving her a young single mother. She missed her husband playing piano while she sang, so my grandfather started taking lessons at age nine to make her happy. He became a jazz musician and later a composer; he played with all the greats. My parents were babies themselves when I came along, so I was raised mainly by my grandparents. My grandfather is one of my favorite people. Which leads me to the envelope you're staring at."

"You've piqued my curiosity."

"When I say that my grandfather played with all the greats, I mean people like Cab Calloway and Duke Ellington. He was as sharp as a tack, until one day, I told him I was going to be in a band with the great Jack Herman. Well he swore he'd played with you, too." Marvin shook his head.

"This was about the time we noticed other things were a bit off with his memory. Anyway, he gave me this envelope and made me promise to give it to you no earlier and no later than this evening. See the date on the envelope? October 22, 1995," Marvin said as he handed Jack the envelope. Some of the tension eased in his muscles as he leaned back against the couch. Jack thought he had the look of a man who was at the end of a long quest.

Jack took care opening the gold envelope. Inside was a smaller yellowed envelope that smelled of grass, almond, and finally vanilla. He held up the smaller envelope. It was addressed *To Jack - October 22, 1995*. Lots of people smelled of almond and vanilla. Hell, it could have been the smell of decaying ink and paper, which are similar, but Beck's handwriting was unmistakable.

Jack swallowed hard and asked, "Marvin, how long did your grandfather say he'd had this?"

"Nearly fifty years. Crazy, right?"

"Yeah, um, I'd like to be alone when I read this."

"Oh man, do you know how long I've waited to know what's inside that envelope? Can you at least tell me who it's from?" Marvin pleaded.

As Jack walked him to the door, he said, "You wouldn't believe me if I told you."

Marvin frowned as he crossed the threshold.

"Wait," Jack said. Marvin turned around, his face full of hope. "Could you please thank your grandfather for me?"

Marvin furrowed his brow. "Sure. If you want you can visit sometime. He's living with me now."

"I'd like that, but for now, please tell him the Red Devil says 'Hello.'"

Marvin stared at Jack, then said, "Yeah, sure thing, Man." Then he headed back to his car.

Jack poured himself another whiskey and grabbed the letter. Rufus was still resting on the rug in the jazz room and gave Jack a sniff as he entered. Up to a year ago, Rufus greeted every guest at the door, but the dog's arthritis had put a stop to that. Tonight, he hadn't even felt like barking at the doorbell. Jack set the letter on the nightstand and shrugged off his suspenders, then made himself comfortable on the rug with Rufus.

"We're on borrowed time, aren't we?" he asked as Rufus put his head in Jack's lap. His breathing was shallow.

Not wanting to disturb his ailing friend, Jack gingerly reached up and grabbed the letter from the nightstand. The first thing he noticed was the date, December 30, 1947.

My dearest Jack,

I'm not sure if you'll ever see this, but I have to try for both our sakes. For nearly two months now, I have been living in the French Quarter circa Fall 1947. I ran into a mutual friend of ours, and I plan to ask him to hold onto this letter until the evening of October 22,1995, since that was the day I left. I don't want you to worry about me a second longer.

I had a bumpy start, but now I have a place to stay, good friends, and a job. I miss you, but I'm keeping myself busy. It's how I carried on when I missed you during our marriage, and so far, it's an effective coping mechanism. Especially now that we're decades apart.

The nights and holidays are the hardest. At first, my nightgown smelled like you, and I'd shut my eyes tight and pretend you were holding me. But, your scent is nothing but a memory now. Sadly, I missed Halloween here and at home, but I spent Thanksgiving and Christmas with the Broussards. They're the family I'm staying with. They're kind and welcoming, but I miss our family. The feasts we'd have at your brother's house every November as he grilled Tri-tip and fried a turkey. I miss the dance we always shared on Christmas night. Soon I'll ring in the New Year without your kiss on my lips. It will be hard to start the year without you.

My dearest friend, I wanted to spend forever with you. We were supposed to be tethered together, and I'm still trying to understand how we unraveled. I've searched everywhere for you, and you're not here. I had hoped I could somehow make my way back to you, but I have been here nearly as long as I was in Harlem, so I think it's not meant to be.

I tried piecing together how I came to be here. But it makes no sense. I was sitting at my desk, feeling very upset after our fight. Thankfully, there was no head injury this time. But, It felt like I had just opened and closed my eyes, and here I was. The scenario has played in my head so many times I just can't stand to think of it anymore. I would have made very different choices if I had known it was my last day with you.

Anyway, the point of this letter wasn't to bring up bad feelings. What we had together mattered. I will always love you, but I'm grieving a man who hasn't even been born yet. The healing needs to start, and I need to follow your example as I did in Harlem. This new life isn't what we had, but it's all I have now, and I need to move boldly forward and embrace it.

My darling, I hope you will do the same. Please give our hellhound extra scratches behind the ears and belly rubs for me. Tell him Mommy loves him. Take time to be with those who love you best. You're going to be fine. You'll keep doing new things and reinventing yourself. Remember, I'll be there, in spirit, always.

I love you now and forever,
Beck

Jack stared at the letter. He couldn't believe that he'd lost Beck a second time. He swapped the letter for the whiskey, trying to process the situation. Why hadn't they traveled together? Was she right? Had they unraveled? She made it sound like something that had been going on for a while. Where was he?

How did I not notice my marriage was in trouble?

It had all been a whirlwind. They were reunited in the summer of 1993 and he had proposed immediately. Despite all the commitments he had Halloween week, he made room in his schedule for the ceremony on October 29th. It had been so much fun to work together on the score of her first movie. To watch her win an Oscar and come into her own.

Life had been good. They were busy. That's an understatement. But it had been incredibly fulfilling. No one could argue that he wasn't a real film composer anymore. He now had a shelf of awards for composing and a healthy net worth to prove it. They both did. Why wasn't that enough for her?

Jack finished the whiskey and re-read his wife's letter. His heart hurt to think he'd never see her again. Having wealth and prestige would mean nothing without her to share it with him. The last paragraph hit him the hardest. *Take time to be with those who love you best.*

Jack began to weep. "That's you, Beck. You love me best. I don't want to be without you," he said. His tears fell onto Rufus' red and cream fur. The dog lifted his eyebrows in an effort to look at Jack. The effort was only partially successful, resulting in a lop-sided stare from his ice-blue eyes. Exhausted by the movement, Rufus' head fell back down as he closed his eyes.

Jack set the whiskey back on the nightstand and scratched his dog behind his ears. "Hey, hellhound, here's some love from Mommy." This time Rufus didn't perk up at the mention of her name. Instead, Rufus' breathing was shallow. Jack pulled him into his lap and rubbed his belly as Beck had requested. All at once, Rufus let out a great sigh. It took Jack a moment to realize that it was his faithful companion's last breath.

"No, Rufus, no. You can't do this, not now. Please, I can't lose you both all in one day," Jack pleaded, but it was useless. His faithful companion of thirteen years was gone, and his wife was lost to him. Jack wrapped Rufus in the quilt from the end of the bed. Then, he returned to the kitchen to grab the bottle of whiskey.

This time, he poured a double; okay, if he was being honest, it was more like a triple. Then, he thumbed through his records until he landed on one of Cab Calloway's. The one with Saint James Infirmary, Beck's favorite. Jack couldn't recall how many times he played it nor how many glasses he poured himself before he had to lay down and close his red, swollen eyes.

CHAPTER 8

Beck read over the letter she'd just completed. The first five drafts lay crumpled at her feet. She wasn't overly confident in this version, but it was late, and she was out of paper. So, this one would have to do. Is there a perfect way to tell the love of your life goodbye?

She washed the fountain ink off of her hands and dressed for bed. Slipping into her nightgown that no longer smelled like her husband.

She hoped for sleep, knowing she'd have a busy night at the 500 Club tomorrow. But today had been a hard day. Her days off were often the hardest because she had plenty of time to think about Jack, their marriage, and where it had all gone wrong.

She usually coped by club hopping with her writer friends on Bourbon Street. Typically ending up at Cafe Lafitte's in Exile as it was friendlier to men of a certain persuasion. But tonight, she had needed to do some writing of her own.

It's time to quit bargaining and accept what I've lost. To look ahead instead of behind. However, the hell that's supposed to work in time travel.

The next evening, Ginny decided it would be fun for them to do each other's hair and makeup. Ginny watched Beck work on her hair in the mirror and frowned. "Poor Beck, I can't believe you have to work on New Year's Eve."

"At least I have a job I get to dress up for," Beck said as she put Ginny's curls in a dramatic updo.

"Well, I think it's perfectly awful. Wouldn't you rather be out on the town with a dashin' fella? We could have had a double date," Ginny said.

"I'm not interested. Besides, I think Sam would prefer to have you all to himself."

"Not interested? I see the company you keep. Spending all your nights off with a gaggle of men. The dark, brooding, and handsome man is a little old, I guess, but so smart. Then there's Mister, tall, blond, and British, and my personal favorite, the little blond boy with big blue eyes. He's so witty. He cracks me up. Why if I wasn't steady with Sam, I'd beg you to make an introduction," Ginny said with a giggle.

"You mean Truman?"

"Yes, that's him."

Beck didn't want to out her friend, so she said carefully, "Truman's spoken for."

"What about the other two?" Ginny asked

"The dark one, Tennessee, is off to New York. His new play is the toast of Broadway."

"Well, I guess that leaves Sir Lancelot," Ginny said, tripping over her Southern accent as she attempted to imitate a British one.

Beck chuckled. Ginny was making her laugh, but after many evenings at Cafe Lafitte's, she was sure that most, if not all, of her writer friends were gay. Which was preferable for Beck as her broken heart had no room for romantic entanglements. However, she knew that in the 1940s, that was considered unacceptable. So, she changed the subject.

"Should I wear the gold satin gown or the black strapless with the bolero jacket?" Beck asked.

Ginny took each gown and held them up to Beck in turn. "It's New Year's Eve; wear the gold. It will attract wolves."

"You're like a dog with a bone. Give it a rest. Will you?"

"I don't mean to push. I just want everyone to be as happy as I am," Ginny said as the housekeeper came in to let her know that Sam had arrived.

The 500 Club was already buzzing with activity when Beck arrived for her work shift. She had taken a job as a hostess at the 500 Club, but quickly made herself indispensable by helping with the dance hostesses and talent. When the manager of the club left two weeks ago, Beck's boss promoted her.

She took in the action, in attempt to prioritize her tasks. The dark cherry wood boards that made up the stage were crowded with musicians conducting a sound check. Many of the tables had been moved out in order to make room for dancing.

Satisfied that the front of house was in order, Beck smushed into the kitchen with the caterers and other servers, watching as small hors d'oeuvres were placed onto trays. Instead of serving full meals tonight, there would be just enough quick bites to keep the alcohol from taking effect too quickly.

Her boss Leon made his way through the melee in the kitchen. "Hey, Rebecca. That's some get-up. You look good. Listen, we may need you to help behind the bar closer to midnight," he said.

"Yes, Sir. We don't have many tables to seat this evening, so that should free me to help out wherever I'm needed."

"We're going to make the tables first come, first served. No meals are being served, so the tables are only there for tired patrons to rest or for the dance hostesses to entertain. Speaking of which, we got several important guests with reservations in the VIP rooms. Make sure the rooms are ready and check on the talent for me."

Beck made her way backstage which was packed with musicians and dance hostesses. She heard a knock at the door that led to the back alley where the black entertainers were required to enter.

They just returned from fighting for their country and still can't enter through the front door. It's ridiculous, Beck thought.

On the other side of the door was a quartet. The tall, lanky leader was an old friend. Beck smiled, "Evenin', Lowry. You know you don't go on until eleven thirty, right?"

"We know, but we're setting up at Famous Door in a few minutes, and our drummer can't find his brushes. Thought maybe they got left behind last night."

"It's crazy in here right now, but you're welcome to look," Beck said as she let the men in. Then, as Lowry passed by, she said, "Could I talk to you for a minute?"

"What's up?" Lowry asked.

"I feel like we need to clear the air," Beck began.

"Listen, if it's about the trouble I caused you and Jack in Harlem, I'm sorry," Lowry interrupted.

"It's forgiven. But I need to ask you a favor. It's a strange but important favor." Beck opened her handbag and pulled out the envelope containing her letter.

Lowry looked around to make sure no one was listening. Then he leaned toward Beck and said quietly, "Does this have something to do with where Jack's hiding out? Cause you know I'd do anything for the Red Devil."

"Yes, it does. I was hoping you could make sure he gets this letter on the exact date on the envelope, please."

Lowry raised his eyebrows as he looked at what she'd written,

"Hold the phone. You want me to hold onto this letter for forty-eight years? I can barely keep up with my hat. That's almost half a century, Woman. I could be dead by then."

"Then make arrangements to pass it down to someone. Please, Lowry, Jack has to get this."

"That cat will be in his nineties. Wait, what if he's dead by then?" Lowry asked.

"He'll be very much alive," Beck said confidently.

Lowry was quiet for a moment. He rubbed his chin, deep in thought. Then said, "All right. I'll take your word for it." Then he pocketed the envelope.

Suddenly, the lights flickered, and Lowry's bandmates stood beside him. "Did you find what you were looking for?" She asked. The drummer held up his brushes. "Great. I'd better check on whatever that was. See you guys later tonight. Lowry? Thank you from the bottom of my heart," she said. He nodded, and the band turned to go.

Beck had yet to learn where the fuse box was at the 500 Club. She preferred to stay out front and stick to her official duties as Club Hostess. The club wasn't big enough to accommodate an orchestra, so her skills as a stage manager weren't necessary. Most nights, she greeted the talent as they came in and ensured they were comfortable in the green room. Then, she would open the doors and seat the guests for dinner. Occasionally, she had helped out behind the bar. She met many interesting people and enjoyed working for Leon Prima, a jazz musician in his own right.

Most people in New Orleans believed Leon Prima to be the owner of the 500 Club, but it hadn't taken Beck very long to deduce that he was only the public face of the joint. The actual owner of the nightclub was Carlos Marcello, the newly minted Godfather of the New Orleans Mafia.

There were two businesses under one roof. Leon Prima's business was out front. A well-known restaurant, bar, and dance hall. If a man came in unaccompanied, he could enjoy a dance or two with a dance hostess who'd be paid for her time and hopefully tipped by the gentleman. It was legal and respectable.

The mafia, however, operated in the shadows. Known only to a particular clientele. Gaming rooms in the back contained blackjack tables and bookies. If the buzz from the bar wasn't enough, one could procure dope, cocaine, and opiates to loosen one's tensions and wallet. If a client preferred the ladies, certain dance hostesses would encourage them to sit a while and have a drink - or several.

It was an illegal practice known as B-drinking, where the bar would serve watered-down drinks, and the pretty lady would entice the customer to keep buying in hopes of a more intimate encounter later. A few of the ladies would cross that line, but Beck had no clue whether the mafia took their cut of that money. In fact, she decided that the less she knew about the underbelly of the 500 Club, the better.

Beck searched for the fuse box on her way to the VIP rooms. Finally, Ella, one of the dance hostesses, emerged from the first of the two rooms. She was a statuesque beauty who reminded Beck of Halle Berry. "Oh, hello, Ella. Everything in place in the VIP rooms?"

"I've only been in this one. It looked fine enough."

"Good, I'll check the other one. Say, do you know where I can find the fuse box?" Beck asked.

Ella frowned and pointed to one of the rooms with a blackjack table.

"I see. Thanks," Beck said as she played nervously with the finger where her wedding ring used to be.

"Miss Rebecca, would it be okay to take my supper break around eleven?"

"But, you're off at twelve. Do you need to go home early?"

Ella said quietly, "I could only get a sitter until eleven thirty."

"Oh, I didn't know you had a baby."

"Shh, I would prefer this stay between us," Ella whispered.

"Of course. I'll make sure you leave at eleven."

Conversations like this one reminded her just how different the times were. Though dance hostesses were expected to be single, they often secretly dated men they met at work and would typically quit once they were married. Beck deduced Ella must be a single mom, which would have been grounds for termination.

She peeked into the room where the fuse box was supposed to be and hesitated by the partially open door. There were several well-dressed men enjoying cocktails.

"I've reviewed the books, and it's not what we hoped. My operations in Florida do just as well with half the traffic," said a man with wavy brown hair and a hooked nose.

"Look, Meyer, I know it has been a rough start, but at least my joints don't get robbed all the time," said a round-faced man with slicked-back hair and a dimple in his chin.

"Yeah, Floridians can be meshuga. Who knew? Nonetheless, Carlos, we need a plan. How are we gonna move these numbers in the right direction before the Five Families meet?" Meyer asked.

"If we had slots that could lure more people back here. Act as a gateway to some of the bigger stuff. Think you could get your hands on some?"

"I could talk to Firelli, see what we got coming outta New York. How about you send some muscle to Florida, and I'll make sure the slots are here in time for Mardi Gras?"

"You know, I gotta few associates that look like they could use some sun. It's a deal," Carlos said as the men clinked glasses.

It was at that moment, Beck decided that all the lights were in working order. No need to hear anymore. If she had learned one thing from Harlem, it was the less she knew, the better. Besides, it was time to open the doors and welcome the revelers.

The evening flew by as Beck bounced from greeting patrons at the door to bartending. She even intervened when a few tipsy customers got handsy with the dance hostesses. In fact, one such unfortunate incident was what allowed Beck to send Ella home on time.

The man was tipsy but still aware of where his head was resting. When Beck saw Ella's discomfort, she made a beeline for the couple.

"Good evening, Sir. You look a little flushed. I'm going to need you to take a seat over here by the window just for a second," she said.

"You're mistaken, Dollface. I'm right as rain," the man slurred and drooled on Ella's chest.

"I'm afraid your sitting is not up for debate. But, I can offer you a seat with a beignet and a cup of coffee, or Bruno over there can help you find a seat out on the sidewalk," Beck said.

The man lifted his head and looked at Beck, then over at Bruno. "Now that you mention it, I am a little peckish."

Beck escorted him to a seat near the door and motioned for the bartender to send a cup of coffee over. "I'm so glad you decided to accept our hospitality. I'll be right back with a fresh beignet."

Before returning to the kitchen, Beck waved to Ella and mouthed, "Go home."

Ella exhaled and said, "Thank you."

Before she knew it, it was eleven forty-five, and Lowry's set was winding down.

She searched for her boss to introduce his band and play the set that would launch the club into 1948. She finally found Leon in one of the VIP rooms. He was green around the gills, while his companion Carlos was completely sober.

Beck said, "Leon? It's time for your band to play. It's almost midnight."

"Get Louie to do it."

"I can't. Your brother's still in New York."

"Excuse me, Doll, do I know you from somewhere?" Carlos asked. He'd been staring at her since she entered the room.

"I don't think so," Beck said, her shaky voice betraying her nervousness. Interacting with the Godfather was the last thing she wanted.

Leon tried to sit up but slid down the leather sofa onto the floor, "You're gonna have to do it, Rebecca, cuz I'm too drunk."

"I'll take care of it," Beck said as she turned to leave.

"Hey, wait," Leon said, "Do you play trumpet?"

"No, but I know someone who does," Beck said as she closed the door behind her. She sprinted to the green room just as Lowry and his band were packing up. "Lowry, do you have another gig tonight?"

"No. Why?"

"Leon Prima is soused. I need a trumpet player right now. Will you fill in for him?"

"You mean ring in the New Year onstage? Sure, that would be swell."

The two headed for the stage when the bass player blocked their way.

"What the hell's going on?" he snapped, "Where's Leon?"

"Your trumpet player's on a bender. I've brought you an excellent replacement. Please step aside," Beck said, struggling to keep her voice even.

"This ain't the Dew Drop Inn. We don't have integrated acts here in the quarter," the bass player protested.

"Well, we do tonight," Beck said as she and Lowry skirted around the man.

While Lowry adjusted his music on the stand, Beck realized that Leon's absence meant she was down a trumpet player and an MC.

She would have to wing it. "Ladies and gentlemen, we are five short minutes away from midnight. Our servers are circulating with champagne flutes. Please grab one as we prepare to toast the New Year. Now, for your listening pleasure, please welcome the Leon Prima Band featuring special guest Lowry Ringgold on trumpet."

Relieved that the party was back on track, Beck surveyed the crowd, ensuring every patron had their glass of bubbly. Finally, she checked in with Nash at the bar, "Great job. Everyone has a glass, and we're good to go."

"Not everyone, Love," said a man with a British accent. Beck turned and saw her friend Victor standing next to her. He was holding out a champagne flute to her.

"You're going to need that," Beck said.

"Mine's right here," Victor said, indicating a full flute sitting on the bar.

"Thank you," Beck said as she accepted the glass. She couldn't help but admire his towering slender form dressed to the nines. The way his blond hair slid down almost obscuring his right eye. "You're so dashing in that tux. Way too classy for this joint. It's not a white tie event, you know, or even a black tie event, really."

Truman popped out from behind Victor, "Oh, we know, Sweetie. We were at a very chic dinner this evening, but Victor wouldn't shut up about how much he missed you."

Victor stammered, "N-no, I only said -- What I said was that it didn't seem right that you had to work while we were all celebrating and we should stop by and cheer you up."

"Your words exactly were, 'Poor Becks, who will kiss her at midnight?' So here we are, Doll. Pucker up," Truman said with a smirk.

Just then, the crowd began to chant, "Ten, nine, eight, seven, six, five, four, three, two, one. Happy New Year!"

Black and gold confetti rained from the ceiling as Lowry led the band in Auld Lang Syne.

Victor had a piece of confetti near his eye, so Beck reached up to wipe it away. As he half closed his eyes and moved his face toward hers, Beck offered him her cheek. Victor gave her a soft peck as Truman stood awkwardly by. Beck gave Truman a quick peck on his cheek, and he stood on his tiptoes and quickly planted a kiss on Victor's cheek.

They're adorable, she thought.

Touched that her friends had shown up for her, she raised her glass and proposed a toast, "To new friends, a new start, and a happy new year." The trio clinked glasses and finished their champagne.

As Lowry and the band finished their set, Beck went to check on them.

"Lowry, thank you so much for jumping in at the last second."

"My pleasure. Happy New Year, Rebecca," Lowry said. He tipped his hat and headed out into the cold, dark alley.

While it was good to see a familiar face, Beck couldn't think of Lowry without thinking of Jack. Every time they spoke, she remembered Harlem and how she first fell in love with Jack Herrman. Especially when Lowry called him the Red Devil. *No, I'm not going to go there. New friends, a new start, a new year. That was the entire reason for writing that letter. To let go of Jack and move on.*

Once the green room was cleared and in order, Beck checked the VIP rooms. One of the dance hostesses emerged with a man who looked Italian. They were both straightening their clothes.

She had accounted for all but two of her dance hostesses, and a "do not disturb" sign was on the second VIP room.

She made her way back to the front. "Hey Nash, have you seen Rita and Betty?"

Nash didn't look up from the glass he was drying as he muttered, "VIP room. You taking off?"

"I thought I might, but I should check in with Leon."

"VIP room," Nash said again.

"Oh, then I won't disturb him."

"Best not to. He's meeting with Mr. Marcello."

The implications were uncomfortable, Carlos Marcello was the godfather. What on earth was Leon mixed up in?

Beck ran a hand through her hair, and confetti littered the floor encircling her. She heard the custodian groan. "I'm so sorry. I'll get it," she said as she went to grab a broom, with each step, she left a shimmery trail. "Aw, grits," she exclaimed.

A loud guffaw came from the far corner of the room near the jukebox. "Stop, stop. You're getting it absolutely everywhere. Where can I find a broom?" Victor asked between bouts of laughter.

Nash offered him one from behind the bar. Then, as Victor walked past Beck, she stepped toward him. "You really don't need to do this."

Victor broke up again and held out a hand for her to stop. Then, he grabbed one of the unclaimed champagne flutes from the bar and handed it to Beck, "Here, have a drink, and don't move. I'll clean up Beck's Comet."

"Thank you. Where did Truman go?" Beck asked.

"Off to another party, I suppose," Victor answered as he handed the broom back to Nash.

Beck tilted her head. "You didn't want to go?"

"I thought I'd see you home and get back to my place for a few hours of shut-eye before the reading tomorrow."

"Your play's finished?"

"Only the first act," Victor explained. "I must admit I've lost all motivation to finish the damned thing."

"Oh no, writer's block?"

"Hardly, I know exactly how it's going to end, but once it's done, I'm afraid my time here will be finished," Victor glanced away then said, "I'm not ready for that."

"I know all about leaving places before you're ready," Beck said.

"Is that so?"

"It's a story for another time," Beck said as casually as she could. "Speaking of stories, I sent the one about the Voodoo Lady into Fantasy Book. So, fingers crossed."

"Brilliant! That's one of my favorites. Say, why don't we cut a rug before we take off?" Victor asked.

"I'm not much of a dancer," Beck said.

"Bullocks, you can follow my lead, and we'll be moving in no time." he fished a nickel out of his pocket and said, "Here, you pick the song. That way, it's one you're familiar with."

Beck walked over to the Wurlitzer and scanned the titles hoping there was at least one she was familiar with that wasn't too fast. She found *La Vie En Rose* in the middle column. A beautiful song with a simple rhythm to it. When she turned around, Victor was waiting in the center of the dance floor, hand extended.

"Excellent choice. May I have this dance?"

"Of course," Beck said.

He led her in a slow waltz which she struggled with, but he was a skilled and patient dancer. "Parlez vous Francais?" he asked.

"No," Beck said apologetically.

"Well, you understood that much," he said with a silly grin that made her giggle. "I wondered why a proper lady such as yourself would pick such a filthy French song."

Beck blushed. "Is it really?"

"I'm only joking. The literal translation is Life in Pink or figuratively life through rose-colored glasses. She's singing about still being able to find love after a trying time," he said as he smiled down at her.

"Thanks for telling me. I love it even more now." The music stopped, and Beck frowned. "I forgot it was such a short song."

"I happen to have more than one nickel, Love. Shall we play it again?"

"I could use more dance practice. In fact, if you're looking for a job, I think it's about time we had a male dance host," she said with a grin.

Victor laughed, putting another nickel in the Jukebox. "Oh, that would be a fun telegram home 'Dearest Mum and Dad, I've traded my prestigious career in the theatre to become... a Taxi dancer.'"

"Hey, don't knock it. Some of the ladies make an excellent living," Beck said.

"We both know that's not all they're doing," Victor said.

"Most of them are on the up and up."

"If you say so," he said as he took her hand, "They're playing our song." As the song played over again, Victor sang along. When the song was finished. She said, "I didn't know you sang."

"I'm a man of many talents."

She noticed he'd not let go of her even though the song was over. It was so comforting to be held that she had taken a while to notice. She gently shrugged off his arms. "We should go. Nash is about to close up."

"Shall I walk you home?" Victor asked.

"Not yet."

"Then where to, Milady?"

"Let's go to Cafe Lafitte's and relax. Maybe we'll catch up with Truman."

"I don't want you to get your hopes up about Truman. The boy has likely found a warm bed for the night. You know he prefers the company of men. Don't you?"

"I think it's rather obvious."

"I've seen many ladies fall for him and the ensuing misunderstandings. I would hate to see you get hurt," Victor added as they reached the cafe.

"I won't. Truman is a pretty boy, and you, my friend, look like his slightly older brother. But I understand the situation, and I'm not looking for anything like that, which is why I like Lafitte's," she said as they walked into the cafe. The party was still very much alive. The perfect place to unwind after a long day.

Around three o'clock in the morning, Beck realized she had relaxed a little too much. She saw a man at the bar with red curly hair about five foot ten inches tall. Her heart raced as she approached. She touched him on the shoulder. "Jack?" she asked.

The person who turned around looked nothing like her husband. "Oh, sorry. I thought you were someone I used to know." Humiliated and sad, Beck retreated to a quiet corner. Trying to fight back the tears.

Victor came over and put a hand on her shoulder."I'm afraid we've gone from happy tipsy Becks to sad drunk Becks. Am I right?" She nodded. "Then, let's get you home, Love."

Bourbon Street was packed with revelers even drunker than Beck was, so Victor cut over to the much quieter Royal Street. They passed the Court of Two Sisters. Yet another man with copper curls was out in front of the restaurant sitting in a chair with his head resting on the iron table. Beck felt a jolt of recognition and wanted to shake Jack awake so badly.

But, then realized how impossible it would be for Jack to be there. She talked herself out of approaching the man as she remembered the sting of humiliation from the other "not Jack" at Cafe Lafitte's. Keeping a steady pace, she walked on by.

CHAPTER 9

The sun streaked the sky with reds, golds, and oranges. Jack might have appreciated the magnificent sunrise if he wasn't so damn sore. He saw the spectacle through one opened eye as he slowly peeled his aching head off the wrought iron table. He had no idea how long he had been sitting there, but if his stiff back was any indication, it had been hours.

He rubbed the sides of his pounding head and found creases in his skin that matched the table that had been his pillow. Instead of fighting with himself over this new reality, he sat up and accepted it. He willed the other eye to open and took in his surroundings. The French Creole architecture was so unique that he recognized New Orleans immediately.

Don't be so sure. Maybe you woke up at Disneyland. He heard his wife joke inside his head. Jack scrutinized the cigarette butts at his feet and noted the strip club across the street. Nope, not Disneyland. This was the real deal.

It was early, but the few cars that drove by were decidedly vintage. The few men he saw were dressed in suits, so it was hard to discern the decade from their attire.

Finally, a woman walked past Jack with a large Standard Poodle wearing a jeweled collar. The lady's jacket had shoulder pads that could put an eye out. He remembered Beck telling him about the trend that would become popular in the Forties back when they were in Harlem. For the first time, he dared to hope that the so called tether the Voodoo Lady said was between them was pulling them back together.

Jack wandered around the French Quarter, trying to remember his way around the landscape, which only bore a slight resemblance to the French Quarter he had just visited for Tom's wedding. His head ached from overindulging in whiskey the night before. The hangover had apparently traveled back in time with him. He was thrilled to find drinking fountains outside a tobacco shop. Yet, he was disgusted to see that the water fountains were segregated, with one designated for "whites" and one for "colored people."

The water certainly wasn't the best he'd ever tasted, but it helped hydrate him enough to ease the pain.

He finally saw a familiar landmark as he made his way up Toulouse Street. It was a large, beautiful American townhome-style building with red-orange paint and creamy yellow trim. The second floor featured an ornate black wrought iron balcony with matching black shutters on the windows. It was The Olivier House Hotel where he and Beck stayed for the wedding.

The hotel looked very much like it did in 1995, but upon closer inspection, there was a different sign by the door. Instead of the hotel's name, it read "Bessy Brown's Boarding House."

A flash of holding Beck the morning of Tom's wedding went through his mind. They were on the top floor, and she had opened the doors to the balcony and climbed back into bed. There was a slight nip in the air that October morning, but their shared body heat was cozy under the covers. He couldn't remember just what they'd talked about, but he could still hear the music of her laughter.

He wandered further up Toulouse toward Rampart Street, sure of his path. As he reached North Rampart, he heard the soothing sounds of a drum circle. Intrigued, Jack crossed the street, leaving the French Quarter, as he entered Congo Square.

The drumming was not an ordinary jam session. Jack soon realized that a Voodoo ritual was taking place. As he watched, a man selling apples approached, "Are ya hungry, Sir? I got two apples for a dime."

Jack fished a dime out of his pocket, confident that the date on it was after the 1940s. He was afraid the man would notice and accuse him of passing him a counterfeit coin. But, the man simply pointed to his wooden apple tray that had a coin box with a tiny padlock on the lid. Jack placed his dime in the slot and chose his apples.

The fruit helped calm his stomach, which had intermittently rumbled since he had arrived, but he couldn't be sure whether it was from hunger or the hangover.

After finishing his first apple, he went to throw the core in the garbage. On top was a freshly read newspaper. He checked the date. Thursday, January 1, 1948. He fished Beck's letter out of his shirt pocket and checked the date. It read December 30, 1947. His heart skipped a beat. Not only had he made it to the time and place where she was, but he had also made it just two days after Beck had written to him.

Distracted by the music from the voodoo ceremony, but not wanting to disturb the sacred ritual, Jack kept to the perimeter of the square. Finally, when it was complete, a man waved him over. "You seemed interested in our ceremony."

"I didn't mean to intrude. The drums reminded me of music I heard when I visited West Africa years ago," Jack explained.

"We use the drums to awaken our ancestors and the spirits in hopes that they will intercede on our behalf with the Almighty," the man explained. "We came here today to call on the goddess Oshun to help settle a feud between our brothers."

"Oshun?"

"The goddess of diplomacy and healing. Among other things," the man said as he strapped his drum to his back and placed a Mandarin orange next to the trunk of the largest oak tree at the edge of the square. "You seem troubled, my brother. I sense an ache in your heart. Trouble with a woman?"

"Is it that obvious?" Jack scoffed.

"You may want to consider making an offering to Oshun. She's also the goddess of love, intimacy, and fertility, after all."

"Well, I certainly don't need that last one. But if I did decide to, you know, at some point, make an offering, how would I do it exactly?" Jack asked.

"You would pray to your ancestors past, present, and future, as well as Oshun, ask them to call on God to fix what's broken. Then, you'd place an offering at the foot of the Ancestor Tree," the man said, indicating the large oak they were standing under.

"Oh, so I could just leave my apple here?" Jack said as he placed it next to the man's mandarin.

"Don't forget to pray."

"Okay, so I pray to all the ancestors and Oshun, then I place my apple at the base of the Ancestor Tree. Is that all?"

"Well, if you've really messed up, you should probably pray to Saint Jude, too."

"Who?" Jack asked.

"The patron saint of lost causes," the man said with a grin. "Be well, my brother," he called over his shoulder as he left the square.

Once the square was empty, Jack thought about how peculiar New Orleans Voodoo was. It was a unique blend of West African rituals and the Catholicism practiced by the French and Spanish settlers. It felt strange at first, but he bowed his head and prayed, realizing that his ancestors were genuinely located in the past, present, *and* future. He asked help from the goddess whose name he had already forgotten and finally asked Saint Jude to please intercede if all was truly lost. He didn't know where his next meal was coming from, but if there was a chance that his remaining apple could help mend things with his wife, he would choose to sate the longing in his heart over the hunger in his belly.

With hope for a blessing from forces he wasn't sure he even believed in, Jack continued his exploration of the area beyond the French Quarter. The faces and buildings changed in this area of New Orleans. It was clear that the inhabitants here were less fortunate than the residents south of Rampart Street.

The street's large potholes and roofs in need of repair from storms dotted the landscape. Old Creole cottages stood next to a relatively new collection of homes. The sign at the entrance read "The Lafitte," which he assumed was an homage to the pirate. *How odd to name a neighborhood after a criminal.* Even the townhomes in the newer housing development were already in need of repair.

"Ain't you on the wrong side of the street?" asked an older black man who passed by with groceries in his arms.

"I'm looking for a friend of mine."

"You ain't from around here, are you, son?" the man asked as he narrowed his eyes at Jack.

Jack didn't want any trouble, so he grinned and said, "You're right. What gave me away?"

"You talk funny, and you don't seem to know that your kind sticks to the east side of St. Louis Street and the South of Rampart. You lost? Most out-of-towners head south to the Quarter."

"Like I said, I'm looking for a friend."

"I done told you this neighborhood is coloreds only," the man said, running out of patience.

"Where I'm from, black and white people are friends. Why is it so hard for you to believe I have a black friend?"

The man scoffed and said, "Now I know you from somewhere far away. That kind of thing don't happen here. White folks only want us across the street to entertain them and then go home."

"Are you a musician?" Jack asked.

"I play bass. You ever heard of **the Three Hair or Four Hair Combo**?"

Jack chuckled at the name before he could help himself. Then said, "I'm sorry. I can't say that I have. Why is it Three or Four Hair?"

"Depends on how many of us are sober enough to play. We perform down at Club Caledonia most nights. Our leader's Professor Longhair."

Jack raised his eyebrows. "You mean Roy Boyd, the jazz pianist?"

The man stood taller. "That's right."

"I'm a musician, too," Jack said.

"Who do you play with?"

"I'm in between bands right now."

"What do you play?" the man asked.

"I sing, play piano, percussion, violin, trombone, and a little guitar," Jack replied.

"Humph, show off," the man said with a smirk, "Where you played at before?"

"I played up in New York City, but it's been a while," Jack said. He was afraid that mentioning the Cotton Club would be seen as further bragging.

"Some fine clubs up there. Name's Oscar Bastien," he said, shifting his groceries to one arm and offering to shake hands.

"Jack Herman," Jack said as he extended his hand to shake.

Oscar's jaw dropped. "Not the Red Devil from the Cotton Club?"

"You've heard of me?"

"I heard the Cotton Club Revue on the radio. You're aces, my man. Bet you have some stories. I was just about to cook up some red beans and rice. Wanna swap some tales over brunch?"

"I'd like that," Jack said. He grinned and followed Oscar into his modest cottage. *Even in the segregated South, music unites,* he thought.

As the men finished their meal, Oscar suddenly looked at Jack and said, "So, you looking for Lowry Ringgold?"

"Yes, I wasn't sure if he was back in town."

"He moved back here after the war."

"I didn't know he served. I thought he was still on tour with the Duke," Jack said.

"They put that new tax on dancing, so club owners stopped booking big bands. Even the Duke's orchestra. Duke packed up and went on tour overseas," Oscar explained.

"I'm surprised Lowry didn't go with him," Jack muttered.

"Say, you should catch our band at the 500 Club tonight. Leon Prima owns the place, so he has the prime time slot, of course. We play after him for the next couple of nights. Lowry's quartet is closing out the evening."

"That sounds swell. I'll see you there," Jack said.

As Jack explored further, the day turned into evening, and Jack found himself dozing under a tree in Congo Square. A lone guitarist playing the blues woke Jack from his slumber. He decided it was time to go in search of Lowry and Beck.

The French Quarter was a musical smorgasbord. Around every corner was a little club or a large dancehall, each with a different genre of music. He heard a steel drum band in a tiny club that smelled of jerk chicken.

A large dancehall two doors down featured a lively crowd dancing to an amplified band with an accordion player, steel guitarist, fiddler, drummer, and two more guitar players. After watching and tapping his toe a bit, he noted that the accordion had the melody with lead lines carried by the steel guitar and fiddle, respectively. The crowd was dressed down. Women wore cotton dresses, men wore jeans, and people of both genders wore overalls.

He finally located Bourbon Street and discovered he was in the red light district. There were strip clubs mixed in among the brothels. Both had music pouring out their windows. Several had "Now Hiring: Musicians" signs in the windows.

After a couple of blocks, the brothels disappeared, and the music clubs mingled with the strip clubs. Even a number of the mainstream clubs advertised burlesque shows on particular nights. In between joints with sex for sale in various forms, there were tobacco shops and drug deals. Any kind of vice could be indulged in the Big Easy.

The exteriors of the clubs grew more opulent as Jack made his way to the place where Bourbon Street intersected with the epicenter of the French Quarter. On the 200 block, he wandered into the Old Absinthe House, an ancient watering hole with a large mahogany bar.

Onstage a band playing what they called Jump Blues, a cross between blues and swing, brought the crowd to their feet. Jack attempted to order absinthe as he took in the atmosphere, but left empty-handed as the spirit had been banned since 1912.

It was getting late, and Jack was worried he had missed the music at the 500 Club. Suddenly, a familiar piece of music from his past drifted out of an open door. He looked up and saw the sign for the 500 Club and took a seat at the bar. He was just in time to watch Lowry play two pieces he had written for the Cotton Club Revue. Jack reminisced while he sipped a whiskey he bought with yet another dime from the future.

As Lowry finished his set Jack ran around to the alley. Oscar had told him that black entertainers were never allowed in the club. Once again, Jack was reminded of how slowly things had changed for people of color after the war.

Fifteen minutes later, Lowry appeared in the alley with his quartet. Offstage, Jack noticed that Lowry was no longer the bright-eyed twenty-one-year-old kid he had met in New York. He was still fit and lean with a handsome face, but it was obvious that the thirty-year-old had been through a lot. His shoulders were slightly hunched, and worry had left light creases on the corners of his eyes and mouth, hinting at the tragedies of the past decade.

One by one, Lowry's bandmates departed, leaving him the last one to emerge from the alley. He caught sight of Jack and ran over to his friend hugging him. As he pulled back and looked at Jack's face, Lowry said, "Well, if it isn't the ole Red Devil himself. Lawd, you haven't aged a day."

"Look at you. You're all grown up."

Lowry looked away and said, "Yeah, well, a lot happens in ten years."

"I heard you served in the war," Jack said.

"The Army, 333rd Division. Hell, of a way to see Europe. You serve?"

Jack looked at his feet. "No."

Lowry narrowed his eyes, then said, "Guess you were too old?"

"Exactly," Jack said as he scrambled to do the math in his head. Lowry would expect him to be almost forty-nine if he had left Harlem when he was thirty-nine years old. Seven years older than his actual age.

"You sure look good for your age," Lowry said, "If you didn't go to war, where did you go? I know you weren't in New York."

The two began to walk towards North Rampart Street in the direction of Lowry's neighborhood. There was so much that needed to be said, but the emotion behind it was so strong that an activity, even the simple act of walking, took the edge off. If the men were required to say the hard things, at least the necessity of facing forward spared them from having to look one another in the eyes.

"I'm sorry I left without saying goodbye," Jack mumbled.

"I figured you were hiding out after what happened with Pipes and Rebecca. I looked for you everywhere, and asked other musicians I met if they'd seen you. Of course, no one had."

"Listen, what happened to Pipes was an accident. I was just trying to save her," Jack said quickly.

"Mr. Burton told me. He was my downstairs neighbor. Saw the whole thing. He thought Rebecca was dead. After a while, we all thought you might be dead, too."

"I'm sorry I couldn't reach out. I mean that I didn't reach out," Jack said.

"I'm sorry I put your lady in danger," Lowry said as he patted Jack's arm. "You here looking for work?"

Jack wasn't sure how to answer that. His main reason for being in New Orleans was to find his wife. Still, if the opportunity to play music and make money presented itself, he certainly wouldn't pass it up. "Looks like there's a lot of places in need of musicians."

"It's easier for folks that look like you."

"It always is, isn't it?" Jack said sympathetically.

"It's worse here than it was in Harlem. It's actually against the law for us to share the stage or live together."

Jack stared at Lowry wide-eyed. "That's crazy."

"That's life in the Deep South," Lowry said with a shrug, "I know quite a few bands that would love to have "The Red Devil" play with them."

"Really?" Jack was surprised and a bit unnerved that so many people knew of him.

"Yeah, a man like you could do well here. It's different. No more house orchestras, but you can work with different bands at different clubs. Why don't we meet up at the Cobweb Club tomorrow at five? I gotta gig there at six, and I can introduce you to some of the other musicians before I go on," Lowry said as they approached the Lafitte Housing Development.

Jack had been hoping for a place to stay but didn't want to cause Lowry any trouble, so he said, "Yeah, I guess we can meet up tomorrow."

"I'm back at the 500 Club later in the evening if that suits you better. But, I guess Rebecca can always introduce you around there."

"Rebecca? My Beck?" Jack asked, unable to hide the surprise in his voice.

"Yeah, I'm surprised that she hasn't already."

"You know where she is?"

"I thought that was why you were at the 500 Club, to pick up your dame. She's just about to close up. You didn't know? Are you two not together?" Lowry asked, but Jack was already heading back toward Rampart Street.

"I gotta go," Jack called over his shoulder.

CHAPTER 10

The last two nights of restless sleep were catching up to Beck. New Year's Day had brought a small yet demanding crowd to the club. It didn't help that the kitchen had run out of black-eyed peas halfway through the evening. She had run to the market, but it was a futile errand. Every Southerner knows that to have good luck going into the new year, one must eat a meal of hog jowl, collard greens, cornbread, and black-eyed peas on January first.

Beck's grandmother had been so desperate for her to safeguard her luck each year that she would beg her to consume at least one single black-eyed pea. But they disgusted Beck, so she'd swallow it whole like a pill.

Naturally, the audience was convinced that she and the staff of the 500 Club had doomed them all to a tragic 1948. But, in the end, her boss offered them half-price beer, and suddenly all was forgiven. Beck finished her duties and headed for the door, anxious to put the night behind her.

"Oh good, I'm not too late," Victor said, holding the door for her.

"Too late for what?"

"I thought I'd walk you home if you don't mind," he said, offering Beck his arm.

The walk from the 500 Club to the Broussard's was only a block up St. Louis Street, but it was well past midnight in the city, and she enjoyed her friend's company. "Thanks, that would be nice," Beck said as she took his arm and led him onto the sidewalk, turning toward Continental Street. "Let's take the long way," she said.

Jack sprinted down St. Louis Street and stopped at the corner of St. Louis and Bourbon, next to the 500 Club. He stopped to catch his breath, noticing the lights were all shut off. Nonetheless, he checked the door. The place was locked and empty. Jack hung his head and sighed.

Then, he heard it. The music of Beck's laughter rang out through the darkness.

Up ahead was a couple walking arm in arm. Perhaps his wife was just beyond the pair. He walked up Bourbon Street, listening for her. Hoping she'd make that sweet sound again so he could find her. As the couple walked under the streetlamp, Jack noticed that the woman had a beautiful head full of auburn curls. It was at that moment that he heard Beck's laugh a second time. That's when he realized that Beck was not beyond the couple. She was the other half of the couple.

Fuming, Jack followed some distance behind them. Was this why she wrote him a goodbye letter? Beck had said that she needed to stop grieving him. Well, it appeared that she damn well had. Jack turned his attention to his rival. The man was tall, blond, and, wait, was he speaking with a British accent?

Ugh. Beck had loved hearing the Brits talk when they were in London. Worst of all was how at ease they seemed with one another. This was not the first time they had walked somewhere together. That was obvious. *Exactly how long had this been going?*

As the two walked, they compared notes about their evening. Beck told Victor all about the Black Eyed Peas Disaster while he regaled her with stories from his rehearsal.

"It's not funny, Becks. The girl is bloody awful, but she's the producer girl, so we can't replace her. The poor cast is being held hostage while she chews the scenery. It's a complete and utter mess. So, our director finally gives her a note tonight to reign it all in a bit, and she goes off and makes a huge kerfuffle."

Beck giggled, "A what?"

"A kerfuffle. You know, crying to her Daddy and whatnot."

"Kerfuffle? We don't have that word here. I love it," she said as they reached the corner of Dauphine and St. Louis. "Would you like to come up for a nightcap?"

"I can come up for a quick one. You sure the Broussards won't mind?"

"They're asleep, and we'll be quiet," Beck said as they entered the house.

Jack really wanted to hit something. Okay, if he was honest, he wanted to hit someone.

That Brit's so damn tall I'd have to run and jump up to punch him.

Jack heard voices on the balcony above as he was about to leave. He flattened himself like a pancake against the courtyard wall and listened.

"Isn't it the most beautiful thing you've ever seen?" He heard Beck ask the man.

"One of, I mean, I-It's spectacular," the man stammered in a breathy way.

After a few minutes of pointing out landmarks and discussing stories, they'd written. The pair disappeared inside. "Great. He's a writer, and he's British, and he's tall," Jack grumbled to himself.

"Oh, pardon me," the man said as he accidentally swung the courtyard door into Jack, knocking him onto the sidewalk, "Are you alright?" the man asked, offering his hand to help Jack back to his feet.

"I'm fine. Just looking for someone."

"I haven't been in the area long, but perhaps I can help. I'm Victor Shadly, by the way. Who is it you're looking for?"

"Her name is Rebecca Herman," Jack said, waiting for a reaction.

"I know a Rebecca, but no Hermans. Sorry."

It took a minute to sink in that Beck might not be using their last name. "Sometimes she goes by Taylor. Beck Taylor."

"Oh. Yes. I know Becks," Victor said with a warm smile.

He has a nickname for her? Who does he think he is?

As Jack fumed, Victor continued, oblivious to his anger: "Ah, I see it now."

"What? "Jack asked.

"The resemblance, the red hair. You must be Beck's father. It's an honor to meet you, sir. Your daughter is remarkable. You must be so proud."

Jack's fists clenched. He felt his blood boil. Through gritted teeth, he said, "I'm not her father."

Victor blushed, "Oh, I beg your pardon. Older brother, then?"

"I'm her husband," Jack said forcefully.

Victor looked like a deer caught in headlights. "Becks never told me she was married."

Jack and Victor stared at one another until they heard footsteps in the courtyard.

"Victor, are you still down here? I thought I heard voices," Beck said as she stepped onto the sidewalk. She stood between the two men and looked up at her husband, astonished to see him. "Jack? You're here?" she asked breathlessly.

"I really think I-I should leave you to it," Victor stammered as he walked hurriedly away.

The two stood frozen on the sidewalk. Beck looked at Jack through tears that threatened to spill from her eyes. There were so many emotions inside her that it was hard to handle.

"I can't believe you're here," she managed to whisper. She reached for Jack, but he leaned away from her. His arms crossed over his chest, jaw clenched.

"Don't touch me," he snapped.

"What's wrong?"

"What's wrong?" Jack scoffed, "I followed you here."

Beck tilted her head. "What?"

Then he added, "All the way from the 500 Club. I saw you hanging all over that man."

"That's not what I was doing. I was just --"

Beck's attempt to explain was cut off by the arrival of a large black Chevrolet. The car pulled up to a stop at the curb, and in the light of the gas lamp, they could read the word POLICE on the side of the vehicle.

"Good morning," the officer said as he exited the car and approached the couple. Jack and Beck returned his greeting. "Are you Rebecca Taylor, Ma'am?"

"Yes, Officer. How may I help you?" Rebecca asked.

The officer immediately threw Beck up against the car, causing her to hit her head on the hood as he cuffed her wrist. Jack flashed back to Pipes nearly killing her in Harlem. Without considering the consequences, he grabbed the officer's shoulder, pulling him away from Beck before he could secure her other wrist.

"Get the hell away from her," Jack shouted. The officer spun so quickly on Jack that he didn't see the man's fist before it connected with his face. Jack fell to the sidewalk for the second time in an hour. He sat momentarily stunned, holding his sore jaw. Then, before he could get up on his own, the officer dragged him to his feet.

"Come on, you twit. If you're so dizzy for this dame, you can wear matching bracelets, the officer said. He cuffed Jack's wrist into the empty cuff.

"What's this about, Officer?" Jack asked.

"Seems Miss Taylor here is a dirty little coon lover. She integrated the New Year's Eve show at the 500 Club by putting her darky boyfriend on stage with an all-white band. The good citizens of this town don't need that kind of indecency in their faces, ruining their holiday."

Red-faced and trembling, Beck said, "So, the nights when we feature half-naked burlesque dancers shaking their asses are a-okay, but the minute we have fully clothed men who happen to be different colors take the stage to play music, the "good citizens" are offended? That's bollocks!"

The officer's eyes never left Jack's, "You better control your broad. She's got quite the potty mouth. Now, ya better both get in the car before I makes ya. It would be a shame if your lady hit her head again."

Jack looked at Beck just in time to see a small trickle of blood escape her nostril. His body tensed, and panic set in as he remembered how she'd tumbled down the stairs in Harlem.

Their eyes met, and he looked at her and then into the back of the police car and back to her. He was relieved as she climbed willingly into the back seat.

They were taken out of the handcuffs at the station for fingerprinting and mugshots. But their freedom from one another was temporary as the officer soon cuffed them together again.

"Hey Copper, what gives?" Beck said as the cold metal pinched her wrist. Jack looked at her, puzzled.

She shot him a look. "Yes, Mister-Know-It-All. I've learned the lingo," she whispered.

Jack shook his head "From a James Cagney movie, maybe."

"Well, you two lovebirds were so keen on getting arrested together, so you can cool your heels in the same cell," the officer sneered as he pushed them inside.

"At least take off the handcuffs," Jack said.

"Don't feel like it," the officer said, closing the cell.

"This is bollocks," Beck said as she sat on the only bed. Jack joined her. As she looked at their surroundings, she took inventory. Three cinder block walls, a fourth with bars, one bed, one sink, and, to her horror, one toilet. As a married couple, she and Jack had been in the bathroom at the same time. However, one was usually occupied with bathing or shaving while the other did their business unobserved. Certainly, never while chained together.

Jack's anger had been on pause since the police officer had hurt his wife. In the back of the police car, he had handed her his handkerchief to stop the nosebleed. He'd relished being close to her after he'd thought he'd never see her again.

But then she'd gone and said something not once but twice that pushed play on the fury he' felt when he saw her with another man.

"So, Bullocks, huh? Where did you get that word from?

"I dunno, it's something people say here." Beck shrugged.

"No, they don't. You learned that from your British boyfriend."

Beck sighed, looking at the ceiling. "Victor is just a friend."

"Don't lie to me. I saw you walking arm and arm. You giggled at every dumb thing he said. I know that giggle. I know what it means," Jack growled.

"You're not making any sense."

"It's your flirty giggle. I know because you used to use it with me," Jack said. He sighed, feeling like such a fool. For comfort, he ran his hand through his copper curls. Frustrated with the knowledge that even now, he wished it was her deceitful little hand with her long, delicate fingers entangled in his hair.

"I never stopped flirting with you. You stopped noticing," Beck said, the volume of her voice growing.

"Not this again. We're both busy and successful. Other people would kill to have the opportunities we've had. What am I supposed to do? Quit?"

"I never asked you to quit. I just asked you to remember that you're married."

"Well, I might ask the same of you."

Beck gasped. "That's low, Jack Herman. I've already explained the nature of my relationship with Victor to you."

"How did you meet this Victor?"

"We met when I got here, which in case you forgot, was over two months ago. I walked into Cafe Lafitte's one afternoon for lunch, and he was at the bar with two of my favorite writers, Tennessee Williams and Truman Capote. So, I introduced myself. Victor is a playwright, but you probably know that already, huh, Professor Clouseau."

"Leave Peter Sellers out of this," Jack grumbled.

"Well, you're the one who was following me instead of coming up to me saying, 'Beck, it's me. I traveled across time for you.'" She stopped and lowered her voice, "Wait a minute. How did you get here?"

Jack furrowed his brow and said, "I'm not sure."

"Ugh, it figures," Beck grumbled as she slumped against the wall.

Jack's eyes flashed at her as he whispered furiously, "Oh, I'm sorry. I guess I missed the part of the vows that said the husband should figure out the fucking time travel."

"Yeah, you missed a lot of vows."

"I'm not the one with the British boy toy. I see you squirming. You're guilty as sin. I can read you like an open book."

"That's not why I'm squirming, Sherlock. I have to pee," she said in a small voice.

"Seriously?"

Beck was frustrated. "Yes, I'm serious. I thought it was nerves cause I've never been in jail before. But I'm more pissed at you than I am nervous about jail. So it must be the real thing."

Jack chuckled. "You said pissed."

"Grow up, Jack."

He looked at the toilet and back at his wriggling wife, "Come on, get up."

"I can't pee over there," Beck said in a panic as she took stock of her predicament. The bars would expose her to any passersby, she was still wearing her long evening dress from work, and one hand was cuffed to Jack.

"Well, I'd rather you not pee on the only bed," He said.

They approached the toilet together. It was shockingly clean.

They shifted their gaze to Beck's evening gown. She said softly, "You'll have to help me."

Jack kneeled on the concrete floor and gathered the full ballgown skirt pressing it into Beck's free arm. He crawled under layer after layer of petticoats locating her underwear with his free hand and pulling it down. Trying not to look at her body as that seemed somehow wrong at the moment. Once he had worked her panties to just below her knees, he said, "Go for it."

"I can't. People will see me," Beck protested as her squirming picked up speed.

Jack stood up carefully, pinning her skirts under his free arm. "Of course, you can. I'll stand in front of you. No one will see. Go on, sit down."

Beck sat carefully on the seat. "Turn around. I can't do this with you staring at me."

Jack turned his back to her slowly, sure to mind her skirt and petticoats. He waited for the tell-tale sound of liquid hitting porcelain. "Why aren't you going?"

"You're practically in my lap. It's weird."

"This is the way it has to be. I can't move away with the handcuffs."

"Fine, but we take this secret to our graves," she said as she finally relieved herself.

When she was finished. Jack had her step away from the toilet and crawled under her skirt to secure her underwear. As she twisted her handcuffed hand and tried to reach her panties, he said, "Don't help. You're making it take too long,"

"I'm not used to you dressing me."

"Yeah, me either. I'm usually doing the opposite," Jack teased.

As they sat back on the bed, she said, "Well, that was quite the kerfuffle."

"Are you kidding me?" Jack said, exasperated.

"What's wrong?" Beck asked.

"You're doing it again. Talking like him."

"Are you going to police everything I say forever, or just until you find something else more interesting to do?"

"What's that supposed to mean?" Jack asked, leaning away from her.

"You couldn't wait to marry me, and as soon as I was yours, you put me on the shelf like one of your creepy dolls. I feel more like a conquest than your partner."

Jack frowned, "Why am I just now hearing about this?"

"Because you're literally bound to me in a cage and have no other choice but to listen. Did you get my letter?"

"Yeah," Jack said as he looked at his feet.

"Good. So you know that in the two months since I came here, I've found myself a job, a place to live, and friends. It was hard to start over without you."

"Well, I'm sure Mr. Tall, blond, and British helped," Jack grumbled.

"Yes, but not in the way you think. I met Victor, Truman, and Tennessee at Cafe Lafitte in Exile. Do you know what that is?"

"A restaurant?" Jack shrugged.

Beck lowered her voice, "Cafe Lafitte in Exile is the oldest gay bar in the United States. They're all gay."

"Then, why were you there?"

"I didn't know at first. I went in for lunch and stayed for the friends. Unlike most people, the patrons there don't insist that everyone has to be like them. They're incredibly welcoming, and I don't have to worry about men coming onto me."

"So, you're not looking to replace me?" Jack asked.

"No one could ever replace you," Beck said as her eyes misted.

"Aw, Beck," Jack said. He closed his eyes and tilted his head, ready to kiss her. When her lips failed to meet his, he opened them again.

"I don't feel right kissing you," Beck said, avoiding his gaze.

"But you just said that you couldn't replace me."

"You'll always be my first love, but -"

"But what?" Jack asked urgently.

"I don't want to go back to the way things were," Beck said.

"The way things were? You mean where you were married to a man who adored you and gave you everything you wanted?" Jack said sharply.

"Not everything," Beck said quietly.

"Are you asking for a divorce?"

"I don't have to. We're not legally married in 1948. But I --"

"Wow! Okay, I've heard enough. Now if you don't mind, I'm going to get some sleep, because I just got your letter yesterday and the next thing I knew, I was here. Then, I spent all day chasing after you like an idiot," he said bitterly.

As Jack lay down on the twin-sized cot, Beck had to make herself small against the wall. "I wasn't done," she said.

Jack didn't bother to open his eyes as he said, "I am."

"Jack, you can't sleep at a time like this."

"Watch me," he said as his muscles relaxed and his breathing became more regular.

After a while, Beck's arm and wrist began to ache from the pull of Jack's weight. Finally, she lay on the bed, wedging between him and the wall. As she laid her head to rest on his chest, she wondered if it would be for the last time.

CHAPTER 11

"Well, isn't this sweet," said a man with a loud, booming New York accent.

Jack opened his eyes and took a quick look around. Finally remembering where he was. Without looking down, he recognized the weight of Beck's head on his chest, her body pressed against his. He supposed she was too tired to care.

"Rise and shine, Jailbirds. C'mon, I'm here to spring ya," the man said. Beck raised her head and blushed. Then, together, Jack and Beck managed a tricky series of maneuvers required to right themselves on the bed and stand up.

"Leon, I can explain," Beck said.

"No need. I know the charges," Leon said.

"Jack, this is my boss, Leon Prima."

Jack wouldn't know the Prima brothers by sight, but he certainly knew their music. He offered to shake Leon's hand with his free hand through the bars. "Mr. Prima, I'm a huge fan of you and your brothers. It's an honor."

"Likewise, Red Devil. Louie's up in your old stomping grounds. When he arrived, he looked all over for you, but no dice."

"I, uh, had a few lost years there," Jack mumbled.

Leon nodded and said, "The war was hard on all of us."

"Thanks for bailing my uh --" Jack looked at Beck. It felt weird not to refer to her as his wife. "Rebecca out. This is no place for a lady."

"I'm here to spring you both. If we can make a deal, that is."

"What did you have in mind?" Jack asked warily.

"I know the right people. So, I can pay to spring you out and wipe your record if you perform for me. Starting tonight, you'll play with my band at the 500 Club three nights a week. Friday, Saturday, and Sunday. Those are my busiest, and they pay the best, but I'll withhold 25% each night until you pay off your bond. Capiche?"

"Let's do a 50/50 split. I don't like to be indebted to anyone if I can help it," Jack explained.

"That's admirable."

"Great! Then, we have a deal," Jack said, shaking the man's hand. The new officer on duty unlocked the door and removed the handcuffs, setting Jack and Beck free from one another.

Jack strolled out of the cell with a slight smile on his lips, only to hear the door close behind him. He wheeled around to see Beck still behind bars, "Hey, I thought we had a deal. What gives?"

"You and I have a deal. Rebecca and I haven't made one yet," Leon said as he smirked at her.

"I'm already your hostess manager. What more do you want?" Beck said, her muscles tense with worry.

"You're a good manager. You're also an attractive dame. I want you to be one of my dancers." Leon said.

"What?" Jack and Beck said.

"Do you not agree that she's stacked? She's good for business." Leon said.

It was enough to make Jack want to smack him, but Beck was in a cage, and he didn't have the resources to secure her freedom. So there was no other choice than to hear the man out.

"Burlesque or Taxi?" Beck grumbled.

"I was thinking Taxi, but if you wanna to shake what God gave ya, be my guest," Leon said.

"I'll Taxi Dance, but no B drinking or any of that... other stuff," Beck said. Then she added with a frown, "I can't believe you're demoting me."

"I'm not. This is extra work to pay off your debt to me. One hour every shift. You can keep the tips," Leon said.

"Keep them. The sooner I pay this off, the better," she said with resignation.

"Don't knock it til you try it, Dollface. Most ladies find a fella that way. But, then, they marry, and of course, I gotta replace them." Leon stopped what he was saying and looked from Jack to Beck and back again, "Unless you already got a fella. I can't have a dance hostess who's rationed. You her fella, Red Devil?" Leon asked.

Beck and Jack looked at each other, waiting for the other to speak first.

"No. Miss Taylor is free to do as she pleases," Jack said evenly as he headed to the front desk to pick up his personal items from the clerk: suspenders and a wedding band. He quickly put his suspenders on and pocketed his ring.

Leon waved at him as he walked onto the sidewalk, "Miss Taylor's free to go. She's just getting her personals. See ya tonight at ten," he said as he turned and walked in the opposite direction.

Jack was half a block away when he heard heels clicking on the pavement behind him. "Jack, wait," Beck called.

He pretended he couldn't hear and picked up his pace. When she caught up with him, he noticed she was holding her heels in her hand. "Jack, please, wait up," she said breathlessly.

He stopped, but didn't turn around. "What?" he asked.

"Are you going to be okay? Do you have a place to stay?"

"I'll figure it out," he said stiffly.

"Here," she said, taking a stack of cash from her handbag, "This will help you get started."

"I don't want your money."

"I don't want you sleeping on the streets."

He walked further down the street, trying to ignore her, but Beck persisted. "I don't want your help."

"But you need it. Please, Jack. I've been staying with a nice family. I haven't had to pay rent. I eat with them or at work most days. So I have it to give," Beck said as she reached out and took his hand.

Her touch burned him. All he wanted to do was get away from her, and lick his wounds. Taking her money would be yet another injury, but he reasoned he could find a dark little room to hole up in and mourn her. Reluctantly, he opened his fingers and allowed her to press the cash into his palm. He shoved it in his pocket, next to his wedding ring. Touching its cold metal was yet another knife to the heart.

"Thanks," he mumbled. "I'll pay you back."

"It's not a loan."

"We'll see about that. See you around," Jack said as he picked up the pace leaving Beck behind to slide her shoes back into place.

CHAPTER 12

Ginny met Beck in the courtyard. Her face was pink and puffy.

Beck went to her friend and embraced her. "Oh Honey, what's wrong. Was it that Sam character because I'll give him what for."

Ginny motioned for Beck to sit down as she pulled away. "No, Sweetie. Sam's wonderful. On New Year's Eve, he gave me this!" Ginny beamed through tears as she flashed a giant diamond on her left hand.

"Oh, my goodness. Congratulations! This is good news, right?" Beck asked.

"It's the best. We're both so excited. It's gonna be a June wedding."

"Then why the tears?" Beck reached across the table to wipe another tear from her friend's cheek.

Ginny whispered, "Mother and Daddy found out that you were arrested. They said you are a Negro lover and a fruit fly. Then, they said that thay can't have someone like that in their home." Ginny sobbed. "Oh, Beck, I'm so sorry. If it were up to me, you could stay here forever. I don't even care about the company you keep. I know you're just one of them modern women, but they say Sam's family might not want him to marry me if they find out you're staying with us."

"It's okay, Ginny. I'll find a place. After all you've done for me, I don't want to make trouble for you and Sam. I'll go pack."

"That's not necessary. I packed your things, and our Butler took them over to Mrs. Bessy's Boarding House. Here's the address," Ginny said, passing her a card. "I made Daddy feel so guilty that he paid for your first week. Ginny smiled triumphantly.

"Will I still see you?" Beck asked.

Ginny looked at her feet, "I hope so, but I got an awful lot of wedding planning to do between now and June."

"I see, "Beck said. She left the courtyard, and took one last look at the lovely Creole townhouse that had been her first home in New Orleans. Then, she stepped onto Dauphine Street and headed to Toulouse Street, just one block away.

Bessy's Boarding House was a charming red townhouse with creamy yellow trim, black shutters, and black wrought iron balconies. Beck recognized it immediately from her most recent stay in New Orleans when she was Mrs. Rebecca Herman, and the boarding house was the Olivier House Hotel.

Beck knocked on the tall yellow door and was greeted by a woman with a pale, round face and jet-black hair pulled back into a smooth bun, not a hair out of place. She stared suspiciously at Beck, who reasoned she probably didn't see many strangers in ball gowns on her doorstep midday.

"Hello, I'm Rebecca Taylor. Are you Mrs. Brown?" Beck asked.

"Yes. So, you're the new girl. Come in," she said, opening the door wider for Beck's full skirt. "You always dress this fancy?"

"No, ma'am. I had a series of unfortunate events after work last night, and I haven't been able to change."

"I see," she said matter-of-factly. "Your room's on the top floor. Last door on the right. Lunch will be ready in half an hour if you want to refresh yourself and join us," Mrs. Brown offered.

"Thanks, I'd like that," Beck said. She made her way carefully up the stairs so as to not trip over her gown. Every step she took was painful. Physically, because her shoes were not meant to walk all over the city, and emotionally because the room behind the last door on the right was all too familiar to her.

The bedding and draperies were different, but there was no doubt that this was the room in which she'd spent her last happy weekend with Jack in 1995. She approached the French doors that led to the balcony taking in the view of the courtyard and the city beyond. The scene from the morning of Tom and Lenora's wedding day played out as though she were watching it on a movie screen.

She and Jack had laid there a tangled mess of limbs and sheets, exhausted after the raucous rehearsal dinner and a night filled with lovemaking. The room had felt a little stuffy, so she'd untangled herself from her husband and tiptoed over to the balcony, opening the drapes and the door, relishing the feel of the crisp October morning on her naked body.

Jack stirred as the chill hit his own naked form. "What are you doing, Darlin'?" he asked as he tried to free himself from the sheets.

"I wanted to let in the sunlight and fresh air. Isn't it a glorious day? There's not a cloud in the sky."

"Aren't you chilly?"

Beck looked down at her goose-bumped skin and back to her lover, "Yes. Yes, I am." With that, she had dove under the covers pulling up the down comforter over their heads. Pulling Jack's body close to hers, she whispered, "You're the only one I want in my blanket fort." Then she kissed him passionately.

They had made love again, and after, as he held her tightly, she said, "I wish we could actually control time."

"Where would you go this time?" Jack asked with a grin.

"I'd stay right here locked in this moment for as long as we wanted," she said wistfully.

"So, no rewinding or fast-forwarding?"

"No. Just pause and play," Beck said, then kissed the end of his nose as he chuckled.

At the end of the memory, Beck shuffled out of her ballgown and washed her face. She was thankful that she had a private bathroom. At Mama Esther's boarding house, there were three women, all sharing one. It could get quite hectic, but she missed her roommates and, most of all, Mama.

Perhaps this place would be filled with wonderful people, like her home in Harlem. Determined to make a fresh start, she fixed her hair and reapplied her makeup. As she slid into her celery-colored day dress, she tried to focus on the prospect of making new friends in her latest home while doing her best to ignore her broken heart.

There were several guest rooms on the top floor. At least six doors by Beck's count. Instead of additional rooms like she'd seen in 1995, the second floor was home to a grand ballroom and a set of ornate double doors with a plaque next to them that read "Owner's Suite." Beck deduced that these were Mrs. Brown's rooms. Downstairs there was a double parlor, dining room, and kitchen. Beck knew the parlors would stay, but the kitchen was destined to become even more guest rooms.

The moment she started her descent from the final flight of stairs, she could smell the combination of coffee and chocolate, slightly burned. Beck wondered if something had gone wrong in the kitchen.

As she stepped into the front hall, Mrs. Brown called to her from a set of French doors just beyond the parlor, "New girl, in here. "

Beck opened the doors in time to see Mrs. Brown and a young black woman setting bowls down on the table in front of the tenants. Starving, she peeked in the bowls and was thrilled to see a dark brown substance with shrimp, onions, and andouille sausage peeking out of it. That smell hadn't meant lunch was burnt at all. It simply meant that Mrs. Brown knew how to make a proper Cajun roux.

"Remind me of your name again, Honey," Mrs. Brown said.

"Rebecca Taylor," Beck said. A man previously hidden behind a newspaper dropped it immediately. Beck was pleasantly surprised to see Victor.

"Becks? What are you doing here? What happened?"

"Um, I'll fill you in after lunch," she said.

"You already know Victor Shadly? Good," Mrs. Brown said. She introduced Beck to two ladies who worked second shift at Higgins Industries and an old man named Nicholas O'Reilly.

With a slight Irish brogue, Nicholas smiled broadly at Beck. "Always a pleasure to meet an Irish lass."

"While you'll be responsible for tidying your room, Addie here will do the deep cleaning, and for a little extra, she can do your wash or take your dry cleaning in for you," Mrs. Brown said as they sat down to lunch.

After eating some of the best gumbo she'd ever tasted, Beck and Victor retreated to the parlor farthest from the dining room. They talked in low voices as Beck didn't want to risk being booted from yet another home.

"Are you going to tell me who that angry man was? Is he actually your husband?" Victor asked in a hushed voice, his brow furrowed.

"His name is Jack Herman. We met in Harlem years ago, and we were together for a while," she explained.

"He said he was your husband."

"It's complicated," she said as she absently fidgeted with the finger on which her wedding ring used to sit. Beck leaned in close, "Listen, Victor, I'm in big trouble. I need you to please keep this to yourself. Don't tell anybody. Not even Truman."

"Oh, bugger. Are you with child?" Victor said as he pressed his fingertips to his lips.

"What? No, not that kind of trouble." Beck proceeded to fill Victor in on her arrest and her night spent in jail, minus the humiliating bathroom incident. She planned to take that tale to her grave. Then, she told him of the deal she'd made with Leon for her bail and, finally, about Ginny's family kicking her out for what she had done. Carefully omitting the "fruit fly" part.

"Life's all gone to pot for you. I'm so sorry, love," he said, placing his hand gently over Beck's, stopping her fidgeting.

"If Leon thinks I have a fella, then he won't let me Taxi dance, and I won't have a way to pay back my debt. Jack promised not to mention our past. Can I count on you?"

"Mum's the word. Oh, Becks, I'm so glad you're here. It's all going to be okay. You'll do a little bit of dancing, and it will all be squared away in no time."

"That's my other problem," Beck said as she bit her lower lip.

"You don't know how to dance," Victor said, nodding, "Well, that's simply an obstacle, not a problem. I'd be honored to be your dance instructor."

"Are you sure?" Beck asked.

"It will be a gas, as they say. There's a ballroom upstairs. Let's get started. I have a couple of hours before rehearsal. We can at least make sure that your waltz is solid for tonight. Then, we'll go from there."

Beck followed her friend up the stairs feeling a bit lighter.

CHAPTER 13

The room had a smell of sweat mixed with vomit. A mattress on a rusted iron frame and a threadbare chair were in the corner. Plywood boarded the hole where the remains of a shattered window used to be.

"I'll think about it and get back to you," Jack said as he tried not to breathe through his nose.

He had spent the first part of his morning walking off angry energy. After an hour of wandering aimlessly, he started hunting for lodging. There were few vacancies in the quarter, and the ones he'd visited so far were either too expensive or disgusting.

There was one more place to try. A place Jack had been avoiding all day due to its painful memories. He let out a deep sigh as he walked slowly up Dauphine Street. His footsteps felt heavier with each step he took toward the red townhouse with the creamy yellow trim and black shutters.

A stern woman met him at the door.

Jack cleared his throat. "Good afternoon. May I speak to Mrs. Brown? I'm looking for a room to rent."

The older woman narrowed her eyes at Jack and looked him over. Her mouth was set in a straight line, but he couldn't tell if her stare was one of apathy or annoyance. "I'm Mrs. Brown," she said at last.

"Oh, I didn't expect someone so young and attractive to own

such a grand home," Jack said. He wasn't above pouring on the charm for a decent place to sleep.

Mrs. Brown's face relaxed, and her cheeks turned pink as she smiled at him. "I inherited the place from my husband, but he's dead now. So I'm single. I mean, I'm a widow."

"I'm sorry for your loss."

"That was years ago," she said with a wave of her hand, "Please come in, Mister…"

"Herman. Please call me Jack," he said as he entered the house. The double parlor looked the same as it had a week ago, back in 1995, with a few cosmetic differences, and of course, the check-in desk was missing.

"I have one room available, Jack. It's a bit small with a shared bathroom. It's more for one person, so if you have a wife -"

"No, ma'am. It's just me," he said quickly.

"Well then, I think you will find it adequate. Why don't we discuss the terms after lunch? I made gumbo. I was just about to put away the leftovers, but there's still plenty if you're hungry."

Jack had learned from Beck that no one ever turns down a bowl of gumbo in Louisiana. He graciously accepted her invitation, and Mrs. Brown's cooking did not disappoint. After lunch and negotiating a reasonable room rate, Jack sat back and enjoyed the rest of his iced tea.

Suddenly, he saw a tall, blond man head through the parlor and out the door. "Who was that," he asked Mrs. Brown.

"Victor Shadly. He's a visiting playwright all the way from London. Such a gentleman. I can't wait for you to meet him."

Jack was exasperated but decided that while one should keep their friends close, it's best to keep one's enemies closer. The stress of the past twenty-four hours weighed on him once again, and with a belly full of gumbo, sleep was close at hand. "Mrs.Brown, I think I'm ready to go up to my room."

"Okay, dear. Head up to the top floor. Yours is the second to last door on the right."

Jack wandered around, searching for the elevator that had been there in 1995. Finally, he opened a door he was certain concealed it and found a coat closet instead. He wasn't thrilled with the walk up to the third floor, but thinking of the bed that awaited him made the climb bearable.

As he reached the top of the stairs, he walked up to the last door on the right out of habit before remembering that his former hotel room was not the one he'd rented. *Probably for the best*, he reasoned, as it would have been haunted by memories.

His little room was charming enough. There was a double bed, a plush green chair, and a small dresser that doubled as a nightstand. He was pleased to find that even though the room was small, it still had access to the wrought iron balcony and a view of the courtyard.

He cracked the balcony door, but the air was too cold to keep it open for long. As he fell asleep, he swore he heard the voice of Cab Calloway singing Saint James Infirmary drifting ever so faintly from the room next door. *At least my neighbor has good taste in music*, he thought as he drifted off to sleep.

CHAPTER 14

Having never stepped foot in the 500 Club before, Jack decided to arrive at nine o'clock instead of his ten o'clock call time. His goal was to check out the stage and the acoustics and meet the rest of Leon's band. However, he was distracted when he saw his wife working the door.

She was all dolled up with her auburn locks tamed into Lana Turner waves. Her dark green velvet dress was pleated and cinched with a sash. The neckline plunged, revealing her ample cleavage, and the skirt was slit to mid-thigh, revealing most of her leg when she walked. As she returned to the door after seating the party before him, her eyes met his, and he quickly looked away.

Beck said, "You're early."

"I thought I'd check out the club and grab a late dinner," he said, trying not to stare.

"I can seat you at the bar or a table. Which would you like?"

"The bar's fine," he said. She led him to an open stool. He couldn't stop his eyes from tracing her velvet-draped curves. "You don't have to dress like that, you know. You agreed to dance, but you shouldn't have to dress so...you know."

"I didn't dress like this for Leon. I wore for it me. The velvet feels good against my skin, and I think it looks sexy. Don't you?" Beck said.

Jack didn't answer her. She already knew the answer.

"Nash," Beck said, waving over the bartender. "This is our newest musician, Jack Herman. Nash will take good care of you. See you around."

The lights dimmed slightly, and Lowry took the stage with his jazz quartet. He'd really come into his own. Part of Jack was sad to have missed his friend's transformation from orchestra member to accomplished band leader.

The set started with some toe-tapping Dixieland Jazz which brought many of the patrons to the dance floor. Not much of a dancer, Jack was content to keep his seat and enjoy his whiskey.

Meanwhile, Beck hurried backstage. "Ladies, the Ringgold Rebels have just started their set. I need every dancer out there right now," Beck said as she waved the dance hostesses out of the green room.

Anxious for the tips, most of the ladies hopped out to the dance floor straight away, but Ella held back, pacing the room.

"What's wrong?" Beck asked.

"I can't go out there now," Ella said.

"I'm okay with letting you go early every now and then, but this has gotten to be a pattern. If you're struggling this much to find a sitter, you may need to consider a job with different hours," Beck said gently.

"No. I need this job. My husband hasn't had steady work in forever. All he does is play gigs, instead of looking for a steady job. I need this position."

Just then, Leon walked through the door, "If you need this job so much, I suggest you get out there and cut a rug," He said.

"Please, Mr. Prima, I just can't. I can go back in an hour," Ella offered.

"That's unacceptable," Leon said as he crossed his arms over his chest. "I need you both out there now. We've got men without partners. That leaves money on the table."

"I can't be seen out there right now. Is there anything else I can do?" Ella asked.

Leon looked at Ella as he took a drag from his cigarette and said, "We got a whale in the VIP room tonight. Do you know what that means?"

"Yes, Sir. He's a wealthy man," Ella said.

"Go in there and be your charming self. Get him to buy you as many drinks as you can to run up the tab."

"But, Sir. I'll get drunk," Ella protested.

Leon chuckled and said, "Not to worry, I have Nash water down all the drinks. It's damn near impossible to get drunk in this place unless you open a new bottle."

With that assurance, Ella disappeared into the first of the two VIP rooms. Leon blew the smoke from his nostrils and turned to Beck, "You better get your sweet patootie out there, or there's another VIP room with your name on it."

Beck's cheeks felt hot as she exited the green room and headed for the dance floor. She arrived just in time for a new number. An older man was the only waiting patron unclaimed, so Beck came over and invited him to dance.

"Back in my day, it was the man who asked the lady," he said as he led Beck to the edge of the crowd.

"Well, next time, you can ask me," she said warmly.

Lowry tipped his hat to Beck as she took to the floor. She had informed him of her predicament, so he had promised to play a waltz for her first dance. As Beck and her companion moved through the steps, she went over and over them in her head. Trying to get them just right.

"What's that, Sugah?" the man asked, "You're going to have to speak up."

Beck hadn't realized that she was mouthing the count as she went. *One, Two, Three, One, Two, Three.* "I'm sorry. I don't want to mess up." As soon as she spoke, she lost count and struggled to get back on beat. She was exhausted and relieved as the song came to an end.

Her partner sank off to the sidelines, and just as Beck breathed a sigh of relief, a man with a New York accent said, "Hey, Dollface, let's cut a rug." Not waiting for an answer, he grabbed her wrist and took her out onto the floor.

The Ringgold Rebels began to play a mid-tempo swing song. Beck was hopeful that the moderate West Coast Swing pace would help buy her time as she struggled to follow her partner's lead. However, it was not to be. She lost count of how many times she stepped on his feet.

Halfway through the song, the man pulled her to him. He breathed in her ear, "You're clearly not good at this. Why don't we go somewhere private and have a drink? Maybe we can discover what you might be skilled at."

"No," Beck said as she tried to wiggle free.

"Why not, Baby? You got a thing against Jews?" he asked.

No longer dancing, Beck struggled harder against the man who only tightened his grip. "What?"

"I gotta to say, I woulda thought a broad in a get-up like that wouldn't be the discriminating type." He sneered as he slid his hand down her neck.

Before his hand could reach its desired destination, Jack reached out and wrenched the man's arm behind his back, "I wouldn't do that if I were you. Take your paws off her. Now."

The man yelped in pain as Beck ran backstage. His voice was strained as he said, "Let go if you know what's good for you, Red Devil."

Jack checked to make sure Beck had made a clean getaway before letting the man go, "Who do you think you are?" he demanded.

"Meyer Lansky from New York City. You don't want to make an enemy of me, Jack."

"Oh really? After you treated my friend so shamefully? I ought to beat you to a pulp."

"I heard you were a hothead," Meyer said with a smile. "I knew good and well what I was doing. I saw that kitten with you up in Harlem. I figured that if I got too friendly, you'd come running."

Jack said as he stabbed his index finger into Meyer's chest repeatedly, "You mean you harassed Beck to get to me? That's disgusting."

Meyer raised his lapel discreetly, revealing a flash of his pistol in its shoulder holster, "You might wanna cut that out. Don't be cross. It worked, didn't it? You came to her rescue - again."

"Next time you want to speak to me, dial direct. Leave her the hell out of it."

"Here, take my card. Better to channel that anger into more productive pursuits. I certainly wouldn't mind having a fellow Jew in the Family," Meyer said as he placed his business card in Jack's shirt pocket.

Meyer turned to head toward the backstage area. Concerned for Beck, Jack followed him. But instead of turning right toward the green room, Meyer entered a hallway on the left.

There was no sign of Beck in the green room, so Jack checked the rest of the backstage area. There was a hallway with two black doors reading "VIP room." They were numbered one and two, respectively. Room two was open and had mood lighting that mimicked candlelight, a curved burgundy leather sofa with black and silver satin pillows, and a round coffee table with an ice bucket in the middle. There were "Do Not Disturb" signs for the door handles. He had a bad feeling about these spaces.

As he continued on, he saw rooms with tables for casino-type games. He could hear Meyer and a few other men with New York and Italian accents playing poker in the third room and decided to keep his distance. Satisfied that Beck was not being held hostage, he returned to the green room.

He sat down in one of the chairs and listened to the last song of Lowry's set. The way his shirt shifted caused the tiny corner of Meyer's card to poke Jack in the chest. He took it out and glanced at its raised black lettering. It read:

Meyer Lansky
Lead Accountant
Worldwide Casinos

He put the card away and began to put the pieces together. Meyer and his cronies were clearly running casino games out of the back of the 500 Club. A practice that Beck had told him was illegal in Louisiana due to Christianity's strong influence on the Deep South. He concluded that there could only be one group organized enough to run a global operation of hidden casinos. Jack had found the Mafia in New Orleans. *No, Meyer Lansky knew who we were*; he corrected himself. *The mafia found us.*

Lowry walked into the green room sweaty but happy. He picked up a small towel and wiped off his face. "What's cooking, Red Devil?"

Jack smiled at his friend and applauded. "You are, my man. I can't believe I have to follow that."

"Aw thanks. I wish for several more gigs like it."

"You and me both."

"Club Coco just shut down, and that's where I played the other four nights of the week. My old lady's busting my chops to get a real job."

"Wait. Old lady? As in wife or mother?" Jack asked.

"Both. I live with both, and now that the baby's here, they're pressing on me to get a day job. But, you know how it is. Music's in my soul. I can't imagine doing anything else."

"Hold the phone. You're married, and you have a baby? Why didn't you tell me? Congrats, man."

"I ain't seen you in almost ten years. I was gonna tell you when I saw you, but you took off after Beck," Lowry explained.

"Sorry," Jack said.

"Did you smooth all that over?"

"Not by a long shot," Jack said as he put his head in his hands.

"She seemed pretty down tonight. I thought it was that trouble with Mr. Prima. Can't believe he's making her Taxi Dance to pay him back. You're a better man than me. I'd never let my woman do that kind of work, and she was a professional dancer with the Duke's orchestra."

Jack looked up at his friend. "What's wrong with Taxi Dancing?"

"Officially nothing. They're dance hostesses that teach the men to dance," Lowry looked around and lowered his voice, "Unofficially, the real owners of the club push those girls into B drinking, and some of them end up doing other kinds of favors for money."

"Wait, what? What's B drinking? Leon doesn't really own this club?" Jack asked in rapid succession.

"Hey, Red Devil," Leon called from the stairs to the stage. "Let's go. It's showtime."

"We'll talk soon. Break a leg," Lowry said.

As Jack ascended the stairs, he looked back to wave to his friend only to see Lowry go down the hall and enter one of the casino game rooms.

CHAPTER 15

The alley was dark and cold, its ground uneven. Beck navigated it carefully in her heels. She could just make out the street lights at the end, like a light at the end of a tunnel. Suddenly she heard a sound from the other side of the dumpster. Blargh, over and over again.

As she rounded the other side, she saw the silhouette of a slender woman with short hair retching in the alley.

"Hey, are you alright? Beck asked. Seeing another human in need momentarily distracted her from her own troubles.

"Miss Rebecca?" the woman muttered.

"Ella, is that you?" The woman nodded in affirmation. "Oh, honey. What's wrong? Are you sick?"

Ella glanced at Beck and quickly looked away, attempting to hide her face with her hands. Beck reached into her bag and handed Ella a handkerchief to wipe her face. When Ella was finished, she said, "No. I'm just not used to drinking that much. Or at all, really. I stopped back when I found out I was expecting, and I just weaned my son. Guess I'm just not used to drinking anymore."

Beck offered her arm and said, "Come on, let's take a walk. You could use some fresh air."

"It's fine. I'll get used to it," Ella said as they emerged from the alley and walked up St. Louis breathing in the cool January air.

"You don't have to B drink, you know. That's not required of the Dance Hostesses. We're supposed to teach the men and keep them company *on* the dance floor."

"I need the money, Miss Rebecca. My husband is, uh, I mean, he has friends in the Ringgold Rebels. I'm just trying to make sure he doesn't find out."

"Why didn't you tell me?"

Ella stopped and looked at Beck. She smirked and furrowed her brow, "Why would I? You're my manager, and you already know I have a husband and a baby. That alone is grounds for dismissal."

"You're my best dance hostess. I'd be out of my mind to let you go."

"I have a family, I'm hiding from the band, which disrupts everything, and I'm an octoroon. It feels like I'm on borrowed time," Ella said as she pulled ahead of Beck, her shoulders slumped, disrupting her normally perfect posture. Suddenly she stumbled. Beck caught her arm to steady her.

"I'm sorry. You're a -- what was it you said? An octoroon? I've never heard the term. I don't know what it means," Beck said apologetically.

"I'm mixed. Octo means eight. Out of eight great grandparents, one was black."

They sat on a bench. To Beck, it didn't seem like a big deal, but as she looked at Ella, her face buried in her hands, she realized that it was clearly significant to Ella. "I can imagine that makes life hard for you."

"Ha! That's an understatement. I'm straddling two different existences all the time. At work, I'm hoping that no one sees my blackness, because one little drop and I'm in jail for dancing with white men. But on the days I'm not working, I don't smooth my hair, I let the kinky curls spring and bounce. I relax my speech, praying that no one in my neighborhood figures out I'm part white."

Beck thought about how hard it was to fit in here. Taming her curls, using just enough slang to get by. It wasn't the same. Beck belonged in 1995. She wasn't able to get there, but a place existed where Beck belonged. For Ella, no such place existed. "It's like you don't have a home. There's nowhere you can relax and be yourself."

"Exactly. The state keeps arguing this 'One Drop Rule,' one drop and I'm a Negro, but if it swings the other way and I'm too white then, my marriage could be annulled, and we'd both go to jail for mixed marriage. Lord knows what would happen to little Jackie."

"Who?" Beck asked.

"Jackie, my son."

"Cute name," Beck said with a smile.

"Thanks, it was my husband's idea." The ladies walked until they hit the northern boundary of the quarter at North Rampart Street. "This is where I leave you," Ella said.

"I just want to make sure you make it home safely," Beck said.

"I'll be safe over there. You won't, at least not until daylight. Go on now. I'll see you at work?" Ella asked anxiously.

"Of course, you will," Beck said. The ladies hugged one another, and Beck watched as Ella disappeared in between the oaks on the border of Congo Square. It was the first time she'd found herself on this part of the quarter since she had traveled back. She wanted to explore the square and compare it to the 1995 version of itself. However, Ella had told her it wasn't safe.

She turned to go but stopped when she heard a rustling sound in the low branches of the large tree in Congo Square. She could just make out the figure of a woman trying to steady herself on the lowest bough. Worried that Ella had stumbled again, Beck crossed the street.

"Ella?" Beck called softly.

A cold wind stirred in the square. Beck found herself hating her dress for the second time that night. The square had been so full of life the night of Tom's reception, but it was vacant and eerie tonight. The oaks' branches cast long, thin, claw-shaped shadows across the desolate square.

The rustling happened again, causing her to gasp. "Ella?" Beck's voice trembled as she called for her.

Suddenly, an old woman in a turban with a long flowing robe burst forth from the tree line.

"You don't belong here," the woman said slowly in a deep voice.

"I know. I'm going," Beck said as she turned and started to walk quickly out of the square.

"Why do you always run away, Rebecca?" The Voodoo woman called after her.

"I don't," Beck said as she stopped and rounded back at the old woman. "Wait, how do you know who -- ?"

"Who you are?" the woman asked. "You're Rebecca Taylor Herman, wife of Jack Herman. Citizen of Topanga Canyon, California, 1995."

"It's you," Beck said, her eyes wide. As she recovered from the shock of seeing the Voodoo Lady from Harlem again, anger bubbled inside her. "Listen, Lady, I'm sick of people telling me who I am and what to do. I've built a life here. I have a job, friends, and a room. Jack and I aren't 'tethered together' like you said. He started to let me go the moment we tied the knot. Maybe it's you who's wrong. Maybe I do belong here."

"Wrong. You ran here when life got too hard," the Voodoo Woman said. "Your job put you in jeopardy tonight, and the jackals are circling. Your friends are not as they seem. The tether is stretched to its limit, but it will pull back. You need your husband as much as he needs you."

"Ha! Jack has never needed anybody. He's all wrapped up in his music," Beck scoffed. Her face felt hot. The words seemed to sting more than ever once she'd said them out loud.

"So, were you once. The first thing that drew you to Jack was his music. You were a fan for years before you were friends and lovers. Do you deny it?"

Beck sighed as she remembered herself as an awkward teenager watching Jack on TV. Infatuated with his copper curls and devilish grin. "No, I don't," she said softly.

"Don't discount music, Rebecca Herman. It existed before language. It's rhythm paired with emotions. It's mighty. That's why Voodoo rituals are accompanied by drums. It opens up possibilities for the departed and those yet to be to reach out from the other world with guidance, blessings, and warnings. Under the right circumstances, it can detach a soul from one plain to the next."

"What are you trying to tell me?" Beck asked.

"The tether's not broken. You and Jack Herman have a shared destiny," the lady said as she stepped back from Beck, partially hidden by the branches.

"What does that mean?" Beck said louder as the woman completely disappeared. "AGH!!" Beck exclaimed as she ran back toward the boarding house.

By the time she reached the front steps, her feet throbbed. She may have been more proficient in heels, but that didn't make them less painful. Beck removed her shoes and started the slow, steady climb to the top floor.

Once in her room, she removed her dress and took a soak in the clawfoot tub. She was on a mission to rid herself of the unwanted touches she'd received that night, only emerging from the hot water when her skin was pink and well-scrubbed.

She slipped into her nightgown and threw on her robe. Her feet hurt, but her dress couldn't stay on the floor. As painful as it was to trod up and down the stairs again, she proceeded to the corner where the trash cans were perched for garbage pick up early the following morning and unceremoniously dumped the velvet dress inside, replacing the lid. A good portion of the dress hung out over the sides, but she didn't have it in her to touch the tainted garment again.

In her white gown and robe, she felt like a spirit moving through the house. There was no doubt that Bessy Brown's/The Olivier Hotel was haunted. The ghosts of Mr. and Mrs. Jack Herman were everywhere.

This thought was interrupted by footsteps on the bottom flight of the stairs. Beck sped up her ascent and slipped inside her room. Not wishing to speak to another soul, she carefully closed the door, trying not to make a sound. Wrapping her arms around herself, her back braced against the door, Beck finally allowed herself to cry.

CHAPTER 16

The sound from the roar of the crowd strummed through Jack, and sweat poured off his body. There was nothing quite like connecting with a small audience. Being able to look them in the face and watch them writhe to the beat. To feel the collective heat of the musicians and revelers. Almost better than sex. Almost.

This last thought led him to search the room for Beck. There was no sign of her. As he walked backstage and looked for her, his performer's high diminished, and worry set in. Not only for Beck but for Lowry as well. What was he doing with those mobsters?

"Hell of a set, Mr. Herman," purred the blonde dance hostess as she passed, rubbing her body against him like a cat marking its territory.

"Um, thanks," Jack murmured.

"Aw, that shy guy act doesn't fool me, Mister. I saw you tear up that stage like an animal. " The dancer winked.

"Believe it, Lola. The Red Devil is a demon onstage, but off stage, he broods in solitude," Lowry said melodramatically as he entered the room..

"Aw, a dreamboat like you. Say it isn't so." Lola pouted her red cherry lips while she attempted to muss Jack's curls.

As he ducked away from her hand, he said, "I'm afraid so. I'd only disappoint you."

"We'll see about that," she said as she turned her back and asked,

"Will you be a dear and unzip this dress for me?" She lifted her light blonde hair away from her zipper.

Jack unzipped Lola's zipper as efficiently as possible, averting his eyes from her body. He looked to Lowry for help. "Hey, Jack, we've got some business to discuss. Wanna walk out with me?"

The men headed out through the alley to St. Louis Street, and Lowry asked, "Hey, remember our chat about needing more gigs?" Jack nodded. "Well, I just booked the rest of our week, and we get to play together."

Jack furrowed his brow. "Together? What's the catch?"

"Well, the only places that will let us play together are owned by Marcello."

"Who?" Jack asked.

"Marcello is the true owner of the 500 Club. He's the one running the games," Lowry explained.

"We'd be working for another gangster?"

"Not just any ole gangster, the Godfather of New Orleans," Lowry said casually.

"Oh my God, Lowry. " Jack sighed. "So we'd be working at other clubs he owns? I'm guessing they're real dives if the cops look the other way."

"They're not dives," Lowry said, "They're very classy brothels."

"Pretty sure that's an oxymoron," Jack said, pinching the bridge of his nose.

"Come on, Man, it will be aces to play together again. We could even try out some new material."

"All right, when do we start?" Jack asked, folding his arms across his chest.

"Tomorrow night at 6pm. The address is 1026 Conti Street. Our contact is Ms. Wallace," Lowry said.

"What instruments will we play?"

"They got a piano and a small drum set. James from my group will join us on bass for part of the evening. When he's not there, we take turns on piano and vocals and give each other breaks."

Jack raised an eyebrow, "A break for what?"

"It's a six-hour gig. We gotta eat sometime. I figured we could take turns breaking for dinner."

"I'm not eating in the same place where people are…"

"No one asked you to. You sure you're up for this?" Lowry asked.

Jack ran a hand through his hair. "Yeah, the sooner I can pay back Prima, the better."

The walk home was cold and lonely. Jack's head hurt from worry. He was concerned about Beck and furious that Meyer had used her to get to him. He considered going over to the Broussard's to check on her, but it was after midnight. He promised himself he'd get up early and check on her in the morning. Now that he had a little cash, he needed to go out and buy a few new clothes anyway.

Once he got to Ms. Brown's, he noticed that the trash had something sticking out of it. As he got closer, he saw that it was a lovely dress. He lifted the lid and took the dress off the top. The velvet dress had a plunging neckline and a daring slit in the skirt. It was no doubt the dress Beck had worn. The one she'd been so proud of until the incident with Meyer. Jack bundled the dress up under his arm and replaced the trash can lid. *Why would she dump her dress a block over from where she lives?*

He pictured a distraught Beck running a block over to secretly dump the tainted dress unseen by her benefactors. With a sad sigh, he entered the boarding house and headed up the stairs. As Jack climbed, he heard a door close at the end of the hall.

At the top of the stairs, he stared at the door to his right and remembered how Beck had pushed him up against the wall as he fumbled for their room key. Both of them were tipsy from Tom's rehearsal dinner.

"Mmm, that feels nice, but if you'd let me unlock the door, we could have some privacy," he had said, partly muffled by her kisses.

"I don't want to stop, not even for a second," Beck had said between the kisses she was applying to his neck. "Privacy is overrated."

Her last sentence was enough of a pause for him to find the key. Jack had turned and unlocked the door while she stood on her tiptoes kissing the back of his neck. As soon he had opened the door, he had whipped around and grabbed Beck, sweeping her off her feet. She reached behind them to shut the door. Then, he carried her to bed. The pair made love like a couple on their honeymoon, and in the morning, he awoke to the crisp October air and his bride's beautiful body standing at the open French doors.

Beck was authentically bold and outgoing. Jack only pretended to be that way when he was onstage. As he pictured her laughing and diving back under the covers, he thought, *I should have given you a honeymoon.*

Alone in his room, the longing grew. He missed his wife so much that he thought he heard her singing. He sat on the bed, his back against the headboard, and listened. His next-door neighbor was indeed singing, she sounded just like Beck, but Beck lived a block over with the Broussards. He closed his eyes, concentrating to see if he could hear the woman better.

"Don't, don't you go..."

As the voice sang through the walls, he thought, *That's my song! A song I wrote in 1986.* All at once It hit him, it had to be Beck. She was the only person in 1948 who would know that song.

Normally, he was far too self-critical to listen to something he wrote, but hearing his words in her voice brought a new appreciation for them. That is until he began to wonder why Beck was in the building. One reason flashed to mind: *Victor*.

Is she actually in that man's room in the middle of the night singing my song?

Jack's cheeks grew hot. He decided to splash some water over his face to cool down. The bathroom that was shared between him and one other boarder was occupied. "Figures," he grumbled.

After a few minutes, the door swung open, and Victor stood before Jack. He wore red and white horizontal striped, button-down pajamas. To Jack, the tall man looked like a candy cane. It would be funny if he wasn't so furious.

Victor raised his eyebrows and gasped, "Jack? What are you doing here?"

"I should ask the same of you," Jack growled.

"I live here. And you?"

That wasn't what Jack had meant at all. He meant what are you doing with my wife in your room at this hour, but at the same time, he realized that Victor didn't know they were neighbors. So before Victor could start shouting about an intruder, Jack said, "So do I."

"No, you don't," Victor scoffed, "I've never seen you here before."

"I moved in this afternoon." Jack pointed toward his door for emphasis.

"Over there?" Victor pointed in the same direction as he

frowned.

"Yes," Jack said, crossing his arms over his chest and trying to appear taller.

"That can't be. Becks would have told me."

"Told you what?"

"That you're living together," Victor said.

"Beck lives with the Broussards. I saw you there with her last night."

Victor shook his head and said, "They booted her out after her arrest to avoid a scandal."

"That's terrible. I just saw her at the club, she didn't say anything. Why wouldn't she tell me?"

"She probably didn't want you to follow her here."

"I didn't know she was here. I looked all over town for a room. This was the only one I could afford where I didn't have to worry about being murdered. What's it to you if Beck and I live in the same place?"

Victor blushed and said," I-I guess it has nothing to do with me. I just c-care about her."

"So do I. I don't know what Beck told you about me, but I love her. She's out to prove her independence right now, and I'm trying to give her the space to do that, but I don't intend to give up on us."

"Oh. Well, good luck with that," Victor said.

"You don't sound very supportive there, Vic." Jack smirked.

"It's Victor, and I'm one hundred percent supportive of whatever is best for Becks. Good night, Jack," he said as he went into the door to the left of the bathroom.

Once he was back in his room, Jack flopped his body onto the bed. He desperately needed a drum to beat, but a pillow would have to do. Jack hit it over and over, releasing the tension from dealing with Meyer and Victor. Pounded his fists into it while he ached to feel the soft fur of his beloved Rufus one more time. Knowing that the love of his life was on the other side of the wall but never felt so far away. Exhausted and pillow well fluffed, he finally fell asleep with his palm on the wall next to his headboard.

CHAPTER 17

The following morning, Jack slipped Beck's dress in with the clothes Addie would take to the dry cleaners. He went back upstairs and knocked gently on Beck's door, determined that he'd tell Beck about being her neighbor before anyone else did.

"Who is it?" Beck mumbled on the other side of the door.

"It's Jack. I need to talk to you."

The door opened, and on the other side stood his wife in a white robe, her hair in curlers. "How did you find me? Did Mrs. Brown let you up here?" she asked with a yawn.

"That's what I wanted to talk to you about."

Beck looked down the hall and said, "Come in. I don't want the other boarders to see me like this."

Once in the room, Jack didn't quite know where to sit. He looked at the only chair and then at the bed before he said, "It's strange to be back in this room."

Beck nodded. "I'm surprised you remember it. Have a seat."

As he sat, he said, "Of course I do. It was only a week ago, and we were happy."

Beck crawled back onto the bed and propped herself up with pillows against her headboard. She bit her lip and pulled her knees to her chest, "I forget that it's only been a couple of days for you. I've been here for months."

"Time traveling hazard," he said with a small smile that faded as he continued, "Beck, I live here. This was the nicest place I could find with the money you gave me. Not saying you didn't give me enough, but the other places were scary. Not fun scary, but scary as in potential murder houses. Please don't be angry. I didn't know you had to leave the Broussards and move here."

"Okay," Beck said.

"Okay?"

"Thanks for telling me."

Jack leaned forward in the chair and studied her face. She smiled at him.

"You're not mad?" Jack asked.

"No. I'm glad you told me."

"I would have told you last night, but I didn't know we were neighbors."

"Wait, how *did* you know I was living here?"

"I was pretty sure I heard you singing through the wall. Then, I ran into Victor, who confirmed it."

"Oh, You're right next door?"

"Is that a problem?" Jack asked.

"Sorry. I know you don't like hearing your songs," Beck said as she hugged her knees closer.

"I didn't mind as much when you sang," Jack said with a grin. "Speaking of last night, are you all right?"

She avoided his gaze and said, "I think so."

"I spoke to Meyer, the jerk from last night. It won't happen again."

"There will be others," Beck said with a sigh, "I manage the dance hostesses, and I see guys try to pull stuff like that all the time. I'm constantly sending the bouncer over, but we're all vulnerable when I'm dancing instead of watching. I've got to pay off Prima as soon as possible."

"It won't be forever. I'll help keep watch, and you'll have him paid back in a couple of weeks," Jack said. Just then, a bell rang downstairs. "Join me for breakfast?"

Beck was still deep in thought, but she nodded. "I'll change and be right there."

She had agreed to spend more time with him. It was progress. Jack practically floated down the stairs. Sitting directly across from Victor brought him back down to earth.

Beck felt hopeful after her talk with Jack. As she dressed, she ran through the figures in her head. Dancing an hour each night for the next two weeks would be enough to pay off her debt. However, if she could somehow bring in more tips, that would shave off some time.

As she entered the dining room, deep in thought, she saw Jack and Victor sitting across from one another. They looked like two chess players locked in a stalemate.

They both looked up as she approached the table and smiled. Then, they both stood up and pulled out the chair next to each of them. Beck looked from Jack to Victor and sat between the two men in the chair at the foot of the table.

"Thanks, but this way, I can see you both," she said with a smile.

"You can sit wherever you like, Becks. No need to explain." Victor flashed her a smile. The morning sun was hitting his light blonde hair, giving him an ethereal look.

"Exactly," Jack said with a wink. His hazel eyes sparkling, a devilish grin on his lips.

What's wrong with me? Beck thought. *If I flirt with Jack, he'll think he's forgiven. We still have a lot to work through. And I really shouldn't be thinking of Victor that way. He's gay, so there's zero chance of us getting together. I'm being ridiculous.*

"So, what's everyone up to today?" Beck asked, trying to distract herself with small talk.

"I'm going out to buy some clothes. I have a new gig tonight, and I want to look sharp," Jack said.

"Where are you playing?" Beck asked.

Jack stared wide-eyed at Beck, then his face relaxed as he said. "It's a very exclusive little club on Conti Street."

"Oh. Well, break a leg," she said.

"As for me, it's my day off. So I thought I'd offer my favorite redhead some dance lessons and maybe dinner after," Victor said with a grin.

"Sorry to disappoint you, but my dance card's full," Jack teased.

Beck cut her eyes at Jack, then said, "I'm pretty sure Victor meant me, and I'd be delighted. But, are you sure you want to spend your day off teaching me?"

"Of course I do. Speaking of dancing, how did it go last night?"

Beck filled him in on her difficult first night.

"Sorry, Becks, that sounds awful," he said quietly.

"It was. I'm determined to pay Prima back as soon as possible. If I can increase the tips, I can return to being manager full-time, but in to order to do that I have to learn to dance or start B drinking."

Jack said sternly, "Well, that last one is not an option."

"Are you sure he's not your dad?" Victor asked with a chuckle.

"Knock it off, Limey," Jack growled.

"Whoa, you two play nice. I wasn't serious about the B drinking." She turned to Victor and said, "But I am serious about learning to dance."

"Well, let's get started, " Victor said as he stood up from the breakfast table.

Beck was both excited and nervous to begin. In her haste to put her new plan into motion, she almost forgot to say bye to Jack. She called over her shoulder. "Bye, Jack. Have fun with the new gig."

CHAPTER 18

The ballroom was awash with morning sunlight splashing across the cherry wood planks on the floor as Beck and Victor opened the drapes.

"So last night was a little tough for you?" Victor asked.

"That's an understatement. I was fine waltzing until my dance partner noticed I was counting and decided to talk to me about it mid-dance, which completely threw me off."

"We'll start with the waltz then and fine-tune it. Then we can move on to a couple of the more advanced dances."

"That sounds awfully ambitious," Beck said as she crossed her arms.

As Victor approached the record player, he said, "Nonsense. We have the next two days while you're off work. Give it everything you've got, and you'll get there.

He wrapped his arm around her waist and took her hand in his. Beck tensed as the music began.

"Remember to relax and let your partner lead," he said as he smiled warmly at her. She gave him a small smile and took a couple of deep breaths as she tried to relax. They were dancing to 'You Made Me Love You,' one of Beck's favorite songs from the era.

The words were soothing and familiar, and she could feel the tension leave her shoulders.

"You have a lovely voice," Victor said.

"I didn't realize I was singing." she blushed.

"Did you realize you're waltzing?" he asked.

Beck gasped. "I am? Oh, my goodness. This is amazing," she said as she accidentally stepped on his toes. "Oops, sorry."

"It's fine. Keep going," Victor said.

After a few more times practicing the waltz, they decided to move on to the Foxtrot. "This dance is popular around the quarter. We can start with a slow song and our way work up to more lively tunes."

The Foxtrot required more challenging footwork. After the first turn about the room, Beck stumbled, but Victor caught her in an awkward dip. The pair giggled as they righted themselves. She'd forgotten how nice it was to be held.

"Maybe we should stick to the slow songs for today," she said, smoothing out the wrinkles in her day dress.

After lunch, Beck was doing much better with the Foxtrot, so Victor suggested they try something new. "Do you like Latin Music?"

"Absolutely. I like anything with good percussion," she said.

"Have you ever tried to Rumba?"

Beck looked at her feet and said, "No."

Victor took her chin gently in his hand and raised her face to meet his gaze, "There now, there's no need to be ashamed. It's relatively new to the States. We'll start slow, like we did with the other dances."

She watched as Victor demonstrated the steps. "That's a lot of hip movement," she said.

"That's one of the keys to Latin dance. Come here and stand in front of me with your back turned. Good. May I place my hands on your hips to help you learn the movement?"

Beck nodded but felt guilty as the thought of him touching her hips excited her.

After a few tries, Victor said, "Good. Now the woman always starts the dance. So come out to the center of the floor. When I start the music, move the way I showed you."

As Victor played a Cuban song with a slow, steady beat, Beck swayed her hips. She glanced back at her dance partner, "Like this?" she asked.

"Yes, but mind your posture. That's it. Oh, Beck, you're stunning," he said softly. His encouragement prompted her to stand up a bit straighter. "This next part is where your partner has accepted your offer and approaches to couple up, as it were."

"The more you say, the more nervous I get. Let's just Rhumba before I change my mind, please?'" Beck said.

Victor agreed, and she watched in the mirror as he danced right up to her back. He placed his hands on her hips and encouraged her to make more prominent movements with them. Her heart began to pound from a combination of exertion and attraction. He moved in close, and she could feel his breath on the back of her neck, and she stopped moving.

"Don't stop, Becks. You've got the idea. Trust yourself," he said as he reached down and lifted her arm above her head. Then, he slid his hand seductively down her side.

Beck shuddered with desire as she felt his hips on her backside, but the face that came to mind was Jack's. She could picture him as clearly as if he was right there in the room with her. That's when, to Beck's horror, she realized, he was.

CHAPTER 19

As Jack watched his wife dance with another man, he felt like he had been slapped in the face. The scene he walked in on looked like all the lies she'd told him laid bare. This was not the behavior of a conflicted woman. Grinding up against another guy could only mean that she was done with their marriage. It also meant that either Beck had either misrepresented Victor's sexual orientation to him, or she was in complete denial.

Suddenly, his eyes met Beck's in the reflection of one of the oversized mirrors that decorated the ballroom walls. Her cheeks were instantly red, her mouth agape at the sight of his reflection. He wanted to yell, smash the mirror, or better yet, smash the mirror with the jerk who had just stroked his wife's body. Instead, he narrowed his eyes at her, pursed his lips, and shook his head before leaving. It was time to go to work.

The exterior of 1026 Conti Street was yet another example of New Orleans's grand architecture. On the inside, however, it was home to Norma Wallace and her stable of beautiful ladies. Norma insisted on a strict code of conduct from the women she hired. For example, they were expected to practice impeccable hygiene, and drug use was not tolerated.

The interior was lavishly decorated yet colorful. There were a couple of monkeys dressed in various outfits and a parrot that would taunt anyone going upstairs. There was a definite carnival vibe to the place.

Tom would love this, Jack thought.

As he set up the drums with Lowry, he couldn't help but notice the steady parade of gorgeous women. Each one was more beautiful than the next.

"What did I tell you? It's a classy brothel," Lowry said with a smile.

"I've got to say, this isn't what I pictured. It feels like we're playing a party for rich people," Jack admitted.

"Yeah, except eventually the rich people go upstairs to get it on."

"That happens at rich people's parties all the time, Lowry."

"Well, damn, I guess I've been running in the wrong circles," Lowry said with a shrug.

"Nah, you've got a wife who loves you. That's everything," Jack said wistfully.

"Yeah, I gotta admit, it was rocky at first. The baby surprised us. We had to get married real fast. But I'm crazy about her. Just wish she had a little more faith in me as a musician."

Norma Wallace glided into the room as the men prepared to play. She was an attractive woman with short brown hair and dressed to the nines in a bar suit and hat. The gossips often said she lied about her age and was pushing fifty, but the woman had a glow about her and could easily get away with it.

"Evening, boys. Are you the musicians Marcello sent me?" Norma asked in a husky Southern drawl.

"Yes, Ma'am. I'm Lowry Ringgold, this here's James Bastien, and Jack "the Red Devil" Herman."

Norma looked them over like a hungry lioness. "Y'all will do nicely. But first, some house rules. You're here to work. Don't fool around with my ladies unless you're a paying customer. Understand?" The men nodded. Norma continued, "Good, you slip my girls drugs or rat on any of my clientele, you won't be able to get a gig at a hog callin' contest. Are we clear?"

The men agreed and started their first set, launching into some Dixieland jazz tunes to bring the customers and the ladies up on their feet. It felt like a regular gig, with more blatant public displays of affection and couples disappearing to other parts of the house as they played.

James had to leave toward the latter half of the evening, so Jack moved from drums to vocals. There were more ladies than customers that late, and most were unaccompanied. They gathered to listen to Lowry play the piano as Jack sang.

Jack had never seen such a diverse group assembled in one place. Madame Norma had indeed hired a broad collection of ladies. They ranged from slender to pleasingly plump. Every hair color and texture was represented. A spectrum of skin tones from the darkest Haitian up to a raven-haired girl who was so pale she looked like a vampire. Their ages ranged from barely legal to probably a grandmother, and everything in between.

He had to admit that there were worse gigs than singing to a group of alluring women. In fact, this boosted the ego of the forty-two-year-old who had put his rock band days behind him. *I've still got it,* he thought as he worked the crowd, taking each woman's hand and squeezing it while holding their gaze. The last woman he came to was a young lady with auburn curls. She had hazel eyes and an upper lip with the perfect cupid bow.

Except for her hazel eyes, she looked like a younger version of Beck. So, innocent and vulnerable. She looked up at him through her lashes and blushed when they made eye contact. As he finished the song, he asked Lowry for his break.

"I just need some air," Jack said as he left Lowry to sing and play. Like a caged animal, Jack paced in the alley, trying to reconcile his attraction to the young woman with his pining for Beck.

The ten-minute break was over all too soon, and Jack joined Lowry in the parlor. He found the same young woman from before, chatting with the pale, raven-haired woman. They looked his way and smiled. Jack gave them a quick wave and walked back to the piano.

"Well, hello, Casanova," Lowry smirked, "Guess I should leave you to it while I grab a quick bite."

"Hey, I can't help it if I have stage presence."

Before Lowry could fire back with a witty retort, the girls came running up to them. The raven-haired one wore a dress with a corset-style bodice, causing her breasts to be lifted and pressed together. The men couldn't help but stare.

"Will you sign my…" she began to say as she reached toward and then beyond him. "Autograph book?" she asked as she grabbed a small burgundy leather book from the table behind Lowry.

"Get outta town. You got an autograph book?" Lowry said as an amused smile spread across his face.

"There are many famous and infamous people that pass through here. It'd be foolish not to keep one."

Jack took the book, desperate for somewhere else to focus his attention. "Who shall I make it out to?"

"I don't need any of that. Just a signature, please."

"Oh. Okay." He signed the book and handed it back. "What about you?" He asked the redhead.

She blushed and said, "I don't have a book, but I wanted to tell you that I love your music."

"Thanks. What's your favorite?" Jack asked.

"Rebecca's theme. She must have been very special."

"Oh, she *is*," Lowry said, "Jack loves her very much. Isn't that right, Jack?"

"Um, yes. Yes, she is." Jack mumbled. As the women drifted away, Jack narrowed his eyes at Lowry, "What in the hell was that?"

"I should ask you the same thing. Why are you chasing that skirt when you got Beck? Madame Norma specifically told us not to do it. Do you want to be fired? Because that, my man, is how you get fired."

"I'm sorry. It's just that Beck has spent the entire day learning to dance," Jack said.

"Good. I saw her the other night, and she needs all the help she can get," Lowry said.

"It's not good. Her dance teacher is tall, blonde, and British. I don't know if I can compete. Beck says the man isn't interested in women if you know what I mean. But I've seen how he acts around Beck. He acts more like a man in love than a dance teacher, and what's worse is that she's enjoying the attention."

"You want her back?" Lowry asked.

"You should have seen the position I caught them in," Jack fumed.

Lowry leaned toward Jack, "Do you want Rebecca back?"

"Absolutely," Jack said.

"What are your chances if you get mixed up with Beck Junior over there?"

"Zero," Jack mumbled.

"Good, now that you're thinking with your big head. Let's figure out what in the heck she ever saw in you in the first place."

Jack smirked. "Gee, thanks, Lowry."

"I'm just teasing, Cuz. You're a catch. I saw how that little dark-haired cutie was all 'Will sign my dot dot dot,' I thought that the 'dot dot dot' was gonna be her biscuits," Lowry chuckled.

"Well. that would have been a first for me...at a brothel, that is," Jack said as he and Lowry laughed.

CHAPTER 20

"What's wrong, Becks?" Victor asked.

"I need a break," she said as she stepped away from him and fidgeted with her bare ring finger.

Victor checked his pocket watch, "I didn't realize it had gotten so late. It's nearly five o'clock. You must be famished from all that dancing."

"Don't you have rehearsal?"

"The theater's always dark on Mondays. I was hoping we could have dinner together."

"I think Mrs. Brown is serving ham," Beck said.

"I'm sure it's lovely, but what if we went out for dinner?"

"Just the two of us?" she asked.

"W-we don't have to. I merely thought a change of scenery might be nice after being in the house all day."

Beck was sick of being indoors. However, after Jack had walked in on her and Victor dancing, going to dinner with him seemed wrong.

This feels like a date, she thought.

"We could invite Truman," she offered.

Victor tilted his head. "I'm pretty sure he has other plans."

"You're right, it's short notice, and he's been awfully busy with his novel," she said.

"Then it's settled. There's a seafood place down by the river I've been wanting to try. Let's freshen up and meet downstairs," Victor said.

Beck cleaned up and dressed in a burgundy dress with a sweetheart neckline and a tea-length swing skirt. Before the full-length mirror, she carefully looked at the fitted bodice as it stretched over her chest, self-conscious that she might be dressing too sexy again. However, before Beck could help herself, she started twirling around the room in her skirt, delighted at how the material flowed. For a moment, she felt like a little girl again.

She met Victor on the stairs, looking dashing in his navy double-breasted suit. "Well, aren't you a vision," he said.

Beck blushed and smiled, "Thank you, you're quite dash -uh dapper yourself." *It's only dinner with a friend*, she told herself. *A well-dressed friend who's definitely not attracted to me.*

Victor took her to a tiny little place overlooking the river that claimed to serve only the freshest seafood, hauled in daily from the Gulf of Mexico. The pair tried everything, including the raw oysters.

"Fascinating," Victor said as he closed his eyes, "These have a taste that's more sweet than salty. I used to spend summers at my grandparent's estate in Brighton, and the oysters were large and meatier. Very salty. These are more buttery."

Beck hoped this esoteric but interesting bit of food knowledge might be further evidence that Victor was not interested in women. "I never thought much about it before, but you're right. The ones in California are more crisp, like a cucumber. I guess they're all a reflection of their environment."

"I didn't know you'd visited California." Victor leaned toward her and smiled.

"That's where we're from, actually," Beck said as she tipped up a shell and slid another oyster into her mouth.

"We?' Victor asked.

"Um, yeah. Jack was born there. I'm originally from Louisiana, but I moved out there to work in the movie business."

"What have you been in?" Victor asked.

"I wasn't acting. I wrote a few scripts, nothing you'd have heard of."

"Oh, come now, I'm a huge movie fan. Try me," Victor pressed.

Beck scrambled to make up a title in her head as a jazz trio began to play. "Oh. Look, they have a dance floor. Want to practice?"

"If you'd like," he managed to say before she dragged him out to the dance floor.

"This tempo works for any of the types you've been learning. Lady's choice."

Beck bit her lip, remembering the heat she felt when they danced the Rumba and the anger and hurt she saw reflected in Jack's face, "Anything but the Rumba," she said.

"Foxtrot then?" Victor asked. Beck nodded.

It was by no means perfect, but as long as she relaxed and remembered to let Victor lead, she managed not to step on his poor toes again. The more they danced, the more comfortable Beck felt. Not only that, she felt confident and at home in her body.

"May I cut in?" asked a man with a Southern drawl.

Beck and Victor stopped and turned, surprised to see their friend Truman.

"You had dinner without me. The least you can do is dance with me," Truman said.

"We thought you were busy," Victor said, with an exaggerated shrug.

"You should have asked," Truman said, crossing his arms.

"You're right. Here you go," Beck said as she tried to join the men's hands.

"We can't dance together. Are you trying to get us arrested?" Victor whispered.

"Or killed?" Truman asked.

Beck was stunned by what she'd done. This wasn't the nineties. Even in the nineties, there were places were two men weren't safe to dance together. "I'm sorry, I wasn't thinking," she said. Just then, a wave of nausea hit her. "Listen, I'm gonna split. You two have fun."

"But Becks..." Victor said, "At least let me walk you home."

"I wouldn't feel right pulling you away from Truman. Thank you for dinner," Beck managed to say before bolting for the door.

One block up Toulouse Street, she had to duck into an alley to vomit into a trash can. She was one block shy of the boarding house when she got sick a second time in someone's bougainvillea bushes.

Beck's condition deteriorated as she trudged up to the boarding house. She trembled as she struggled to open the door. Her skin felt cold and rubbery as she lay on the cool tile floor and dozed momentarily before attempting the three-flight journey upstairs.

The third wave hit as she made the last few steps to the top of the stairs. There was no time to fumble around in her handbag for her room key, so she made a beeline for the bathroom at the top of the stairs. Thankfully, making it to the toilet. As she was getting sick, someone walked in and wordlessly held her hair.

CHAPTER 21

After the gig, Jack's thoughts bounced back and forth between longing and betrayal. Perhaps Victor was gay. Maybe they were performing a dance that just happened to appear sexy. Both could be true. But the thing he knew for sure was Beck's body language. She'd enjoyed Victor's touch, and Jack had seen the undeniable flash of guilt in her eyes when she met his gaze.

The scene played on a loop in his mind, as hurt and anger rooted in his soul.

Jack walked briskly, his hot breath freezing in the mist before him. He rehearsed everything he'd say to his wife as he clenched and unclenched his fists.

A list of her faults and past transgressions seemed to line the path back to the boarding house.

Beck had hidden being a columnist who published hurtful things about him, allowing him to believe she was dead for an entire year. She'd said she understood how important his music was to him. Another lie. Now, she was being dishonest about her relationship with this British guy. It wasn't a matter of if she was lying, simply a matter of the manner in which she was lying.

She's going to hear what I have to say, dammit.

As he marched up the stairs and reached the third floor, Jack noticed a river of light pouring down the stairs from the bathroom he shared with Victor. *Great, the last person I want to see right now,* he thought.

His first inclination was to avoid the bathroom entirely, but he caught a glimpse of a burgundy skirt splayed out on the floor. "Blaargh!" Came the unmistakable sound of someone retching into the toilet. He stepped into the doorway and saw that his wife was the one hurling into his commode. The move was instinctive as he walked over, gently took her auburn hair into his hand, and held it out of harm's way.

After a few minutes of inactivity, he said," Do you think that's it?"

Beck only nodded. So, he stepped over to the sink and wetted a washcloth for her. She cleaned her face, and Jack offered to help her up. Once on her feet, he noticed how pretty she looked in her swing dress. He had a fleeting urge to twirl her but immediately dismissed that idea.

"Too much booze?" he asked.

"Bad oysters," she said weakly.

"Want some help back to your room?"

Beck shook her head no, and tried to walk forward but lurched and had to hold onto the bathroom counter to steady herself. "Actually, yes," she said.

He carefully lifted her into his arms and walked over to her room. "Are you able to unlock the door?"

Beck gingerly grabbed the key from her black leather handbag and leaned toward the lock. Once inside the room, Jack laid her on the bed, helped her change into a nightgown, and pulled the covers onto her still-trembling body.

He sat beside her and helped her get to and from the bathroom over the next two hours until her stomach settled and she could finally sleep.

Jack stroked her red curls as they extended out over her

pillowcase. Her hair was incredibly soft. His eyes traveled over her form hidden under the covers and replayed how the moonlight held her breasts as he helped her into her gown. Despite all she had done to him, she was perfect.

Jack shook his head. He'd planned to read her the riot act. He'd seen so clearly how wrong they were for one another. But sitting in the room where he had loved her so passionately, dancing in the river of moonlight that cut across the wool carpet, he saw stretched out before him everything lovable and unique about his wife. The way she had cared for marginalized people and put herself on the line to fight for others. How she managed to put people at ease, making them feel like she had known them her entire life. Rivaling only his mother, she had cheered him on tirelessly in all his endeavors.

Beck was more of a cat person, yet she loved Rufus with all her heart. A lover of celebrations and travel, she'd agreed to put their honeymoon on hold when his work crowded the schedule around their wedding.

"The best wedding is the one that ends with us being married to one another," Beck had said. Before their trip to New Orleans, she had done her best to be patient with his workload. Maybe he had asked too much of her.

Jack knew that he'd been given a gift. However, he wondered if it was possible to balance the inspiration that inundated his brain several times a day with the company of the woman he loved.

As Beck rolled over and turned her back to him, Jack eased off his suspenders and removed his dress shirt leaving only his undershirt. He eased himself down next to Beck as she made soft noises. He pressed his body against her back, breathing in the lovely, familiar scent of almond and vanilla as he nuzzled her neck. Delighted in the soft sleepy sigh that escaped her throat, Jack gently pulled her close, and her body melted into his.

As he drifted off to sleep, he began to outline a plan to bring her home.

CHAPTER 22

Beck woke up content for the first time since she had come to New Orleans. A muscular arm was wrapped around her waist, a large calloused hand at the end. There was no doubt that Jack was there, and not a dream as she had initially thought.

"Jack?" she whispered.

"Mmm?" he moaned. His breath warmed Beck's neck, raising goosebumps on her skin.

"You stayed?" Beck asked sleepily.

"You were pretty sick."

"I think it was the oysters," she explained. "As if the creepy decor wasn't enough, they had to go and try to kill us, too."

"Us? As in, you and Victor?" Jack asked with a smirk as he sat up in the bed.

Oops, Beck rolled over to face him. "We went to dinner after the dance lessons. Truman joined us later. Please don't look at me like that."

"Did you want your freedom so you could see other people?"

"I wanted to see if I could make it on my own. Living in your shadow isn't easy, you know?"

"Is that how you feel?" Jack asked.

Beck stared past Jack out the window and sighed. "Sometimes, your music fills all the available space in your head. There's no room for me."".

Jack fidgeted with his fingers and said, "I told you that my career occupies a lot of my time. You said that you loved my music, you promised you'd support me."

Beck sat up and put her hand on his arm. "And you promised to share your life with me, but I've been on the outside looking in ever since we finished our movie. You promised to love and cherish me, but I don't feel loved or cherished."

"It seems an awful lot like you're trying to replace me," Jack grumbled.

"I'm not," she said, annoyed that he hadn't addressed what she'd told him.

"I saw you in the ballroom with Victor. The way he stroked your side - "

"We were doing the Rhumba, that's part of the dance," she snapped.

Jack exited her bed and crossed to the window, glancing at the city before turning back to face his wife, "Stop lying to me. I saw the look on your face when he touched you. You loved it."

"You're right. I'm attracted to Victor, but he'll never be interested in me. Which is fine because I'm not looking for that."

He ran his hand through his hair and huffed, "What *are* you looking for, Beck?"

"At first, I wanted to build a life on my own. I've done a pretty good job, but it's lonely. I'd like to share it with someone who appreciates me and who's interested in what I'm doing instead of always focusing on their own thing. Someone who will walk arm in arm with me and hug me. It sounds silly, but it's better than sitting in a lonely bed hugging myself. That sounds pathetic when I say it out loud." She could feel the warmth in her cheeks and worried she'd said too much.

"It doesn't sound pathetic. I could use a hug myself," Jack said.

"Come here," she said as she opened her arms.

He crossed over to the bed and embraced her. "I don't want to let go," Jack said. He took a deep breath. "It feels like I'm home again."

When she eventually let go, he took her hand and asked, "Beck, are we ever going to be 'us' again?"

She wanted to tell him what he wanted to hear, but she knew better than to settle again. "I'd like for us to be a better version of ourselves. There's a lot we need to work through. Things that would be easier to work through if we were back home."

He nodded and said, "I'd love to go home."

"Have you seen the Voodoo Lady?" Beck asked.

"The one from Harlem? No. Have you?"

"She appeared the other night while I was walking one of the dance hostesses home. She was across the street in Congo Square. She spoke to me about us."

"What did she say?"

Beck recalled how the woman had chastised her for running away and had pointed out that she needed Jack as much as he needed her. But she wasn't ready to share that. Instead, she said, "She called me Rebecca Herman and knew we were from Topanga Canyon 1995. Then, she told me that music had existed as a sort of pre-language. It's basically emotions set to rhythm."

Jack smiled. "That's why music is crucial to Voodoo rituals. They believe it allows the dead to communicate with us."

Beck nodded. "That's not all. She told me that it can detach a soul from one plain to the next under the right circumstances."

Jack paced at the end of the bed and furrowed his brow. "Music and emotions. That might be a clue."

"To what?" Beck had been pretty sure the old lady was just rambling.

"To return to 1995. Maybe we need to do some sort of ritual or something. I need to find this lady." Jack said.

"She was in Congo Square," Beck said.

"That makes sense," he said.

"It does?"

"Congo Square is where the slaves gathered to practice their rituals from West Africa and the Catholicism they had learned from their masters. Eventually, two faiths were combined, and New Orleans Voodoo was born. People who practice it believe in God, saints, and ancestors who intercede on our behalf. The largest oak there is called the Ancestry Tree. Believers leave fruit as offerings and pray."

"I remember some of that from Tom's wedding. A guy swung a sword at the border near our seats. He said he was letting the ancestors in from the underworld, and they made an offering."

"I'm playing a gig near the square tonight. I'll look for the Voodoo Lady after I'm done," he said, "What are you up to today? Wanna grab some brunch at Cafe du Monde?"

Beck bit her bottom lip and said, "I have dance lessons all day today."

Jack frowned. "I see."

"We could eat breakfast here together and go to Cafe du Monde tomorrow."

Jack seemed to brighten at her offer. "Sounds good."

"Great. I'll freshen up and see you downstairs," Beck said as she got up and headed toward her bathroom.

Jack gently touched her arm. "Beck, I love you. You know that don't you?"

The words felt good, especially after he had been so quiet. "I love you, too, but words aren't enough, Jack," she said, placing her hand over his.

"I know," he said as he crossed the threshold and closed her door.

She could tell her words had been painful for Jack to hear, but Beck required action, not words. For once, instead of running away, she had stood her ground. Determined to fight for the life she deserved.

CHAPTER 23

On the nights Jack and Lowry worked for Norma, the men would walk to the northern boundary of the French Quarter. Once Lowry was out of sight, Jack would sneak across North Rampart Street and into Congo Square. Night after night, the tree-lined square was cold and deserted. The Voodoo Lady was nowhere to be found. Without her guidance, he felt resigned to life in 1948.

In early February, Mardi Gras season was in full swing. The quarter sparkled in purple, gold, and green decorations. Parades would come through the quarter almost every day in the two weeks leading up to Fat Tuesday, and elegant balls were planned all over the city.

"If we hang the bunting from the rafters, will it hold?" Beck asked the crew preparing for the ball at the 500 Club. The men nodded. "Great, let's get to it."

Jack stood near the door unnoticed for several minutes by design. Watching her work was one of the best things about working at the 500 Club three nights a week. He loved to watch her take command of a crew. She was a fair but firm leader. Beck turned around, and he was soon discovered.

"What do you think?" she asked as she gestured around the room.

"They're pretty good," he said.

"They have to be better than pretty good. The ball's in three days. Everything has to be perfect."

"It will be. I have every faith in you," he said. Beck turned to him and smiled, looking genuinely radiant. Then over his shoulder she saw something that alarmed her.

"Look out!" Beck grabbed Jack pulling him to her as a large Mardi Gras mask ornament came loose on one side and swung for him. After he was safely out of the way, she looked at the fallen decoration. "Oh no, it's broken." She let go of Jack and gathered the larger-than-life beads that had once adorned the side of the large mask.

Jack looked at the damage. "I can fix it."

"You can?" Beck asked eagerly.

"Do you have any Super Glue?" he whispered.

"It's not super, but there's glue behind the bar."

"I'll make it work," Jack said

As she held a bead in place, Jack applied the glue. They continued in silence until the work was complete.

"Are you coming to the ball?" Jack asked

She nodded and said, "I'm working."

"I thought you had Mondays and Tuesdays off," Jack said with a pout.

"It's the biggest party of the year. They want me here in case something goes wrong," Beck explained.

"So you're on-call?"

"Yes, but without a pager. Aren't you performing?"

"A short set at the end of the night. Prima has booked a lot of special guests. So, I'm free until the end of the evening. Will you save me a dance?" Jack asked.

"I told you, I'm not doing that during the ball."

"I didn't mean in your professional capacity. I thought we could dance together, for old time's sake."

"Oh," Beck said, caught off guard. Then she smiled at him, "I'd like that."

Jack's eyes grew wide as he said, "Okay. I look forward to it."

He practically floated back to the green room, excited to tell Lowry of his progress with Beck. When Lowry wasn't in the green room or the alley, Jack had a nagging suspicion. He peeked into one of the gaming rooms and found his intuition correct. Lowry played Blackjack with another man wearing a yellow-gold zoot suit and a large matching hat.

"Lowry? What are you doing?"

Both Lowry and the man in the yellow suit turned to Jack.

"Why, Hi-de-ho there, Red Devil, I feel like I've seen a ghost. Lowry mentioned he'd found you, but I thought maybe he was pulling my leg."

Jack hurried over to his old friend. "Hello, Cab," he said with a sad smile. It was strange that Cab said that he'd felt like he had seen a ghost because, in 1995, Cab had been dead for almost a year. "Slip me five," Jack said as he shook the man's hand and pulled him into a hug.

Then, Lowry and Cab finished their round of Blackjack, which the house won. "Wanna play Red Devil?" Cab asked.

"No thanks," Jack said as he wrung his hands and watched helplessly. He knew Lowry's financial situation wasn't great, and being a huge fan of Cab's, Jack was painfully aware that his gambling habit would soon cause his band to split. However, he had to remind himself not to interfere. The breakup of Cab's band would free him up for other projects.

Jack was not as sure about Lowry's future. All he knew was that Marvin had said very little about his grandfather, and Jack had been concerned that he'd give himself away if he'd pressed too hard for details. What if the gambling was destined to hurt his friend's career or, worse, his family?

While Jack was lost in his thoughts, Lowry won big on the second round of Blackjack and was poised to play another. Jack couldn't help himself. "Hey cuz, maybe you should quit while you're ahead."

"What's it to you?" Lowry asked with a frown.

"You're up right now, and you need the dough. Why not quit while you're ahead," Jack suggested.

"Why don't you scram?" Lowry asked.

"You need that money for your family," Jack said.

Lowry got off the bar stool and narrowed his eyes at Jack, "You got some nerve talking to me about my family. Your woman's taxi dancing and drooling all over her dance teacher. She's gotten to be quite the hoofer. That limey must be her workin' overtime."

All at once, Jack felt heat rush to his face as he bared his teeth and raised his fist. Cab quickly jumped between him and Lowry.

"Now, gentleman, Let's not flip our wigs. Why don't I buy us a round, and you can fill ole Cab in on all this," Cab said as he motioned for the cocktail waitress. Once the men had their drinks, Cab looked at them and said, "Alright, what's buzzin', cousins?"

"Well, Jack and Beck are -" Lowry started.

Cab held up his hand, "Hold it now, I wanna hear each story straight from the horse's mouth. What's this I hear about you having a family, Lowry?"

Lowry smiled. "Yes, Sir. I got hitched right after the war to a beautiful dancer that I met while touring with the Duke. We have a baby boy."

"Congratulations, my boy!" Cab jumped up and hugged Lowry hard. "I have a few ankle biters myself. All girls, though. There's nothing in the world like being a daddy. What about you, Jack? You and Rebecca must have a few rug rats by now."

Jack looked at his feet and cleared his throat, "No, no rug rats. Beck and I aren't actually together at the moment."

"I don't follow," Cab said.

Jack rubbed the back of his neck and sighed. "It's complicated."

"I'm sorry, man. I thought for certain that you two were in it for the long haul, but then again, that Rebecca can sure be a pistol."

"It's not all her fault," Jack said, "I wasn't the most attentive husband."

Lowry snapped to attention. "You didn't tell me you two was hitched."

Oh shit, I've got to learn to keep my mouth shut around Lowry.

Jack whispered furiously to his friends, "Hey, don't spread that around. She could be fired if Prima ever found out."

Lowry smirked and mumbled, "Yeah, only single ladies can taxi dance."

"Hold the phone. Why is Rebecca doing that?" Cab asked.

Jack and Lowry filled him in on Beck's arrest after she had Lowry play with Leon Prima's band on New Year's Eve and how they'd been working feverishly to pay off the debt they owed Prima for their bail.

Cab smiled. "I always liked her gumption, but she's lucky all she got was a nosebleed. A few years back, I went to see a friend play in St. Louie. It was a whites-only show, but most places will allow a fellow black musician to attend another's shows. Especially if you're famous, but the doorman claimed he didn't know me, and before I could grab my ID to prove it, he beat the shit out of me with the butt of his gun."

Jack gasped and said, "Oh my God! That's awful."

Cab tipped back his yellow hat, "Yep, eight staples to the head and a broken pinkie finger. See, I still got the scar."

Leon peeked in. "There you are. I've been looking all over for you, Mr. Calloway. The paper is here to do an interview and take some publicity shots for the Mardi Gras Ball."

Cab got up from his bar stool. "I'm right behind you, Mr. Prima. See you soon, boys."

"Had you heard that story?" Jack asked Lowry.

"It was big news. How did you *not* know that story?"

"Um, I must have missed it somehow, I guess." Jack said.

"Sure you did," Lowry said as he headed back to the Blackjack table.

"Lowry, please don't do this."

"You fix your family your way, and I'll fix my family my way."

"How is gambling going to fix things? Jack asked.

"I'm gonna double this money. You'll see it will last twice as long."

"It doesn't work like that, Lowry."

"The hell it don't. I doubled my winnings last week." Lowry sat down at the table.

A voice behind Jack said, "Mr. Ringgold, is this man bothering

you?"
Meyer Lansky stepped in between the men, staring Jack down.

"I'm trying to keep my friend from making a big mistake," Jack said.

"Mr. Ringgold is a big boy, I'm sure he's capable of making his own choices. Now, I suggest you go back to the ballroom. It'd be a shame if something were to happen to that cute little cookie of yours while she was left unattended," Meyer sneered.

Jack took one last look at Lowry, who looked back at him and defiantly laid all of his cash on the table.

Jack sighed, then narrowed his eyes at Meyer. "This is your last warning. Stay the hell away from Rebecca," Jack growled, then he hurried back to the ballroom.

He hurried out front and was relieved to find Beck unharmed. "Aren't you supposed to be onstage?" she asked.

"Yes, but can I please walk you home after the show?"

"Sure, is everything okay? You look flushed."

"I had a rough time earlier. I'll be fine," Jack mumbled as he stroked her upper arm to reassure her and headed for the stage. Looking back at Beck as she reluctantly headed over to the area where the available hostesses stood and was soon asked to dance by a young guy.

Ever vigilant, Jack watched over her and the other dancers as he sang. As he turned his attention to Beck and the boy, Jack noticed that the kid could barely look at her as she guided him through a swing dance. Stealing glances only when she wasn't looking at him. It was sweet in a way. The dance Beck was performing was new. *Victor must have recently taught her,* he thought, with a pang of jealousy.

As soon as the young man seemed at ease, Jack noticed that Beck was watching him play. Invigorated, he sang more passionately than he had in years. His voice rang out across the hall, and his spirits lifted as he watched her move about the floor to his song.

Beck switched partners for the following number, dancing the waltz with an older gentleman. Once again, Jack caught her looking at him over the old man's stooped shoulders. As their eyes met, she quickly shifted her gaze toward the bar. But when the old man turned her back toward the stage, she glanced Jack's way. He met her gaze with his signature devilish grin and saw her cheeks redden as his own skin grew hot.

As he sang and watched the bodies glistening with sweat as they moved about the dance floor, he felt at home for the first time in 1948. As the band switched songs, his eyes scanned the floor until he once again found his wife's auburn locks. Over the next two numbers, he watched her, admiring how confident she seemed in her own skin. The refined gracefulness in how she moved her body. He wondered if she could feel the change that he saw. He wished for her sake that she could, yet knew she was always hard on herself.

Then again, so am I, he thought.

Jack's bass guitarist danced over and gave him a gentle nudge, reminding him not to fixate entirely on Beck. He re-engaged the crowd, only to drift back over to watch her curvy body move in time with the rhythm of the music again.

Half in shadow, Jack tried to read her expression, hoping he'd been able to keep her attention the way that she'd held his. But with her face half in light and half in shadow, he couldn't be certain. Into the darkness, Jack flashed her one more "Red Devil" grin. Hoping that he might capture her heart once more.

CHAPTER 24

The weekend leading up to Fat Tuesday flew by as it was packed with parties and parades. It seemed like every organization and establishment had its own celebrations. In fact, parade season had begun weeks before Mardi Gras as the citizens and tourists alike were determined to wring every ounce of revelry and indulgence out of the season before Fat Tuesday gave way to Ash Wednesday, which ushered in the Christian season of Lent. A time of denying one's self of certain vices for the forty days that preceded Easter.

"I think I should give up drinking for Lent," Victor mumbled to Beck at the breakfast table on Sunday morning. "I'm absolutely knackered after last night."

"Are you Catholic?" she asked.

"I was raised Anglican, but I'm clearly not practicing. Sitting here nursing this bloody hangover."

"Sorry. I was raised Baptist. We didn't really do much for Lent, but I've always loved Mardi Gras. It's one of my favorite holidays," Beck said wistfully.

"You told me your favorite holiday was Halloween," Jack said with a smirk as he entered the dining room.

"It is. Mardi Gras is a very close second. I love the parades, the costumes, the parties, and of course, the food."

Victor turned slightly green, "Oh, Becks, please don't mention food right now."

"Sorry," she said as she reached across the table and gently squeezed Victor's hand.

At that moment, Mrs. Brown entered the dining room with a tray of plates. As she served Victor, she said, "Here you go, dear. An egg and spinach omelet light on the cheese. That will pink you back up in no time."

"Thank you," he said, leaning back away from his plate. As Mrs. Brown headed back into the kitchen, Victor scrunched his nose. "I'm afraid I'm going to chunder if I eat this."

Jack said, "It's actually a decent hangover cure. It's saved me many times."

As Victor brought the first bite to his lips, he looked at Beck, "Please tell me more about Mardi Gras. I need the distraction. Did you come here to celebrate as a girl?"

"We had our own celebration up in Shreveport, but it was much smaller. We only had two krewes, so there were only two parades and balls. I've never seen anything like this. It's incredible," Beck said.

Jack looked up from the newspaper and said, "It says here that there's a record-breaking forty-nine krewes in New Orleans this year."

"I wish I could see everything. Lafitte's Krewe was amazing last night. It must have been fun riding on a float," Beck said as she smiled at Victor, who was gradually returning to his normal color.

"Absolutely, but If I had to do it again, I think I'd prefer to wear something a little less revealing," Victor said.

"But you and Truman were stunning. I loved your mermaid costumes."

Jack laughed. "You were a mermaid?"

"It was a part of the theme," Victor said, narrowing his eyes at Jack, "And Beck's right; we did look stunning in our costumes. It was a bit chilly, is all."

The ringing phone interrupted the lodgers. Mrs. Brown called from the kitchen, "Rebecca, your boss is on the phone."

Beck stood, her brow furrowed. "Leon's never called me before. I hope everything's alright," she said as she entered the kitchen.

Jack watched her leave and then smirked at Victor, "A mermaid," he snickered, "Was pirate wench taken?"

Victor was perfectly poised as he said, "As a matter of fact, all the pirate wench roles were taken by men closer to your age, who were less comfortable showing some skin."

Jack was at a loss. He couldn't care less what anyone chose to wear and had just wanted to needle Victor to get a rise. He didn't expect an expertly delivered barb at his expense. As he tried to form a clever retort, Beck came bounding into the room with a huge smile on her face.

"I'm the queen!" she shouted as she jumped up and down. "I'm the queen."

Victor didn't miss a beat hurrying over to her while Jack lagged behind, completely confused.

"You positively rule, my dear. But what do you mean?" Victor asked with a chuckle. "Did you pull off a coup in the kitchen?"

"The Prima family runs the Krewe of Persephone, and their Queen was caught doing something less than queenly, I guess. So, Leon wants me to do it. I get to be in their parade and wear a fancy costume. I'm so excited," Beck said rapidly. She grabbed Victor's hands and jumped up and down as he tried to steady himself.

Jack finally managed to say, "Congratulations, Darlin."

"Thanks. Oh, Leon wanted to speak to you, too."

Jack went into the kitchen, grateful for a reprieve from the glee in the dining room. Unlike Beck, Leon called Jack every time he wanted to tweak the setlist. "Morning, Prima. What's cooking? You thinking of switching things up for the post-parade show tonight?"

"My band's on a float tonight, so the Ringgold Rebels are taking our spot for the finale," Leon explained.

Jack's mood brightened a bit. "Oh? What are we playing on the float?

"You ain't playing nothing 'cause I need ya elsewhere."

"Where do you need me?" Jack asked, feeling deflated.

"Our King had himself a little accident last night, so we need a new one. How about it, Jack?"

"You want to make me king of your parade?"

"It looks bad if I make myself king, and let's face it, Jack, you're the most famous face playing the club next to me."

"I'm not as famous as Cab Calloway," Jack argued.

Leon sighed, "Let me rephrase that, next to me, you're the most famous white guy."

"I see," Jack said. After Prima's revelation, he wanted to refuse, but the offer to be king to Beck's queen was too good to pass up.

"I'll take that as a yes. Lemme give you the address for the tailor. They'll alter the suit and crown to fit ya. We line up at five for the parade on the corner of Bourbon and Conti. Capiche?"

"Yes, sir," Jack said as he grabbed a pen and paper.

He emerged from the kitchen with a crooked grin and said, "I have some news, too. Guess who's king?"

"You're my king?" Beck asked.

"That's right, Darlin," Jack said as he scooted in between her and Victor. He took her into his arms and twirled her around.

"This is going to be fun," she said.

"I have to go to the tailor so they can alter the costume. You wanna come with me?" he asked as he cut his eyes to Victor, who looked a bit ill again.

"I'm afraid I'm off to see the seamstress for the same reason," she said with a shrug.

"Oh, that's a shame," Jack said as he took her hand and bowed dramatically, "Until tonight, then, your Majesty." He noticed a definite blush as he kissed her hand.

CHAPTER 25

It had been months since Beck had seen the southwest corner of the French Quarter. As she turned the slip of paper with the address for the seamstress over in her hand, she thought about the circular nature of life and how people and places had a way of coming around again.

Today, she was headed back to the train station she'd arrived in back in November, but this time, Beck was dressed in clothes she had purchased, not stolen, as she rode the streetcar named Desire instead of walking.

As the city breezed by, Beck recalled her early days in the quarter. The fun she'd had meeting Tennessee and reading scenes with him as he finalized the edits to his now famous play. Beck wondered if he would return to ride the streetcar he'd immortalized before they shut the Desire line down permanently in the spring.

When the streetcar stopped at Bourbon and Canal, Beck headed across Canal Street to New Orleans Union Station. The seamstress shop was adjacent to the dress shop where she had stolen the much-needed supplies when she arrived suddenly in 1947. Her stomach hurt as she walked into the shop, which looked much more cheerful by the light of day. An older lady with a round pleasant face was humming to herself behind the counter.

"Good morning. May I help you?" the woman asked with a smile.

Beck took a deep breath and walked up to the counter, "Are you the owner?" she asked.

"Yes, I'm Dottie," she said proudly.

"I came to give you this," she said as she handed an envelope of cash to Dottie.

The woman opened it and thumbed through the bills. "I don't understand."

"Months ago, I arrived at this station with nothing but a nightgown. I was scared and cold. I needed clothes, and your shop was unlocked. I took what I needed, but I didn't have a cent to my name. I've been working and saving a portion of my pay every week until I could return and pay you in full."

Dottie furrowed her brow. "You stole things from me?"

Beck lowered her head in shame. "I'm sorry," she said softly as tears filled her eyes.

"This is a terrible location, but it's all I can afford. You see, lots of people are passing through. They steal stuff from my shop all the time. But, you came back. That's never happened in the twenty years I've been here. Don't cry, Sugar. I forgive you," Dottie said as she reached across the counter and patted Beck's hand.

Beck felt like a burden had been lifted. She'd wanted to simply slip the envelope under the door anonymously, but owning up to what she'd done had been the right thing to do.

I didn't run away that time, Voodoo Lady, she thought.

Entering the seamstress's shop, she marveled at all the Mardi Gras gowns on the dress forms waiting to be worn over the next few days. She wandered through the gorgeous costumes and wondered which one was hers.

"You Rebecca?" asked an unseen woman with a strong New York accent.

"Yes, Ma'am," Beck said, trying to locate the woman among the gowns.

"Great, walk straight back and turn left. I had to do a last-minute fix on one of your attendants. I'm just making sure it's perfect," the woman said.

As she rounded the corner, Beck was shocked to see the booming voice was coming from a tiny Jewish woman. She was even more shocked when a baby with light brown skin and a head full of black curls crawled out from the gap underneath the dressing room door.

A woman's voice inside said, "Oh shoot, he's awake."

Without missing a beat, the seamstress tilted her head toward the escaping toddler. She asked Beck, "Be a doll and pick that up, would ya?"

Beck scooped up the adorable baby just as Ella emerged from the dressing room. Beck gasped at the statuesque dancer dressed in a long sleeveless deep purple gown with black opera gloves. "Ella, you're breathtaking."

"It'll do," the seamstress said.

Ella smiled shyly and said, "Thank you, Ms. Rebecca."

"Please call me Beck." The baby wiggled in her arms as he reached for Ella. "I'm so excited to finally meet little Jackie," she added with a smile as she struggled to keep him on her hip.

Ella flashed Beck a worried look and said, "Yeah, I've told you so much about my *nephew*, but I guess you two haven't met."

"Go ahead and take that off, and I'll deliver it to the club. Just hand it over the top once you get it off," the seamstress said impatiently as she undid the zipper.

Ella went back into the dressing room to change into her street clothes.

The seamstress leaned toward Beck conspiratorially and said, "I don't believe for one damn minute that she's that baby's aunt. Look how attached he is to her. She just doesn't want everyone to know she was with a black man. This little one is obviously a Negro."

"I've known Ella and her family a long time," Beck lied, "This is her nephew Jackie. She's told me a million stories about him."

"Here's the gown," Ella called, handing it over the top of the dressing room door.

At the sound of her voice, the drowsy baby began to cry. Jackie reached his arm toward the sound of Ella's voice, opening and closing his tiny fist.

"Mmm, Mmama, Mmama," he cried.

C'mon Jackie, work with us here, Beck thought as she bounced him up and down, trying to soothe him.

The seamstress smirked at Beck and said, "Hmph! Nephew, my eye." Then she went to the back room to hang Ella's dress. "I'll be out with your gown in a minute, Queenie."

Jackie laid his head on Beck's shoulder and yawned. He took his little fist and rubbed his eyes. By the time Ella was dressed, the baby was fast asleep on Beck's shoulder.

"You're a natural," Ella said as she tousled her son's curls.

"Thanks, I've had lots of practice," Beck smiled and cuddled him closer.

"I didn't know you had children," Ella said.

"I don't. But, I was the oldest grandchild on both sides of my family, and I babysat for most of my neighbors."

"Do you wanna be a mom someday?"

Beck thought about what a mess things were with Jack. He'd been too busy for her, much less a baby. Besides, the only time the subject ever came up was when Miriam pressed them for grandchildren, and they both agreed that it wasn't the time.

Ella was staring.

"Someday," Beck admitted, "but I don't think it will ever happen."

"Sometimes, they surprise you," Ella said, indicating her sleeping son.

The seamstress returned with a dress even more elaborate than Ella's. It was olive green with a train and had an intricate hand-beaded design on the full skirt down to the train. Gold flames and purple blooms illustrated the two worlds Persephone occupied in Greek mythology.

"Is that for me?" Beck asked as her mouth fell open.

"Try it on," the seamstress said.

Beck reluctantly parted with the sleeping babe, gently placing him into his mother's arms. "Bye, Jackie. It was nice to finally meet you," she whispered as she smiled at Ella. "See you soon."

The dress would have to be hemmed, but thankfully, nothing too drastic was needed. Beck left even more excited for the evening. Exiting the station, she saw Ella resting on a bench with Jackie still asleep against her chest.

"You two okay?" Beck asked.

"He's just getting too heavy for me to carry, and we can't afford a buggy."

"I was just about to take the streetcar back into the quarter. Why don't you join me? My treat."

Ella smiled. "Thank you. I haven't been on the streetcar since the war. I'd like that."

As the two approached the streetcar, they strode confidently into the "whites-only section." At first, no one said anything. Ella passed easily enough. However, as they began to move, Jackie raised his little head and let out a shriek of delight, thoroughly enjoying his first trip on a streetcar. Ella smiled and talked to her son about everything they were passing while the men and women in the section started whispering amongst themselves.

A man at the front tapped the driver's shoulder, "Aren't you going to do something? That negro lover and her abomination can't be allowed to ride up here with the rest of us," he shouted, pointing at Ella and her baby.

The street car crossed Canal Street and halted, and the driver stood up and scowled at Ella. "That negro baby needs to go to the back," he said forcefully.

Ella's cheeks were flushed. "Oh, okay. Yes, sir," she said as she stood up and started toward the back.

"Where do you think you're going," he asked.

"I'm taking my son to the back. Like you asked," she said, flustered.

"I can't let no white woman back there. It's obvious you can't help yourself around negro men."

"You need to quit hassling, my friend," Beck said as she stood up, fists clenched, "She obviously isn't going to just leave her baby unattended in the back. So, what in the hell would you have her do?"

"Get her darkie lovin' ass out of my streetcar. You stand up for her; you're probably a negro lover, too," the conductor said, narrowing his eyes.

Beck desperately wanted to stay and fight or refuse to move, but as she regarded the crowd of angry white people, she noted that two of the men had their hands on the butts of their guns. The best way for the ladies to protect themselves and the baby was to exit.

As the streetcar pulled away, Beck reached for Jackie to give Ella's arms a break. "I know you haven't ridden a streetcar in a long time, but does stuff like that happen in other places?"

"Well, looking the way we do, Lowry and I stick to the restaurants, theaters, and clubs in our neighborhood. People assume I'm a white woman, and sometimes they'll say ugly things, but if we went to whites-only places on a date we could be arrested, or my husband could be killed. At first, Jackie had my complexion and very little hair. Now that he's a little darker and his curls are growing in, we're having to stick more and more to our side of North Rampart," Ella said sadly.

"I'm sorry," Beck said. It was hard to imagine living a life where one's family was never entirely accepted because of physical appearance. As Beck processed what Ella said, she stopped, "Wait, did you say your husband's name is Lowry? As in Lowry Ringgold? I remember you said that he played with the Ringgold Rebels."

Ella looked at her wide-eyed. "Lowry can't know I'm working at the club."

"Okay, but you should know he and I go way back. He worked with Jack Herman and me at the Cotton Club."

"You're *that* Rebecca? That's why everybody's making a big deal over Jack down at the club. He's the Red Devil. So, y'all aren't dead. Lowry was so worried."

"We're very much alive." Beck smiled.

"But not together?" Ella said, disappointed. "When Lowry told me the story. I told him y'all probably ran off to live happily ever after."

"It's complicated," Beck said.

"Do you know you're holding Jack's namesake?"

"What?" Beck asked.

"Lowry idolized Jack. Said he was his mentor. So, he insisted on naming our son after him."

Beck smiled as she gazed at the sleeping baby. Her arms ached, but she hated to hand him back to Ella. Over the mile they walked to Congo Square, the ladies took turns bearing the sweet burden of the baby.

CHAPTER 26

The entirety of the 500 Club was abuzz with activity. The musicians crowded into the dining room and onto the dance floor for a quick sound check before filing out the door to load onto their floats.

Next, the additional float riders were checked in backstage and sent up front to await their assignments. Beck sat in a chair, having her hair and make-up done, taking it all in when Ella passed by.

Beck smiled and waved as Ella nodded and said, "See ya out there."

Since there was no way of slipping into the ball gown on her own, Beck had one of the attendants assist her. While she was being zipped up, the seamstress walked in, holding a stiff jeweled collar in one hand and a step stool in the other. She ascended the stool and attached the collar to two small buttons hidden in the thick shoulder straps of Beck's gown.

The gold-colored beads were arranged in a pattern that resembled flames, like the ones on the skirt of her olive green gown.

"I'll meet you back here after the parade to take off all the extras so you can dance during the Krewe-only party tonight. I've hidden snaps to form a bustle for your train," the seamstress explained.

Beck was familiar with this type of bustle because she'd had one built into the train of her wedding dress. "Oh, good. By extras, do you mean the collar and the crown? Beck asked.

The seamstress whipped out a pair of opera gloves. "And these, and of course, your cape."

"Oh, nice, I like capes."

The seamstress chuckled, then yelled, "Bring me the cape."

As three women walked in struggling with something encased in a large bag, Beck knew she was in trouble. The ladies revealed a cape that was seventeen feet long. It was a deep purple with additional beaded blooms and flames.

Beck furrowed her brow and asked, "How am I supposed to move in that?"

"That's why you have attendants, Queenie," the seamstress explained.

With some difficulty, the attendants positioned the cape behind Beck as the seamstress carefully moved her hair to one side. Then, she lifted one of Beck's dress straps. "There's another set of buttons on the collar and your shoulder straps. I'll attach the cape now, and you'll move out to the dance floor slowly and carefully".

Beck felt the weight as the cape was attached to her gown. Behind her it rustled and shifted as the attendants worked to arrange it perfectly.

Once the seamstress was satisfied, she said, "There's slow music; use the tempo to guide you. Your king will be there to meet you and crown you as his queen. Then, with the help of a small army, you'll take a turn around the room, and we'll load you onto a trailer and drive you two to your floats, Understand?"

"Why will it take a small army?" Beck asked.

"His cape's just as long," she explained.

"Oh my." Beck chuckled, "Did you say floats as in more than one?"

"The King and Queen always have their own floats," the seamstress said.

"That's right," Beck said, remembering the other Mardi Gras parades she'd seen.

"Tomorrow night at the public ball, you're allowed to wear your own formal attire, but we will do your hair and makeup, and you'll wear the crown briefly when you're presented."

Beck nodded as she struggled to stand up straight under the weight of the cape.

"I know it's a lot to take in, but I'll keep reminding you," the seamstress said.

Then the attendants filed in wearing their ball gowns and opera gloves. Some of the dresses featured dark purple with gold beaded flames, and others wore a slightly lighter green with beaded flowers.

"Wait, what's the theme here exactly?" Beck asked.

"No one told you? You're Persephone, that's the lady the Krewe's named after. He's Hades, her husband. Do you know who they are? Because I had to look it up."

Beck's eyes were wide as she nodded. *I can't believe it, we're Hades and Persephone all over again,* she mused.

The seamstress said, "Good, saves me time. The theme this year is 'No One Lives Forever.' Now let's move out."

It took four women and the seamstress directing traffic to get Beck to the edge of the dance floor. While waiting in the shadows to be announced, she caught sight of Jack before he saw her. His outfit was deep purple, accented with beaded gold flames. He looked dashing in his medieval-style doublet with a small but dramatic collar on his equally long cape.

But as her eyes traveled down his body, she noticed he was wearing poofy pants that ended in cuffs at his knees. It appeared as though he had gold and purple striped pumpkins on each thigh. Below the knee, he wore tights. She giggled a bit before her name was announced, and it was time to cross the dance floor to greet him.

Jack felt ridiculous all trussed up in this medieval torture device. He assumed that when Leon had said "suit," he would be wearing an actual suit, not playing dress up as King Arthur. Had Beck known? Surely she must have. She'd been to Mardi Gras several times growing up. When he saw her, he would give her a piece of his mind.

The spotlight shone on his wife as she was announced. It was still strange to hear her referred to by her maiden name. But, as he looked at her in her green gown and purple robe, he was awestruck. Everything was so formal. It felt like the wedding they didn't have. Theirs had been more like a classy Halloween party where two people happened to get married.

As Beck reached him, he said, "Darling, you look incredible."

"Thank you." she smiled radiantly at him, looking up through her lashes and saying, "Why are you wearing pumpkin pants?"

"They're not pumpkins," he said defensively. "They are pained slops. Medieval kings used to wear them."

"I didn't know you were so touchy about them," she said.

"I said nice things about your outfit," he added.

"I'm sorry. You're very dashing."

"Thank you."

"For a man in pumpkin pants," she said as she grinned, crinkling her nose at him playfully.

Prima came over and handed Beck's crown to Jack, "Go ahead," he said.

"Insult my pants one more time, and I'll get my four attendants to help me march over to some nicer lady, and I'll crown her queen," he said and they both chuckled. Then Jack touched her hair with his empty hand. "Now hold still, 'cause this thing is heavy, and I'm tired of holding it."

Beck bowed her head slightly, still smiling. Jack carefully placed the large crown on her head, and the attendants rushed over to secure it to her head with a multitude of bobby pins.

The two carefully took their turn about the room while blinded by flashbulbs from the press. "So much for keeping a low profile," Jack quipped.

"I think that ship sailed in Harlem, Red Devil. Have a good parade," she said as they were loaded onto their individual floats.

Though they talked about it often in the 90s, Jack and Beck had yet to make it back to Louisiana for Mardi Gras. While Beck at least had some idea of what to expect, Jack had almost none.

As the float rolled into public view, an attendant thrust several strands of beads in his hands. "What am I supposed to do with these?" he asked as he raised his voice to be heard over the roar of the crowd.

The attendant tilted his head at Jack and shouted, "Throw 'em."

Jack did as he was told. He threw all ten strands at once, accidentally smacking another attendant in the back of the head.

"Ow, what the hell, man?" the guy said as he bent down to pick up his hat and Jack's beads.

Jack pointed at the first attendant, "He told me to throw them."

"I didn't say all at once into the back of Gary's head," the first attendant argued, "Now throw one or two at a time into the crowd. You can't move in the cape, so I'll give you more when you run out. Do yourself a favor; listen for the ladies yelling, 'Throw me something, Mister."

"Why?" Jack asked.

"Trust me," said the first attendant with a wink.

Plenty of little kids were yelling the phrase, but It took a while for Jack to come across grown women yelling for him to throw them something. As he looked over for his target, he was surprised to see a few ladies baring their breasts. As his float rolled along Bourbon Street, many more pockets of drunk women flashed their breasts for the cheap, plastic beads. Jack had never seen so many at once.

And I've played rock concerts and brothels, he thought.

Once he and Beck were reunited in the dancehall, Jack said, "You didn't tell me there'd be boobs."

"What?" she asked as they were helped backstage.

"Women flashed their tits at me for beads," Jack said.

"Oh, that." Beck nodded as her cape was carefully removed.

"Yes, that," He said as he came to a sudden realization, "Hey, wait a minute. You have tons of Mardi Gras beads. Rebecca, what did you do?"

"Nothing. Mardi Gras is way more conservative where I'm from," she explained, "Say, you look a little flushed. You must have seen some you liked."

Jack felt his cheeks grow even redder, "Well, it has been a while," he mumbled.

"Now we know why they gave you pumpkin pants," she teased.

"You're never going let me live this down, are you?"

"You agreed to be my king." She shrugged as her gown was bustled. Once they were alone, she said, "By the way. I met your namesake today."

"My what?" Jack asked.

"I know Lowry's wife. Please don't tell him I told you. She works with me, but he doesn't know."

"Secrets in a marriage are a bad idea," Jack said.

"I know, but it's none of our business. Anyway, their baby's name is Jack, but they call him Jackie. He's precious," she said with a wistful look that Jack tried his best to ignore.

"That's so nice. I didn't realize I had made that much of an impression," Jack said, wondering what Lowry would have named his son if they had never met. Perhaps there wouldn't have been a son, but Jack wasn't certain that they had impacted the future enough to cause a person to be that didn't previously exist.

"Hey, Maestro," Beck said, "It's time for our dance."

The first dance was very slow and posed for the press. After they were done, Jack and Beck sat at a table, and the club fed them dinner, which included a fair amount of alcohol.

Beck sipped on a Grasshopper, while Nash suggested that since the cocktails were complimentary, Jack should branch out a bit from his typical whiskey neat. He offered to make Jack an Old Fashioned, and in his already tipsy state, that sounded like a very amusing proposition given his current predicament.

The drink was still primarily whiskey, but first, Nash added a sugar cube, bitters, and water, which he muddled together. Then he added the whiskey and ice cubes. Finally, finishing it off with an orange peel and a cocktail cherry.

"So it's a fancy whiskey?" Jack asked.

"Just try it," Nash said.

By the third one, Jack was in an excellent mood. He let Beck lead him in a couple of dances. Then asked, "What was that sexy dance? The one I caught you doing with Victor?" he teased.

Beck looked away, "It's called the Rumba. I told you Latin dances are often sexy. I didn't make it up."

"Teach me," he said.

Jack loved holding her close. Pulling her to him, raising her arm, and stroking his hand gently down it, tracing the side of her breast. "I think this dance is my favorite," he whispered in her ear, slurring his words slightly.

"Mmm, mine, too," Beck said as he spun her around to face him and drew her close. "Jack?"

"Mhm?" he said, losing himself in her olive-green eyes.

She took his hand and held his gaze as she said, "Take me home."

Jack flashed her a devilish grin and said, "I thought you'd never ask.".

The two separated backstage to change into their street clothes. Jack dressed and waited for her by the back door. Moments later, Beck emerged in an overcoat and her soft pink shirtwaist dress. As soon as they were in the alley, she pushed him up against the wall and asked, "How drunk are you?"

"I danced most of it off. Why?" Jack asked.

She pressed her body against his and said, "Because I don't kiss drunk boys." She grinned mischievously and stroked his cheek.

"I'm not drunk, I swear," he murmured as she pulled him into a passionate kiss. He kissed her back with equal enthusiasm.

The walk home took longer than it should have as the tipsy couple kept doubling over in laughter and stopping for more kissing. They tiptoed up the stairs and stopped at Beck's door.

"Thank you for tonight," she said. "I had forgotten what it was like."

"Kissing?" he asked.

"Not only kissing. I've missed doing fun things with you. Laughing and talking without constantly looking at a clock."

"You realize that we'll never be able to keep that up all the time, right?" Jack asked. "We still have to work to pay the bills and feed our creative monsters."

Beck looked at her feet, "I know, but somewhere between being reckless free spirits and workaholics, there has to be some balance."

As she unlocked her door, Jack said, "Maybe we could find it. Good night, my queen," he said as he turned to go.

"Don't go," she said as she stood in her doorway.

"Are you sure?" he asked.

Beck pulled him in, shutting the door behind him. "I asked you to take me home," she said, then pulled him into a passionate kiss which she stopped abruptly, "Wait, are you sure?"

"I'm sure I want you to keep kissing me."

She kissed him again, trailing from his lips to his jawline, then down his neck. Nipping his flesh gently, raising goosebumps on his skin. Jack felt his temperature rise and shrugged off his coat. Beck looked him over, "Mmmm, you know how I feel about you in suspenders."

"That's why I wear them," he said as he winked at her and pulled her in for another kiss. "My turn?" he asked as he continued down her neckline.

"Don't stop," she moaned as Jack planted a trail of kisses down to the V in her dress collar.

He reached for her buttons, then paused and looked up at her. She nodded enthusiastically, so he unbuttoned the top of her dress, kissing as he went. Once enough buttons were undone, Beck removed her dress. Jack's eyes traveled from her bra to her garter belt and thigh-high stockings. "Ooh, sexy 1940s underwear," he said.

"One of the advantages of time travel, my love," she added, "but I'd wear it for you anytime, anywhere."

Her feet were still in the thick Cuban heels she'd worn all night. They made her legs look sexy, but he was sure her feet were sore. Jack led her back to the bed and sat her down. Beck stretched her curvy body onto the bed as he picked up her foot and removed the shoe.

He took her foot in his hand, rubbing his thumb firmly over her arch, focusing on the tender spot where the arch ended, and her heel began causing her to moan in pleasure. Then, he gave the same treatment to her other foot.

While he rubbed her feet, he admired how the glow from gas lamps danced across her breasts and her belly, the way her red hair splayed out onto the sheets. He wanted more than anything to hold her close, so he quickly kicked off his shoes. Beck attempted to pull him down on top of her, but he chose to land on his side next to her.

"Not yet," he whispered. "We have time."

"Do we?" Beck smiled sadly, "I'm never sure."

"We don't have to stay here, Darlin. I'll find a way to get us home, I promise," he said as he traced her hairline with his finger and stroked her cheek.

"I don't care where we are as long as we have time together," she said, kissing him again. As the kiss ended, she gazed at his body and said, "I think you're overdressed."

She undid the first of his buttons, and he joined in helping her complete the task. Her eyes studied him as she slid the suspenders off his muscular shoulders and removed his shirt.

His undershirt was the next to go as Beck used her fingers and lips to reacquaint herself with his broad chest.

He wrapped his arms around her, reaching for the clasp of her bra. After he had undone it, she gasped. "I'm sorry, I should have asked," he said.

"You're fine. It was a good gasp. An anticipatory gasp," Beck said as she bit her lip and laid back down.

He slid off her bra, watching how the lights and the shadows changed as he caressed her breasts. He took his time kissing her body and feeling her writhe against him. It was interesting how being a part for months made actions that they'd repeated many times seem brand new again. Yet, at the same time, there was already a deep love and comfort between the two. As though they had just begun but had always been.

For the first time since she'd dropped into 1947, Beck felt safe, cherished, and loved. She gave herself over to Jack, body, and soul. Oh, how she'd missed the touch of his long, deft fingers. The weight of his body on hers. She smiled as she thought about how the powers that be had brought them back to the same room where they'd last made love in New Orleans.

In the afterglow, she lay Jack's arms, her head resting on his chest. She reflected back on her time in 1940s New Orleans. Being independent was a worthwhile goal. She'd proved to herself that she could make a life on her own, but it might be nice to go back to being interdependent. Was it possible? Jack was the love of her life, but that wasn't enough. She wasn't content to settle for what they had before. This time would have to be different.

CHAPTER 27

Jack opened his eyes as the sunrise painted the sky. He felt the weight of his wife's head on his chest, listened to her rhythmic breathing, and thought he was back in 1995 for a moment. That it had all been a dream somehow.

Confronted with the reality that he had once again woken up in 1948, he wondered if he'd ever be able to control what was happening to them. Wouldn't it be nice to control when and where they could travel? They could return to the weekend of Tom and Lenora's wedding. This time he'd ignore the piece of music he'd started writing during the ceremony and walk with Beck arm and arm to the reception in the square.

They'd dance and party all night. Perhaps he'd take her back to this room and make passionate love with her, or maybe they'd hop from club to club and roll onto the Los Angeles-bound plane, still in their wedding party clothes after a crazy all-nighter. Either way, he wished that they stayed. That he'd finally given Beck that overdue honeymoon.

At the very least, he'd rewind time and not throw Beck's headphones. Then she would have stayed. Together, they would have realized Rufus was ill and taken him to the vet. Their dog would have been saved. Their little family could have thrived safely in Topanga Canyon's hills. If only. It was all beyond his control. Without the wisdom of the Voodoo Lady or some sort of divine intervention, all he could do was be present and try to love Beck the way she deserved. He prayed it wasn't a case of too little too late.

In the distance, Jack heard percussion music. He listened carefully and realized it was coming closer. He embraced Beck and gently rolled her to the other side of the bed, then got up and dressed quickly, anxious to find the source of the music. As he buttoned up his shirt, he walked out onto her balcony, intrigued to see a group of men costumed as skeletons with drums approaching.

He ran downstairs and found Mrs. Brown sitting at the dining room table, sipping coffee as she gazed out the window. He could hear the group approaching. The musicians beat their drums as the skeletons knocked on doors. "Wake up! It's Mardi Gras Day," they shouted as they moved along. He studied their round white papier mache masks and their all-black attire with painted-on bones. The masks made them look incredibly similar to the character he voiced in the Halloween Musical he wrote with Tom. Especially the skeleton who walked on stilts.

He glanced back at his landlady, who looked perfectly calm. "What's happening out there, Mrs. Brown?"

"That's the Skull and Bone Gang. They've been waking up people on Mardi Gras for over two hundred years. I just love their dances. If you're going out for a closer look, would you take this tray of drinks out to them? The red mugs are coffee, and the blue is hot cocoa."

Jack took the tray to the porch and leaned against the pillar, watching as they approached. One skeleton knocked on a door and said, "We come to remind you before you die you better get your life together.
Next time you see us, it's too late to cry!"

Jack heard another skeleton say, "If you don't live right, the Bone Man is comin' for ya!"

The band of drummers and skeletons was flanked on either side by Voodoo priestesses dressed in white dresses and turbans. They fanned their skirts to create a border around the performers. The skeletons danced as the drumming intensified. The priestesses chanted until the activity reached a crescendo and stopped. Save for a man swiping at the ground with a sword. It was the man Jack had met in Congo Square.

"Happy Mardi Gras, Bone Daddy," the man said with a smile.

"Bone Daddy?" Jack asked.

"I cut through the veil between the world of the living and the dead. The ancestors of the past, present, and future have told me who you are, where you're from, and why does your soul feels different," he said with a painted-on grin.

"Um, I have coffee and cocoa from Mrs. Brown. Would you like to sit for a spell?" Jack asked, wondering if what the man had said was true.

The crowd gathered for the drinks to warm themselves from the chill of the morning. Jack studied their faces, finding one that he recognized. The older Voodoo priestess from Harlem, the one he'd searched for, was standing right in front of him.

"Morning, untethered one," she said with a warm smile.

"You remember me?" Jack asked.

"Course I do. Jack Herman of Topanga Canyon, California. You're Rebecca Herman's Jack."

Jack was astonished. "How do you know all this?"

"Like the Bone man said, ancestors will speak if ya listen. I know you've just come from her bed. The tether is snapping back. I told Rebecca it would."

"Can you help us get home?" Jack asked.

"I've already told your wife. Didn't she tell you?"

"She said something about music and emotions, but I've felt

things, and I play music every day. You'd think I'd be hopping all over the place, but I'm stuck here."

The old woman shook her head. "It takes primal emotion and meaningful music. Think about the music that played when you traveled. Ask Rebecca what was playin' in her ears," the Voodoo Lady said.

Just then, one of the skeletons tapped Jack on the shoulder and handed him an empty coffee cup. When he turned back around, the Voodoo Priestess had vanished, and the crowd was advancing down the street.

Jack returned the tray to the kitchen. He was deep in thought when Addie tapped him on the shoulder, causing him to jump. "Oh, sorry, Addie. I didn't see you there."

"Pardon me, Mr. Herman. Here's the dress you sent out to the cleaners," Addie said as she handed Jack a garment bag.

"Thanks, Addie. Your timing is impeccable," he said as he went upstairs to Beck's room.

She was in a dressing gown with her makeup half applied. "You were gone when I woke up," she said as she frowned.

"I know. I'm sorry," Jack said.

"What's in the bag," she asked.

"I'll get to that in a minute. First, I need to fill you in on what I saw this morning. May I come in?" Beck hesitated. "Come on, at least let me explain why I wasn't there when you woke up."

"This better be good."

As she returned to the mirror, Jack followed. He told Beck all about the Skull and Bones gang and his conversation with the Voodoo Lady.

"So we need to what? Make ourselves really angry or sad?"

"Or feel really good," he said, nibbling her neck.

Beck glanced over her shoulder at him and smirked, "Well, I don't know about you, but I felt incredibly good last night, yet here we are."

"I know. I was drinking whiskey both times I traveled. I'm kinda disappointed that there's no connection to that and time travel either."

"At least we can rule out head trauma," Beck said with a smile, then she added, "So what's in the bag? Did you buy me a new dress?"

"More like I repaired an old one," he said as he unzipped the bag with a flourish revealing her green velvet dress.

"I threw that in the garbage after that night with Meyer," she said.

"I know. I found it sticking out of the trash can and had it sanitized," Jack said.

"You wasted your money. I don't think I could ever wear it again."

"You look incredible in this dress, and wearing it makes you happy. Don't let that scumbag ruin that for you." Jack said.

"But what if it happens again?" Beck said quietly, "Isn't it my fault for dressing that way?"

"No, Beck. You should be able to dress however you want, and as men, we should behave ourselves. Please wear this to the ball tonight as my Persephone. Don't let him take this from you."

Beck was silent for a moment. Jack noticed her fidgeting with the finger where her wedding ring used to be. "I'll think about it, but no promises."

"All I ask is that you consider it, Darlin. I'm headed down to breakfast. Will you join me?"

"I'll be right there," she said, taking the rollers out of her hair. Her face set in a frown.

Jack put his hands on her shoulders and said, "It's going to be alright, Beck. I love you."

She turned to face him. Looking up at him with enchanting olive-green eyes, she said, "I love you, too." Then kissed him gently.

Jack went downstairs to reserve seats at the breakfast table and found Bessy's was a hive of activity. People were coming and going from the parades whose music drifted over from Bourbon Street. He couldn't wait to take Beck over after they ate, but just as he was about to take his seat, one particular phone call altered the course of his day.

"So I might have forgotten to tell Ms.Wallace that we needed yesterday *and* today off," Lowry said sheepishly.

"You might have?"

"I thought I had it all squared away, but after the conversation, I just had with her, I definitely did not."

"Well, I can't be there tonight, can you?"

"I know the timing stinks. You're 'King Mardi Gras,' and I wanna take my wife to the party at the 500 Club, too. To smooth things over, I offered to come in and play for a few hours this afternoon, but she has insisted that we both come in."

Jack sighed deeply, then said, "Alright, if it's what we have to do to keep our gig, then I guess we have no choice."

Jack returned to the dining room to find Beck waiting for him. As he settled into the seat next to her, Victor entered.

CHAPTER 28

Beck smiled at Victor as he entered the dining room, but followed Victor's gaze to Jack who was scowling. She wished the two could somehow get along.

Jack turned his attention back to her. Kissing her cheek, he said, "I'm sorry."

Beck tilted her head and asked, "For what?"

"I have to go to work," Jack said with a frown.

"But it's Mardi Gras. We were going to watch the parades together."

"I know, but there was a misunderstanding with our boss at the other place we're playing, and we'll lose the gig if we don't show up today."

Of course, he was ditching her to play. "Who is 'we'?" Beck asked, narrowing her eyes at him.

"Lowry and me," Jack said as he quickly looked away.

"What about the ball?"

"I'm playing now so I can be done in time for the ball. Don't worry, I wouldn't dream of standing you up, Darlin'." Jack said warmly. He attempted to reach for her hand, but she decided she'd rather grab a biscuit.

"I'll go with you," Beck said, looking up from her biscuit to gauge his reaction.

"But-but what about the parades? You were so excited. I don't want you to miss them," said Jack urgently

"If there's a place with the good sense to let you and Lowry play together, I want to see it. Watching you two play together again would be just as much fun as the parades."

"It's not a great place. It's a very smoky dive. You'd hate it," Jack said as he picked at his eggs.

"But I love watching the two of you play. If the smoke bothers me too much, I'll step out for some air like I do at the 500 Club."

Jack stared at her wide-eyed, and then blurted out, "We're going to play the 500 Club together."

Victor looked up from his paper. "What?"

"I talked to Leon, and he's going to let us do it," Jack said, his typically deep and even voice squeaking at the end of his sentence.

Beck stared at him, her arms folded across her chest. Something was definitely up with her husband. She tried to get him to look her in the eye, but all he could manage was to glance briefly at her and then at the door.

"What's going on, Jack? Why are you acting so strange?"

"I'm about to be late for work. If you don't let me go now, you'll be king-less later," he said as he ran upstairs to grab his things.

Beck stood in the dining room archway and watched him run back down the stairs, pursing her lips. Why would he lie to her?

As Jack passed by, Victor stepped up behind her and put his hands on her shoulders, resting his chin on the top of her head. He said loudly, "Don't worry, Becks. I've got the entire day off. I'd be honored to escort you to whatever parades you desire."

Jack didn't look back at them, but slammed the door on his way out causing her to jump. Victor didn't flinch, allowing her to relax for a minute. As she leaned back against him, he moved his arms to rest on top of hers. There was a calmness to being held that way. After a moment, she asked, "When would you like to leave?"

"I'm ready when you are," he said cheerfully.

The first parade they watched was the Zulu Social Aid and Pleasure Society. The all-black krewe dressed in native African costumes consisting of grass skirts, colorful feather headdresses, and bone jewelry. Their bands played traditional African music, heavy with percussion. As one float passed by, a young musician was playing the balafon.

Jack would have loved this, Beck thought sadly.

"I'm confused," Victor said.

"About what?"

"If some people object to black-face, why are all the Krewe members wearing it?"

Beck shrugged and said, "From what I understand, it's a tradition the group started a long time ago."

At that moment, the king's float arrived. This was the first year the Krewe had a female queen, so instead of having her own float, she sat on a balcony with the mayor of New Orleans. The Zulu King's float stopped, and he paid tribute to her and the mayor. Suddenly a character known as the "Big Shot" challenged the Zulu King and a hilarious mock battle for dominance played out before the crowd, with the Zulu King once again victorious.

"What a marvelous piece of theatre," Victor said as they clapped for the performers.

As the parade wrapped up, Victor and Beck meandered through the performers on their way to the riverside for lunch. "I'm picking the place this time," Beck insisted. She stopped short of colliding with the Voodoo Lady, who took Beck's hands in hers.

"Happy Mardi Gras, Rebecca. I understand that the tether is snapping back," she said as she raised her eyebrows.

"I'm not so sure about that," Beck said defensively.

"Dear Child, there are always bumps in the road," the Voodoo Lady said as she cut her eyes to Victor and back to Beck again, "But those detours along the way only serve to make you realize the treasure you already have." The Voodoo lady reached into her satchel and pulled out an ornately painted coconut. "A gift for you. This is a Zulu coconut, one of the most sought-after treasures of Mardi Gras in New Orleans. It represents the perseverance of the Krewe. At first, they couldn't afford to buy beads, so they bought what they could afford and made it beautiful. What you have was once beautiful, and it can be again."

With that, the Voodoo Lady let go of Beck's hands and walked away.

Victor put his arm around Beck. "Are you alright? Who was that?

"Let's go. I'm starving," Beck said.

Beck chose a little sandwich shop serving various Po Boy sandwiches.

"This shrimp is scrummy, Becks," Victor said after the first bite of his sandwich.

"One of the best parts of Louisiana is the food," Beck said.

"It's one of the things I'll miss most about this place," he sighed.

"Miss?"

"I'm afraid I've gone and finished the damned script. After previews and opening night, I have to go back across the pond,"

Victor said with a sad smile.

"Oh. Congratulations. New Orleans won't be the same without you," Beck sighed.

"Just New Orleans, then?"

"Of course not. I'll miss you dreadfully. First Tennessee left, tomorrow Truman, and in a week, you leave. All my writer friends will be gone," she said as she buried her face in her hands.

Victor gently removed her hands from her face, "What about *my* writer friend? Are you planning to stay in the Crescent City?"

"I don't know. Things are up in the air for me right now," she said. *If only he knew,* she thought.

"If you could go anywhere in the world, where would it be?"

"Well, there are lots of places in the world I'd love to visit. It would be nice to see London."

"Oh, Becks, I would love to show you London," Victor said wistfully.

"That would be fun. I'm sure you'd be the perfect guide." Beck smiled. Her thoughts drifted to Jack and how busy they had been when the Halloween musical premiered. Seeing a city she had always wanted to visit from taxi windows and hotel balconies was frustrating.

"Where did you go just now?" Victor asked, waving to get her attention.

Feeling the heartbreak and frustration of her situation, Beck began to tear up. "I am sorry. I'm just so homesick."

"I thought this was your home, Louisiana, I mean."

"I grew up here, but in my heart, I belong in California. I always have. Right now, I just feel so lost," Beck said as she wiped a stray tear from her cheek.

"There now," Victor said, handing her his handkerchief, "You've been on edge since that odd woman spoke to you in the car park."

"Victor," Beck said as she reached across the table and squeezed his hand, "You're the best friend I have here. I wish I could tell you everything, but I can't."

"Oh, Becks, I feel the same about you. You can tell me anything, you know."

"No, I can't. You'd look at me differently," Beck said as she looked at their hands. She couldn't risk losing another friend. She still missed Ginny. Of course, this relationship felt different than her friendship with Ginny, but there was Jack to consider. She couldn't tell her secret because it also belonged to him.

Victor leaned in close once again. She thought he looked like an angel as she watched the midday sun highlight his light blond waves and pale blue eyes. His smile was kind, with a hint of mischief at the corners. It was a very kissable mouth if the circumstances were different.

"I have a secret, too," he said quietly as he squeezed her hand. His tone sounded husky, almost sexy, but the content of his sentence snapped her back to reality.

While Victor was not an option for her because of Jack. She wasn'tt even on the menu for Victor. He was attracted to men. Not only that, but she was sure he was about to tell her out loud in a crowded cafe. She couldn't let him take that risk.

"Victor, I know," she said.

He sat up and raised his eyebrows, "You do?"

"I've known all along."

"And?" he said, letting go of her hand and using his to hide his face.

She stood up and crossed to his side of the table. It was her turn to gently remove his hands. Meeting his gaze she said, "It doesn't change how I feel about you. Not one bit." Then she pulled him up and hugged him.

"And how do you f-feel about me?" he stammered, his cheeks red.

"Don't you know, Victor? I adore you. I always have. Now, let's get some beignets before the Rex Parade," she said, grabbing his hand and pulling him toward Cafe du Monde.

The Krewe of Rex was all that Beck had imagined Mardi Gras would be like when she was a little girl and dreamed of spending the holiday in the French Quarter. The parade had the longest and most elaborate processions of the Krewes.

"This is amazing, Becks. Look, I caught a couple of coins," Victor said, holding aloft three coins.

"They're called doubloons. Almost all of the Krewes throw them now, but Rex was the first. They even set the official colors of the holiday. Each color represents a value. Purple is for Justice, Gold for Power, and Green is for Faith," Beck explained.

Victor looked at the beads they had collected and pulled out a beautiful dark green strand. "Well, then, I think this one is for you, love."

Beck blushed and said, "I don't deserve it. I'm afraid I've been lacking in the faith department lately. I used to be so much better at it than I am now. Probably why the Voodoo Lady was so cross with me earlier."

"You're still a person of strong faith. I see it. It's not lost, only hidden," Victor said.

At that moment, Beck was thankful Victor wasn't interested in women because she could see herself falling for a man who talked like that.

CHAPTER 29

"Hey," Jack grumbled as he shuffled into 1026 Conti Street.

Lowry looked up from the piano keyboard and said, "Well, hello, Sunshine. You ready to play music for the rich and the horny."

"It would appear I don't have much of a choice."

"Well, considering your charming personality this afternoon, I'll let you choose whether you want to start on the keys or croon to the lovely ladies lounging before us," Lowry said with a wave of his hand, indicating the dolled-up residents of the brothel as they relaxed on the plush sofas and chaise lounges that decorated the large parlor.

Before Jack could respond, Norma Wallace strutted into the room wearing a scandalously low-cut evening gown, "Come on, Jackie baby, sing one for me, would ya? We were all so miserable without you yesterday. Weren't we, girls?"

As if on cue, the ladies flocked around, pleading, "Please, Jack. We love it when you sing. Your voice is so sexy."

The young woman who resembled Beck sauntered up to Jack, "Come on, Red Devil. Undress me with those sexy pipes of yours," she said as she looked over his body, her eyes stopping between his legs. Then, she slowly ran the tip of her tongue over her ever so slightly parted lips causing a warm feeling to pool in his lower body.

Regaining his senses, Jack jumped back from her like a snake had bitten him. Raising his hands and stepping further back, he said,

"Okay, I'll sing, I'll sing."

As Jack approached the piano, Lowry muttered, "Jackie baby? That's what I call my kid. 'Undress me with your voice.' That's just nasty."

Jack smirked at Lowry and said, "Now, who's grumpy?"

"I liked you better when you was spoken for," Lowry grumbled.

"Well, I'm working on that," Jack flashed Lowry a devilish grin. "We took a huge step forward last night."

"If you're freshly shagged you oughtta be able to behave yourself, Red Devil," Lowry admonished.

"It was all them. I didn't do anything," Jack said, holding up his hands again to appear as innocent as possible."

The set could have been better, but the combination of two grumpy reluctant performers and a bunch of day-drunk tourists didn't make for a festive atmosphere. The code of conduct usually present was abandoned entirely when Norma decided to disappear to her room to entertain a powerful politician.

The room was full of distracting displays of flesh. Not-so-discreet sexual acts played out in every corner. Not to mention that the drunk, entitled men were prone to heckling the musicians.

"A ginger and a darky onstage together? Man, has this place gone downhill."

"Ladies, watch out. Black men will do whatever it takes to bed a white woman." A man hollered as Lowry stood up to sing.

He started to lunge for the man, but Jack jumped up from the piano and wrapped his arms around his friend. He led him back behind the drum set.

"Lowry, this isn't worth it. If Norma thought it was so damn important for us to be here, she should have had a better hold on her customers. Let's split," Jack said in Lowry's ear.

"Norma didn't insist that we play. I need the money," Lowry admitted.

"Why? What happened?" Jack asked.

Lowry sighed. "I shoulda listened to you. I lost it all and then some at Blackjack."

"You're broke?"

"Close to it. I bet my whole check and the money I was up."

Jack pinched the bridge of his nose and closed his eyes. "After I begged you not to?"

"Yeah, thanks for pointing that out. Look, you don't need to be here. Why don't you split, and I'll wrap things up."

"If you needed the money, why did I have to come?" Jack asked.

Just then, the man who had yelled about what "all black men wanted" threw a beer bottle that barely missed Lowry's head. Lowry glanced at him, then raised his eyebrows at Jack. He had never seen Lowry scared before.

"Come here, Darlin'," Jack said, motioning to the pretty redhead Lowry referred to as Beck Junior. Instantly, she was at his side, "I need you to go upstairs and bring the boss down before we have an incident."

"Right away," she said. She ran up to retrieve Norma.

"What do we do now?" Lowry asked.

"We stay and play," Jack said resolutely.

They ducked and dodged slurs, insults, and the occasional projectile for the next ten minutes as they did their best to keep playing. Finally, the three men were the only customers left in the parlor, and the five women left refused to serve them.

"You better do your job," one of the men said to the young redhead who had just returned from upstairs without Norma.

"I have the right to refuse service to ignorant bigots," she said with a scowl. The man's face turned bright red as he grabbed her arm.

"You're nothing but a whore. If you don't do what I tell you to, I'll beat your face, then no one will want you," the man growled as he raised his fist. She tried desperately to pry his fingers off her arm.

Hearing the threat, Jack stopped singing, grabbed the nearest vase, and smashed it over the man's head, knocking him out cold. One of his companions jumped to his fallen buddy's defense by punching Jack in the face. The impact of the large man's fist caused him to stumble backward over a red velvet chaise. He smacked his head against the wall, seeing stars.

As he gathered his wits about him, Jack tried to assess the chaos that had overtaken the parlor. The second companion was tall and wiry, an even match for Lowry. However, Lowry hesitated, and the man grabbed his shoulder and punched him in the gut. Jack watched his friend double over in pain. However, Lowry recovered quickly. As he stood up, his nostrils flared. He charged the man and punched him in the ear. The man howled in pain, alerting his friend who was fighting off the women who were throwing things at him for hitting Jack.

He pushed the women out of his way and spun Lowry around, hitting him square in the mouth, splitting Lowry's bottom lip. Jack sprang back up to help his friend by tackling the large man from behind, bringing him to the ground.

The shrill sound of a whistle screeched through the cacophony of the fight. "What in tarnation is going on down here?" Norma yelled. She was standing at the top of the stairs.

The redhead spoke, "Ms. Norma, I can explain."

"Well, let's hear it, Scarlett," Norma said as she narrowed her eyes at the crowd.

"These men," Scarlett said, indicating the three hecklers, "Were saying horrible things to Jack and Lowry. One of them threw a beer at Lowry and hit the wall over there. That's when I tried to get your attention."

"So that was you." Norma smirked and crossed her arms.

Jack spoke up, "We asked her to get you when things started getting physical. When she returned without you, that man grabbed Scarlett and threatened her."

The big guy sat on the floor holding his head, "Your whore refused to serve me."

"My *ladies* have the right to refuse any Vidalia they choose," Norma said.

"Vidalia?" Jack asked Scarlett quietly.

"It's our code name for customers, Sweetheart," she whispered, her breath hot on his ear.

"What kind of business are you running?" the man scoffed.

"A damn good one. Where I have a certain code of conduct for my ladies and an expectation that our customers will behave in a manner that doesn't get the police called. Now, Jim Bob and Billy, you know you don't want your wives or your pastor to know where you're spending your lunch hours. And you, Clyde," she said, pointing at the tall thin guy, "No self-respecting woman is going to marry you if she knows you been prowling around these parts. Now, I suggest y'all git in case my neighbors called the cops."

The bruised and angry men shuffled out of the brothel snarling at Jack and Lowry as they went. Norma shook her head and returned with cash from her back room. "Here's what I owe you for the days you played this week."

"But, we're not done, Ms. Norma, let us finish our set for the ladies," Lowry said.

"I'm sorry, gentleman, I'm going to have to end our arrangement."

Scarlett rushed over, "They were only trying to protect us."

"I realize that," Norma said sadly, "But the police may still come sniffing around here, and they'd love to get me on anything, even something as silly as having a mixed act in my parlor." Norma rolled her eyes. Then she turned to Jack and Lowry. "I'm sorry. If there's anything I can do for you in the future, anything at all," she added as she played with the lapel of Jack's coat, "Please don't hesitate to call me."

As Jack and Lowry walked onto the sidewalk at 1026 Conti Street, Lowry said, "Well, phit."

"What was that, cuz?" Jack asked.

"Phit! Phit! Phit," Lowry exclaimed.

Jack looked at his friend, who was drooling blood from his swollen lip,he patted Lowry on the back. "Let's find you some ice, my man."

CHAPTER 30

"What on Earth?" Ella said as Jack and Lowry dragged themselves into the Ringgold's modest townhouse.

"Now, don't you start," Lowry said, "Jack and I've been through the wringer this afternoon."

"Jack? As in Jack Herman? As in the Red Devil Herman?" Ella asked excitedly.

"The one and only," Lowry said, thankful for the distraction, "Jack, this is my wife, Ella."

"It's a pleasure to meet you," Jack said with a smile.

"We have your record. Yours and Lowry's from the Cotton Club Revue. I just love it," she said, pulling it out of the stereo cabinet. "Would you sign the cover for me, please?"

"Woman, can't you see I'm bleeding?" Lowry asked.

"Oh, I see it, and I'm waiting for an explanation. Did you let each other have it?"

"Why would you think that?" Jack asked, slightly offended.

"You're both bleeding," Ella said simply. Alarmed, Jack looked down at his body. "No, it's your cheek," she said.

Jack brought his fingers up to his tender, slightly swollen right cheekbone. He touched it cautiously, but even the slightest touch caused it to throb. As he pulled his fingers away, he noticed some blood on the tips. The man who'd slugged him had a mean left hook, and Jack had expected a bruise, but the man's wedding ring had cut him as well.

"Looks like y'all could use some ice," Ella said.

Lowry sat down, "Can ya fetch some for us?"

Ella sighed. "I guess." She sauntered into the kitchen. Just then, baby Jackie began to cry. Ella left the kitchen and began to climb the stairs.

"Where you going?" Lowry asked

"Isn't obvious," she said. "You're a big boy. You can get your own ice."

"Isn't Mom up there?" Lowry asked.

"Your mother's napping. I don't want him to wake her," Ella explained as she continued her ascent.

Lowry sat down on the couch with two ice packs, his brow furrowed, "Here you go, cuz."

"Thanks. You okay? You sound like you got the weight of the world on your shoulders."

"I don't how we're gonna make ends meet now," Lowry said softly, "I'm gonna ask Cab tonight if he's got any room for me on his tour. I don't wanna leave my family, but I can't think of anything else."

Jack thought of the guys in Ah Ooga who had wives and kids, "Maybe you don't have to. In my younger days, I toured for a bit, and some of the guys brought their families with them. You could do that."

"Get outta town. Who did you tour with?" Lowry asked.

"No one you'd know," Jack said.

"Try me," Lowry said.

"Ah Ooga."

"Like the sound a car horn makes? That's a terrible name," Lowry said as he and Jack laughed, "No wonder nobody ever heard of 'em. Did you name that group?" Jack shrugged. "If we're ever in a group together. I'm gonna name it."

"Well, you were among the first people to call me the Red Devil, so I guess that's fair." Jack turned his head to better position the ice pack on his sore cheek. A clock on the wall read five thirty-seven. "That clock can't be right," Jack said, "Is it really that late?"

"It's right. See? The sun's going down."

"I'm going to be late to the ball," Jack groaned.

"It's just around the corner. If you leave now, you'll be fine," Lowry said.

"I can't go like this. I have blood and lipstick- Lipstick? How'd that get there? Anyway, we both have to change. I better call Beck and let her know."

At that moment, Ella came downstairs with Jackie on her hip, "We *all* have to get ready," she said, handing the baby to Lowry. "Ladies first."

"Why can't Mom take him?" Lowry asked as the wiggly boy reached for his mother.

"Your Mama just woke up. Said she'll be down in a minute. Now, go on and make your son some supper. She can finish feeding him while you get ready."

Lowry grumbled as he struggled to pull out the things he needed to prepare Jackie's dinner. The baby seemed to have velcro hands as he tried to grab everything within his reach.

"Why don't I hold him while you're doing that?" Jack asked.

"I thought you were going to call Beck."

Jack scoffed, "I can make a phone call and hold a baby."

"Oh, you think so? Be my guest. Here we go, little Jackie, meet big Jackie," Lowry said as he handed his son to his friend.

Jack heard Lowry chuckle as he went back into the kitchen. While Jackie squirmed and reached for his father. Jack bounced him on his hip and said in a sing-songy voice, "Well, hello, little Jackie. I like your name. Yes I do." The baby turned to look at Jack. He had the most enormous brown eyes Jack had ever seen. Jack cooed, "Oh, look at you. You're so handsome. I guess all Jacks are. Isn't that right? You want to help me call a pretty lady? Do you?" The boy nodded his head so fast his little curls bounced. "That's my boy. And if she is mad at me, maybe *you* can talk to her," Jack mumbled. He reached for the phone on the dining room wall, and Jackie immediately put the slack of the coiled cord into his mouth.

Beck paced in the front parlor of the boarding house, fidgeting with her bare left finger. Last night, as she drifted off to sleep, she'd thought of asking Jack to place it on her finger when he awoke. However, she had opened her eyes to find an empty spot where he should have been. The ring resided now inside her royal purple clutch. However, Beck was hopeful that with her debt freshly paid to Prima and things on the mend with her husband, she could once again live openly as Rebecca Herman.

Eyes closed, Beck replayed the moment from last night when he crowned her queen. Then, she imagined standing onstage with Jack tonight at the ball while he lovingly replaced the ring on her hand. Footsteps interrupted her daydream.

"Jack?" she said hopefully as she turned around. She looked at the spot where she'd expected to see his fiery hazel eyes, but instead, she saw the tuxedo shirt of a much taller man.

Victor smiled, "No, but maybe I can help -- w-what are you wearing?" he stammered as he looked at her low-cut green velvet dress.

"Do you like it?" Beck asked.

"It's st-stunning. You're breathtaking. All in green, I see."

Beck felt her cheeks grow hot as her eyes met his. She couldn't help but notice that the pupils in his pale blue eyes were more prominent than she had ever seen them. It was too much. She looked at the floor and mumbled, "Thank you." Her eyes traced back up his long, lean body taking in the sight of his perfectly tailored white tie and tails. "You're quite dashing, yourself."

Victor's pale face turned pink, "Thanks. What do you need, Becks?" he asked.

"Need?" she asked as she tilted her head and furrowed her brow.

"You were looking for Jack," he reminded her, "but maybe I can stand in?"

Don't tempt me, Beck thought as she met Victor's gaze again. Neither one seemed to want to look away.

The ringing phone shattered the silence. Startled, the two turned toward the sound coming from the kitchen. The phone call had broken the spell. Especially when Mrs. Brown said, "Rebecca, Jack's on the line for you."

Beck picked up the receiver and heard *Dada, Dada, Dada.*"Jack? Is that you?" she asked, "Where are you?"

Jack wrenched the phone away from the baby, "It's me and my little helper. I got out of work late, and I still have to come back and change."

"We'll be late," Beck protested.

"You won't be if you leave right now," Jack said.

"I thought we would go together," Beck said as her shoulders drooped.

"Ow! Not the hair," Jack said.

"What?"

"I'll be right behind you. We'll still spend most of the evening together," Jack said as he tried to cradle the handset between his ear and his shoulder while he tried to wrestle his hair from Jackie's fingers.

"Most?" Beck asked. Then she said, "Oh, that's right. You and Lowry are playing together. I can't wait. Any chance Cab will be up there, too? It would be just like old times."

"Ow, ouch, come on, let go," Jack said. Jackie started to cry as he freed his curls from the baby's fat, sticky fingers. "I'm not sure about Cab, Darlin'. I guess I can ask." He started bouncing the baby again, then, as Jackie settled, Jack put his chin on top of the baby's curls and swayed, which seemed to calm him. *I'm not so bad at this, after all,* he thought. Suddenly, he felt the baby jerk, and something warm and wet spread over his shirt. "Uh, Beck, I've gotta go so I can get back there and change. I'll see you soon," he said before hanging up.

"Lowry!" Jack cried out. "Your baby did something to me."

Lowry howled as he took his son from Jack and offered him a dish towel, "Not as easy as you thought, huh? Here wipe up."

Jack took in the sight of his friend tenderly cleaning his baby's chubby cheeks. He remembered that Marvin had told him Lowry wasn't around much when he and Jackie were growing up. The uncertainty of their family's future twisted his stomach into knots. "Hey, Lowry. Promise me you'll talk to Cab tonight. Please?"

Lowry ruffled his son's black curls. "Dada, dada, dada," the boy cooed.

Lowry flashed a sad smile at his son and said, "Okay. Now, run along. Rebecca's gonna be madder than a wet hen if you're much later."

Jack felt far from kingly as he left Lowry's home, reeking of sour, milky spit up. As he crossed the threshold, Lowry began to sing "Swinging On A Star" to his child, a precious sound that followed Jack down the block.

CHAPTER 31

Victor was right by Beck's side as she replaced the handset of the telephone and frowned.

"Is everything alright?" he asked.

"Jack's running late. He told me to meet him there, but I don't want to go by myself," Beck said.

"No need, my dear. I'd be honored to escort the queen to the ball. Your Majesty," he said as he offered Beck his arm. She took it gratefully.

Beck brought Victor into the 500 Club through the Artist's Entrance. "Who's this?" Leon asked as he narrowed his eyes at the blond.

"This is Victor Shadly. He's my escort this evening."

"No. Only the king escorts the queen. Where the hell's Herman?" Leon asked.

Beck pursed her lips and squared her shoulders. Who was this man to tell her who she could and could not be with? "He's late. Victor graciously offered to keep me company until he turns up," she said as she linked arms with Victor.

A man ran up to Leon, "There's a problem. I need you to come with me," he said. Leon followed him to one of the gaming rooms.

"Your boss doesn't seem to like me," Victor said.

"He doesn't like anybody. He's only nice to Jack because he draws a crowd." Beck said with a smirk.

As more people headed back to the gaming and VIP rooms, Victor asked, "What's going on back there?"

Beck leaned in and whispered, "The ones in the very back are for gaming, and the two close to the bar are rooms where men can have a...private audience with a dance hostess."

"Oh Becks, you mean that you have --"

"No, never have, never will."

"Right. So, prostitution over there and racketeering in the back. The seedy underbelly of the 500 Club, as it were."

"The women in the VIP rooms don't necessarily engage in that sort of thing. Most of the time, they're only B drinking."

Victor furrowed his brow, "I'm unfamiliar with the term."

"It's when a dance hostess convinces a man to go into one of the private rooms and buy expensive drinks for them. Nash waters the ladies' drinks down so they're not drunk. At the end of the night, the man gets a huge bill. The club rakes in the dough, and the dance hostess gets a cut," Beck explained. On his look, she crossed her arms and added, "I don't do that either."

"Sorry, dear. It's just that you know so much about everything."

"I'm the house manager. It's my job to know what's going on." At that moment, the first act of the night started to play. Beck smiled and said, "Or who's going on. I didn't know we had a swing band tonight."

Victor raised his voice to be heard over the music, "What do you say, your Majesty? Shall we cut a rug?"

Beck glanced around backstage. Still no Jack. "I thought you'd never ask." She took Victor's arm and hit the dance floor, determined to push away her disappointment.

Jack arrived about forty-five minutes late. He immediately searched for Beck backstage but ran into Leon Prima instead. He called across the room to Jack. "I need you and Rebecca to meet me back here in fifteen minutes. We'll promptly present the king and queen at the top of the hour." Before Jack could respond, a large Italian man called Prima to one of the gaming rooms.

"Hi-de-ho, Red Devil," Cab's voice rang out behind him.

Jack turned to greet his friend. "Hi-de-ho!"

"Woo-wee, what happened to your face?" Cab asked.

Before Jack could respond, Lowry came in the backdoor, dressed to the nines. Cab looked from Jack's purple cheek to Lowry's fat lip, "Dag nabbit, Now, don't tell me you two mixed it up with each other," Cab said as he stood with his hands on his hips.

"That's not how it went down. There were some jerks at our other gig, and we had to work together to take them down," Lowry said.

"I hope your boss appreciated that," Cab said.

Jack and Lowry exchanged a look as Ella entered through the backstage door. Jack cleared his throat and said, "Cab, I don't believe you've had the pleasure of meeting Mrs. Ringgold."

Lowry's face brightened as he put his arm around his wife's waist. "Oh, I'm sorry. This is my wife, Ella. Ella, this is --"

"Cab Calloway, It's an honor. I've always loved your music," Ella said.

"The pleasure is all mine, Dollface," Cab said as he gently kissed Ella's hand.

Ella smiled at him, but turned to Lowry and said softly, "We should probably be a little more careful about who sees us together."

"Nonsense, tonight's Mardi Gras. Anything goes!" Lowry said, "Now why don't you grab us a table, Sweetheart. I'll be right there."

Lowry turned as if to resume speaking with Cab and Jack, but before the conversation could get underway, Meyer Lansky came over to the men.

"Just the gentlemen I wanted to see," Meyer smirked.

"Oh?" Jack asked.

"You know what you three have in common? You owe money to the club," Myer said.

Cab and Lowry looked at their feet, but Jack puffed out his chest and said, "I don't know what you're talking about. I've never gambled here."

"True, but you did have that unfortunate run-in with the law, and Leon bailed you out."

"Rebecca and I've gotta deal with Prima already," Jack said as he crossed his arms.

"This isn't about Miss Taylor. She and Leon are square. But the club needs you to pay in full tonight. All of you."

The three men protested that none of them had that kind of money. Lowry looked particularly distraught as he ran a hand through his curls.

"Yeah, yeah, I know you don't. So, here's what we're gonna do. The boss has a special delivery coming in tonight. It cannot be intercepted by the authorities. I need you to create a diversion when I gives ya this signal," he said as he tapped his temple three times.

"What kind of a diversion?" Cab asked.

"Gentlemen, you're all entertainers. I'm sure you can think of something," Meyer said.

"What's in it for us?" Lowry asked.

"All of your debts to the 500 Club will be forgiven."

"Wait a minute. I don't know about Cab but Lowry and I only owe you about two hundred and fifty apiece. I assume that you're bringing in new gaming equipment that will make you a lot more money," Jack said.

"What's it to you?"

"We want you to forgive our debts and give each of us $250," Jack said confidently.

"Why, you've got some nerve," Meyer said, grabbing Jack by his lapels.

"It's a deal," said the sizeable Italian man standing behind Meyer.

Meyer released Jack, then wheeled around to face his boss, "But Marcello, these men are in our debt. We don't gotta pay them."

It was Marcello's turn to grab Meyer by his lapels as he said, "If we can get the machines loaded in without the cops noticing, they'll be the only slots in the Quarter. It'll be like printing our own money. Capiche?"

Meyer frowned and mumbled, "Capiche." Marcello released him, and Meyer retreated to one of the gaming rooms.

"Cab, I'm looking forward to your set. Good luck in Hollywood."

Cab raised his eyebrows, "Uh, thank you, Mr. Marcello."

"Lowry," Marcello continued, "Ella is one of our best dance hostesses. I'm sure she'd be happy to help distract the authorities. If you know what I mean,"

Lowry clenched his fists and made a step toward Marcello. Jack put an arm around his slender friend holding him in place.

Marcello looked amused at the trouble he'd stirred up, "Oh, and Jack, you should've asked for a lot more money," he said as he turned to leave, his shoulders shaking with laughter.

Jack held onto Lowry until the man went into the same gaming room Meyer had entered. "That's the Godfather of New Orleans. Do you want to sleep with the fishes?" he asked Lowry.

"I don't care if he's the Queen of England. He doesn't get to say stuff about my wife," Lowry grumbled.

"No, the Queen of England came through here with Rebecca on his arm about an hour ago," Cab quipped.

Jack had no love loss for Victor, especially since Cab had confirmed that he was by Beck's side instead of Jack. However, Cab's joke didn't sit well with him. He decided to change the subject. "So, you're going to Hollywood?"

"Marcello must have found out about my movie deal. My band ditched me because of my little problem. So, I'm gonna try my luck in pictures."

"Oh. So you're not touring anymore," Lowry said as he wrung his hands.

"I'm afraid not," Cab said, "Live nightclub music isn't what it used to be. That small stage out there would never hold an orchestra, and if you really want to know where we're headed, look at that shiny, new jukebox near the stage. That's the future."

Lowry buried his face in his hands. "I can't believe it. I came back from the war, and everything's changed. No more orchestras, no more tours. No more music, not for me anyway. I got a mom, a wife, and a baby to feed. I gotta figure a whole new way to make a livin'," Lowry said as his voice trembled. Tears seeped from between his fingers. Jack clapped a hand onto Lowry's shoulder as Lowry continued, "It's not that I don't love them. It's that I love them so much. What if I'm not enough?"

"Hey, little cuz, all us family men worry about being enough from time to time. Don't we, Red Devil?" Cab asked.

Jack thought about Beck and how much he'd let her down, especially today. "Cab's right. We just keep trying until we get it right. Then, we'll screw up in some new way," he grumbled.

Cab furrowed his brow at Jack, "Yes, but we learn how to fix that, too. Love's a journey. Now, take this hankie and dry your eyes because I need you and your band, young man."

"You want the Ringgold Rebels to back you up?" Lowry asked as he wiped his face. Cab smiled broadly and nodded. Lowry's eyes widened. "It would be an honor."

Jack felt another stab of jealousy. His friends would play without him, and his wife was dancing with another man. Jack excused himself and headed to the dance floor.

It was easy to spot the Brit as he stood taller than everyone on the dance floor. As Victor spun around, Jack saw Beck. She appeared to be having the time of her life. She was breath-taking in the lights of the club. The green velvet dress he had dry cleaned for her clung to her curves.

CHAPTER 32

"Beck," Jack shouted over the music, "We need you backstage."

Beck felt a bit guilty. She had been having so much fun dancing that she momentarily forgot she was waiting on Jack. But she frowned as she noticed the purplish-black bruise on his cheek. "What happened?"

"I'll tell you backstage," he grumbled.

Oh, he is not striking the proper tone for someone who waltzed in here almost an hour late with a banged-up face. Beck looked back at Victor. "Save a dance for me?"

"Anything for you, your majesty," Victor said with a smile.

Jack took her hand and led her backstage.

"You don't have to drag me. I know where I'm going," she said as she pulled her hand away from his and sat at a vanity to touch up her makeup.

"I'm sorry," Jack said. "I'm just stressed. There's a lot going on tonight."

"Well, you can start by telling me about your face. It looks bad."

"Thanks, Darlin," Jack said as he looked down.

"I meant that it looks painful. You're as handsome as ever."

"There was a fight at my other gig, and I had to intervene."

Beck stood up and placed her compact back into her handbag

beside her wedding ring. "That's all the explanation I get?"

Jack had never felt so relieved to see Prima appear.

"That's all we have time for, your majesty. Our subjects await," Jack said, motioning to the attendants who had followed Prima holding their crowns.

The pair was presented with great fanfare. It was easier to move without the ridiculously long parade capes, but they still had to steady their crowns on their heads long enough to descend the stairs and share a dance. The blinding flashbulbs of the cameras made it tricky, but the pair finally made it to the center of the floor as the band played "Come Home" from the Cotton Club Revue.

Beck smiled. "Did you put them up to this?"

"No, but I can't think of a more perfect song," Jack said, his eyes shining as he carefully waltzed with her.

In the corner, he saw Ella and Lowry sitting at their table. Lowry whispered something in her ear, and Ella went to kiss her husband, which caused him to wince as she planted a kiss on his swollen lip. Cab was watching from the corner of the stage as Jack caught his eye. Cab winked and nodded in approval.

Jack carefully turned to Beck and was facing the bar. Victor was leaning against it, their eyes met, and Victor quickly shifted his gaze to his drink. The attendants took their crowns as the song ended, and the other revelers joined them on the dance floor.

To Jack's relief, a single piano began to play yet another slow ballad. He pulled Beck to him and inhaled her almond vanilla scent. He half-closed his eyes and attempted to memorize her touch. She began to let go of him, but he held onto her and asked, "Please, one more song?"

"Of course. I love this song. It's the one Victor first taught me to dance to."

A woman with a sultry voice began to sing in French. Jack recognized the song from his brother's first wedding. It was "La Vie En Rose."

"You danced to this song with Victor?"

"He said it reminds him of me." Beck grinned.

"Do you know the lyrics?" Jack asked.

"You know I don't speak French. Victor says it has to do with a rosy outlook on life. I guess he appreciates my positivity," she said with a shrug.

"My brother and his first wife danced to this at their wedding. You remember, his *French* wife?"

Beck nodded. "Yes, your mom showed me pictures of all of Robert's weddings when we were planning ours."

Jack continued, "Well, allow me to translate. They're singing to the person they love. The lyrics say their voice is so angelic that everything they say sounds like a love song. Come on, Beck." Jack stopped dancing. "When will you admit that Victor wants you?"

Beck turned pink, but a young redhead sidled up to Jack before she could respond.

"Scarlett? What are you doing here?" Jack asked, as his cheeks burned.

She wedged her way between him and Beck, then gently took his chin in her hand and turned his bruised cheek to where she could examine it. "You poor thing." she purred.

Jack backed away from Scarlett, "Oh uh, it looks worse than it feels."

"You're so brave. I'm not used to having someone defend my honor," she said, positioning herself closer to Jack. He tried again to back away, but the more he tried, the closer Scarlett followed, and the further away he moved from Beck.

Beck folded her arms and smirked at them. "You want to introduce me to your little friend?"

"Uh, this is Scarlett. We know each other from work. Scarlett, this is my uh, Beck, I mean Rebecca, this is Rebecca," Jack said.

"You work together?" Beck asked.

Scarlett laughed and said, "Yeah, I guess you could say we each entertain the customers in our own way." She winked at Jack.

"What the hell does that mean?" Beck asked as she narrowed her eyes.

"I play music, and Scarlett, uh, well, she serves the guests," Jack said, his voice getting higher with each word.

"You're a cocktail waitress?" Beck asked.

Scarlett laughed, "No, honey. I'm a whore."

Jack squeezed his eyes shut tight. He opened them and peeked at Beck. If looks could kill, he'd be a corpse by now. She said through gritted teeth, "You didn't tell me you and Lowry worked at a brothel."

"It's not just any brothel. Miss Wallace runs a very upscale house. Isn't that right, Jackie?" Scarlett asked as she ran her fingers through his curls while he stood there too shell-shocked to resist. "Oh, I'm sorry. I'm being very rude. I should've asked if I could cut in. I'm used to men asking me to dance."

CHAPTER 33

Beck felt like she'd had the wind knocked out of her. She glared at Jack, expecting an explanation, but he only stared at the floor. "Be my guest," Beck snapped at Scarlett then stomped away, determined not to look back.

She looked over at Victor, who was speaking with Nash. Could Jack be right? Was Victor attracted to her? Not ready to dwell on the possibility, she headed toward Ella and Lowry's table.

As Beck approached, she heard Lowry say, "All this time, I judged Rebecca for taxi dancing, and my own wife was doing it right under my nose in the very club I play in. Everyone must think I'm a damned fool."

"You're a fool? At least dancing is all I did. God knows what you were up to in that whorehouse," Ella protested.

"I never laid a finger on those women. All I did was play music to feed my family. You can ask Jack. He was the one flirting, not me," Lowry said as Beck walked up behind him.

Ella looked away and cleared her throat, "What? You getting sick or something?" Lowry asked. Ella kicked him sharply under the table. "Ow, what the hell's gotten into you, Woman?"

Ella sighed, "Hello, Rebecca."

"Oh shit," Lowry muttered. He turned and flashed a fake grin at Beck, "Oh, hi, Rebecca," he said sweetly, then he turned to Ella and whispered a bit too loudly, "Why didn't you tell me she was behind me?"

"So, Jack and this Scarlett. Are they happy together?" Beck asked as she tried desperately to control the tremble in her voice.

Lowry said, "Oh Honey, there ain't no Jack *and* Scarlett. He only likes her because she looks like a younger version of you." Ella kicked him even harder this time, "Ow! Sorry. I ain't explaining this right."

"It's okay. You shouldn't have to tell me. Jack should have told me," she said, fighting back the tears.

"Becks, do you have room for me on your dance card?" Victor asked.

"On my what?" Beck asked as she quickly wiped her eyes.

"Go away, Fancy Pants, we're having a conversation," Lowry snapped at Victor.

"Pardon me," Victor said.

"You'll have to excuse, Lowry, Victor. He didn't realize that we'd said all there was to say. Let's dance." Beck threaded her arm through Victor's.

"Rebecca," Ella called after her, "Are you sure this is what you want to do right now?"

Beck looked at her friend over her shoulder, "Absolutely," she said.

As they reached the dance floor, Victor said, "Becks, I think we need to clear the air."

"I'm all talked out. Can we just dance, please? At least for one song."

"As you wish," Victor said as he slid his arm around her waist, and gently moved with her to the music.

As they danced, Jack looked over Scarlett's shoulder, scanning the room for Beck. As he did, he caught a whiff of Scarlett's hair which smelled of candied apple and cigarette smoke. It was much different than his wife's scent. If he was honest, the cigarette smell made him crave one.

That's silly. I haven't smoked in twenty years.

Doing his best not to step on his partner's toes, he steered her around so he could search the other side of the room for Beck. Once again, he spotted Victor first, heads above the crowd, and his wife was once again in the Brit's arms. He abruptly let go of Scarlett, determined to cross the dance floor and set things right.

However, before Jack could reach her, he spotted Meyer giving him and Lowry the signal. Lowry grabbed Cab, and Ella followed.

As they approached Jack. Lowry asked, "What are we going to do?"

Jack looked at Beck, desperate to get her attention. After a few moments of trying to signal her, he looked to the stage where the current band's set was winding down. "We do what do we best, gentlemen. Let's get up there and play".

"Together?" Cab asked warily.

"I can't think of a better distraction. Can you?" Jack said.

"How can I help?" Ella asked.

Jack looked at Lowry, who shrugged."She made me tell her everything." Turning back to his wife, he said, "Would you and the other dance hostesses offer to dance with any of the officers that look like they're trying to get backstage?"

"Are you sure?" Ella asked.

"No more secrets, right," Lowry said.

"No more secrets," Ella agreed and gave Lowry a peck on the lips.

"Ouch," he said as he touched his swollen lip.

"Sorry, I forgot again," Ella said. Then, she headed off to rally the other dancers.

"You sure you're okay with this plan?" Jack asked.

"At some point, you either trust each other or you don't," Lowry said with a shrug.

"Come on, boys. It's showtime," Cab said, moving the men towards the stage.

Cab hopped onto the stage and solicited a round of applause for the Metairie Swingers, who were miffed to have their last song cut short. However, Cab was not to be denied. When he called Lowry and Jack to the stage, the crowd screamed.

Beck turned to the stage, astonished. "Oh my goodness, they're actually going to do it."

"I thought you knew everything that went on around here," Victor said.

"Jack said that he and Lowry were going to do this, but after tonight, I thought he was just trying to keep me from following him to the brothel."

"Jack was at a brothel?" Victor asked as he raised his eyebrows.

"He and Lowry have been performing there for weeks. He never told me," Beck said bitterly. "Apparently, that redheaded harlot over there is his new girlfriend." She pointed at Scarlett, who was perched as close to the edge of the stage as possible.

Victor studied Scarlett. "Oh my goodness, she, um..."

"Yeah, I know. Jack has a type."

The dance floor filled to capacity as Cab sang the first song. The hot, sweaty crowd overtook the dance floor. Beck shut her eyes tight and moved with the beat. Floating on Cab's voice and memories of Harlem.

After the thunderous applause died down from their opening number, Victor said, "Becks, I'm sorry, but what I have to say can't wait."

"Okay," she said. She felt her stomach tighten a bit as Victor steered her gently off the dance floor. Beck looked over at the stage just in time to see Cab launch into 'Minnie the Moocher.' Jack emerged from backstage wearing his trademark horns, and the crowd roared. The Red Devil had returned.

Victor patted her arm softly to get her attention. "I've been trying to tell you something for m-months, and I, well, I'm going to come right out with it. I love you, Becks."

He couldn't mean what she thought he meant. Beck said, "Aw, I love you too, my friend."

Victor leaned his head back and looked up at the ceiling, "I don't think that I am. Ugh, why is this so bloody hard." he took a deep breath and looked her in the eyes, "Becks, it's like this. There's no one like you, you're the bee's knees, and I'm hopelessly *in* love with you."

Beck felt as though the room tilted. This wasn't possible. Victor was her friend, her gay friend, "You can't be in love with me."

"Because of Jack, you mean? I can love you better than Jack. I do love you better than him. While he was at a brothel, I've been by your side."

"But you're gay," Beck said quietly.

Victor tilted his head. "No, I'm not."

"You hang out at Lafitte's with Tennessee and Truman. They're gay. It's a gay bar."

"It's an inclusive bar. I was there for the same reason you were. To meet fellow writers."

"But, but you wore a mermaid costume on a float. Everyone saw you," Beck sputtered.

"Well, I take excellent care of my physique. Did it ever occur to you that I was trying to show off?" Victor asked.

"Yes, I thought you were showing off for the other men."

Victor blushed and put a hand on either side of Beck's face, "My darling, I was trying to get your attention." Victor moved his face towards Beck's and closed his eyes.

He's not going to kiss me, is he?

Before she could finish the thought, she had her answer. His lips were on her's, kissing her softly, and she was letting him. Not only that, she was kissing him back.

Adrenaline pulsed through Jack's veins as he played with his friends. It was like old times as the sweaty throng danced in front of them. It was difficult to keep in mind their true purpose while having so much fun, but too much was at stake. By the end of 'Minnie,' he noticed that a few cops had filtered in. As they'd planned, the police were distracted by their integrated act, and those that weren't jazz fans were definitely enjoying the company of the dance hostesses.

Cab, Lowry, and Jack gave each other a quick nod. They had all seen the police. Hopeful that they'd get in one more song before the officers advanced, Lowry played trumpet while Cab and Jack did a duet of "Saint James Infirmary."

Jack searched the audience. Even more officers had gathered now, but they were either watching the show or paired off successfully by Ella. He saw a flash of red curls as an officer twirled Beck, or so Jack thought. But, when he saw the dancer's face, it was obviously Scarlett who had jumped in to help the cause. Even his former boss Norma was chatting up a detective.

He realized at that point that Beck likely had no clue of their plan, but he thought she'd still be watching the show. At the precise moment, he sang the words, "You may search this whole wide world over, but you'll never find another sweet man like me," Jack saw Victor and Beck kissing in the corner. He whispered to Cab, "I need you to bring this one home." Cab nodded while Jack danced over to Lowry.

Jack hoped that whispering in Lowry's ear wouldn't distract him, "You're singing next. We need a song to bring the house down." Lowry gave him a quick wink. The audience barely had time to applaud before the men launched into "When The Saints Go Marching In."

A deafening cheer went up from the crowd as the unofficial anthem of New Orleans played. The officers tried to rush the stage, but the crowd, lost in their revelry, blocked the way. Then, the police attempted to get backstage. Cab and Lowry were still singing, Jack was on trombone, and the rest of the Ringgold Rebels entered the audience. Meyer peeked around the corner and gave them a brief nod. They'd successfully kept the police from discovering the slot machines, but they weren't able to keep the officers from moving in on them.

The music ground to a halt as the police cuffed all six of the men. Ella came running around the corner with Leon as the cops attempted to move the men through the crowd.

"Evenin' officers, what seems to be the trouble?" Leon asked.

"You had a mixed act on your stage. That's what's the matter," one of the officers said as he narrowed his eyes at the musicians.

"It was my fault," Jack said, "I was excited to see my friends from the Cotton Club, and I guess I just forgot when, I mean, where I was."

"Yeah, you did," Leon smirked at Jack and the others. He

turned to the officers, "Gentlemen, this was all a terrible misunderstanding. These men are used to playing up in New York City. They just needed a warning, and you certainly have given them one. Now, would you please take off the bracelets?"

"The law is the law, Prima," the detective started to say when Jack saw his eyes move to a prominent figure over Prima's shoulder.

"Of course, the law's, the law, but I bet there's some way we could come to an understanding," Marcello said as he cracked his knuckles, and several men in suits emerged from backstage and assembled beside him.

The police were outnumbered and began removing the cuffs from the musicians. Beck had ended her kiss with Victor as the band had started their closing number. She had watched in the shadows as the drama unfurled. Relieved that Jack and their friends were being set free, she ran up to him.

"Are you okay?" she asked.

"Get away from me," Jack growled.

"I'm tryin' to take your cuffs off," the officer grumbled. He stopped and looked at the two redheads. "You two again?" He motioned for his detective to come over.

"What's the trouble?" his boss asked.

"I can't let this man go. He's the jerk that assaulted me. That makes him a repeat offender. If you ask me, the dame's in on this, too. I had to arrest her for arranging a mixed act here in January."

Beck began to fidget with her bare ring finger. She couldn't bring herself to look at her husband.

Victor hurried to Beck's side and placed his arm protectively around her shoulder. "I can assure you that Miss Taylor had no prior knowledge of tonight's events."

"That's a load of bull," the officer cried. "She's the house manager. She had to know this was going down."

Jack said, "I waited until she was distracted," he said as he motioned at Victor, "That's when I made my move. I acted alone."

The mob had retreated when the police released the other musicians. Leon alone was left to defend Jack, "Like I said, gentleman, he's not from around here. He doesn't understand how things are done. After tonight, I'm sure he's learned his lesson. Ain't that right, Jack?"

"Yes, Sir," Jack said emphatically. He certainly didn't want to go back to jail.

The detective shook his head, "Alright. Here's what we're gonna do for you, Prima. We'll leave the black musicians and your house manager for you to deal with. However, Mr. Herman assaulted one of my men. He's a repeat offender. I can't let him go. He'll get into more trouble if we let him off with a slap on the wrist." The detective turned to Jack. "I think another night in the slammer's just what you need."

Beck gasped as she watched helplessly while Jack was dragged roughly away by the officer that had arrested them previously. "Isn't there something you can do?" Beck pleaded with Leon.

"Yeah, I'll let you keep your job so you can bail him out. I ain't doing it again. He may be talented, but he's too much of a liability. You too, Mr. Ringgold. Both times I've had a mixed act on my stage, you were involved. You're outta here."

Ella stopped their boss from walking away and said, "But Mr. Prima, please, my husband needs this job. We have a baby to feed."

"Ella," Lowry said sharply.

Leon looked from Ella to Lowry and back to her, "You mean to tell me you lied to me? You're married? To a negro?! That's against the law. You two make me sick. Now get out and stay out, or I'll turn you in, and your baby'll be declared a bastard. And as for you, Mr. Calloway - "

Cab turned and raised an eyebrow, "Oh, no need to address me, Leon. I'll never play this dump again." he said as he laid one hand on Ella's shoulder and the other on Lowry's, leading them backstage.

"Well, it's always good when the trash takes itself out." Leon smirked. He looked at Beck and said, "Well, I suggest you make yourself useful and tell the next act they're going on early. I don't pay you to stand around looking pretty."

"Tell them yourself, Leon," Beck said, "I quit." With that, she turned and walked out of the club with Victor hot on her heels.

CHAPTER 34

There was a cold mist in the early morning air. The breeze was enough to cause the gas flames in the lanterns to flicker, casting odd shadows on the stark gray building that housed the Night Court. Beck, still in her evening gown, shivered.

Victor pulled off his sports coat and draped it around Beck's shoulders. "That officer has really got it in for Jack." He sighed, and his breath crystallized into a mist. "Where is the poor fellow going to get that kind of money?"

Beck thought about how Jack looked in the courtroom. He'd kept his head down but had a fresh bruise above his eyebrow. She noticed he was limping as they led him back to the cell. Tears stung her eyes as she imagined how he had come by the injuries. She reached into her purse for a tissue, but her wedding ring brushed up against her fingertips before she could get one.

"I can get the money," she said as she held up her ring. "I'll sell this."

"That's beautiful. I don't remember you wearing it," Victor said.

Beck looked at her feet and said quietly, "Jack gave it to me when he asked me to marry him."

"You can't sell that. You have to return the ring when you break an engagement."

"He won't take it back, and right now, he needs the money more than -- will you please help me find a pawn shop?"

"No pawn shops are open at this time, Darling. Let's get you home. You can change and rest up for a bit. I promise I'll take you to Clarence's in the morning. It's an upscale shop right across from the theater."

As they entered the boarding house, Beck said, "I don't think I can sleep."

Victor led her into the parlor. "Fancy a chat? A lot has happened tonight."

"You said you love me," Beck said.

"I did. I do. How do you feel?"

Beck fidgeted with her left ring finger. "I care about you."

Victor said, "I know. But, oh god, this is embarrassing. Are you -- I mean, have you ever found me attractive at all?" He looked away and bit his knuckle.

Beck felt her cheeks grow hot, "Of course I have. But I thought I wasn't your type. Can you understand my confusion?"

Victor smiled and said, "Of course, my darling. I understand how it may have seemed. In England, we don't have quite the stigma, I suppose. We're a bit freer to mix our company as it were."

"That sounds like heaven," Beck said wistfully.

"Then why don't you come with me?" Victor asked.

"To England?"

"My play opens tonight, and then I'm off tomorrow. Please, Beck, let me show you London. Let's see where this takes us."

Beck looked at Victor's hopeful face and thought about her and Jack's struggles. Was love supposed to be that hard, or she wondered as Victor smiled at her, was love supposed to be this easy?

"Alright, I'll go."

"Really, Becks?" Victor beamed at her and embraced her tightly.

As promised, Victor brought Beck to Clarence's pawn shop when it opened. As the shopkeeper counted the cash, Victor whispered softly in her ear, "Just enough to grant Jack his freedom."

Beck did her best to give him a small smile through her tears. *He has his freedom In more ways than one,* she thought glumly.

As she paid Jack's bail, the guard told her it would be a minute before he could release Jack as he was processing a large group of drunk and disorderly people from the night before. She asked to see him and was allowed to go back to his cell. He lay on the cot staring at the wall opposite him.

"Jack, are you okay?" Beck asked.

Jack rolled over. Beck couldn't help but tear up at the sight of his bruised face. He sat up slowly and winced in pain. When he saw that it was her, he gave her a weak smile that faded almost immediately when he noticed Victor standing behind her. "What the hell are you doing here?"

Beck put her hands on her hips. "I bailed you out."

"Why? What do you care if I rot in here? You've already replaced me."

"Replaced you? You're the one who constantly put your music first, and then you had the nerve to go find some floozy."

"I'm not with Scarlett. She'd like me to be, but unlike you, I shut that down."

"Unlike me?" Beck asked.

"I saw you playing tonsil hockey with Victor last night."

"Excuse me, I'm not familiar with that term, but it sounds vulgar," Victor said.

"He means kissing," Beck said.

"Oh, well yes, we were kissing," Victor said thoughtfully.

"You're not helping," Beck said through her teeth at Victor. Then, she turned to Jack, "Yes, I finally kissed someone who appreciates me after years of coming in a distant third to your music and the dog."

"Well, the dog's dead. So, you got a promotion," Jack snapped.

Beck gasped. "What? Rufus is...Rufus died! Rufus is dead, and you didn't tell me? That's just cruel."

Jack felt a pang of guilt as Beck began to cry, "I didn't mean to blurt it out like that. He died right after you left, and I just never found the right moment to --"

"So you waited for the moment when it would hurt the most? Congratulations."

"I'm hurt too, you know," Jack protested as the guard came over to release him.

"Well, I won't hurt you anymore. Victor has asked me to go to London with him, and I've accepted. Enjoy your freedom, Jack," Beck said through tears as she walked away.

Jack felt as if he'd been punched in the gut. As he exited the cell and caught his breath, he looked up at Victor. "Did you stay behind to gloat? I didn't think you were the type."

"Jack, you should know that Beck's been very concerned about you. She had me up at dawn to go to Clarence's for your bail money."

"Is that a bail bond place?" Jack asked.

"No, it's an upscale pawn shop near Pirate's Alley. They gave her a good price for her ring."

"What ring?" Jack asked.

"A heart-shaped opal with a tiny diamond on each side. She wept as she handed it over, but she said you needed money more than you needed her. When she saw your injuries last night, she couldn't stand the thought of you being abused."

Jack was stunned. He looked up at Victor's kind blue eyes. The man Beck had chosen seemed to be a good one. His heart was breaking, but there was one thing he had to know. "Do you love her?"

"Utterly," Victor said with the look of a lost puppy dog.

Jack knew the feeling well. He nodded and said, "Take care of her." Then, he walked past Victor and left the station.

CHAPTER 35

After he had spent hours walking around the French Quarter taking mental pictures, Jack entered Congo Square. Something he always wished he'd had a chance to do in New York. Last time, it was impossible as he and Beck fled Harlem to save her life, only to be intercepted by Pipes McGhee. The memory of her body at the bottom of the stairs still haunted him. He thought he'd lost her. This time, it was a slow, painful exit. Beck had chosen a new life, and he'd lost for her good.

He shook his head to stop the music of her laughter from ringing in his ears. His eyes shut tight as he tried not to imagine her by his side, dressed in her Mardi Gras dress. *Maybe this walk wasn't the best idea.* He ached physically from the injuries inflicted by the crooked cop and emotionally from wounds inflicted by his wife. If he was honest, a few of those internal aches were likely self-inflicted - perhaps most of them were. The defeated man sank slowly onto the cobblestone ground under the Ancestry Tree and covered his face with his hands.

"Hey, Africa thought I might find you here," Lowry said.

Jack looked up and saw Lowry holding Jackie on his hip while Ella stood beside him. A lovely sight, he couldn't help but smile.

"How'd you know I'd be here?" Jack asked.

"I know how you feel about all this," Lowry said with a wave of his hand, indicating the square. "You been talking my ear off about Voodoo this and Voodoo that ever since I've known you. You okay? I have your money. Cab and I tried to bring it to you, but they said you'd already made bail. You look like you found some more bruises." Lowry handed Jackie to his mother and sat on the ground next to his friend.

"It looks worse than it is," Jack fudged the truth, not wanting to talk about it, "Why don't you hold onto my share. You're going to need it until you get a new gig."

"We're going to be fine. After that nasty scene at the 500 Club last night, Cab made us an offer we couldn't refuse."

"Oh really?"

"He's got some work lined up in Hollywood and wants me to play in his band and compose for him. Says there's work for Ella as a dancer if she wants, too. So the Ringgold's are moving west," Lowry said with a broad grin.

"That's great. You've always wanted to write music for the movies. And, Ella, you'll be great dancing on the silver screen."

"I might do a couple of pictures to build up our savings, but I want another baby," Ella said as she blushed, "In California, a family like ours isn't hassled by the law."

"Another little Ringgold, huh?" Jack asked, looking at Lowry.

"I told her we'd work on it," Lowry said with a wink and a chuckle.

Jack smiled. "No harm in trying."

"Speaking of family, where's your woman?"

"She's not my woman anymore," Jack said, his eyes stinging.

Lowry patted him on the back. "Don't give up hope, my man."

"It's over. Beck and Victor set sail for England in the morning."

"Oh, no way. She's going with Mr. Fancypants to England? They barely know each other. You two have history."

"Maybe that's our problem. Too much history," Jack said.

Lowry stood up, catching his wife's eye. They shared a meaningful look, and Ella gave him a quick nod. The man turned back to Jack, offering him a hand. "Wanna go back to California? We'd love to have you there to show us around," Lowry said as he pulled his friend up from the cobblestones.

Jack turned the idea over in his mind. He wanted to go home, but California 1948 wasn't it. Besides, his parents were living in Baldwin Hills, anxiously awaiting the arrival of his older brother. The risk of running into them wasn't one he wanted to take.

"Well, I'd better go home and feed Jackie," Ella said as she produced three small oranges from her bag and placed one at the base of the Ancestor tree. She kissed Lowry softly on the lips and handed him an orange. She turned to Jack and hugged him. "God bless you, Jack, wherever you go," she said, then they chuckled as her baby reached for the redhead.

"Thank you," Jack said as he ruffled the baby's curls. "Bye, little Jackie, you wear our name well."

Ella placed the third orange in Jack's hand. "I think you need this more than Jackie does." As she walked away, Jackie waved at him over her shoulder.

"Well?" Lowry asked.

"I appreciate the offer, but there's somewhere else I belong," Jack said, avoiding his friend's gaze.

Lowry nodded, "I understand, and I have a feeling that where you're going, you're gonna need this." Lowry reached into his pocket and retrieved Jack's Casio watch circa 1992, discreetly handing it to his friend.

Jack opened his hand just enough to confirm what he was

holding and raised his eyebrows, "How long have you had this?"

"I found it years ago when you and Beck went missing. It was in the top of my closet when I cleaned out the place. It's dead. Sorry, but I don't think the batteries have been invented yet."

"You knew? Why didn't you -"

"I've wanted to say something, but never found the right moment. When's a good time for the 'So you're from the future' talk?"

The men chuckled, "Wait? How do you know that? With this technology, maybe I'm from Mars or something."

"I can read, Jack. The back says 'Made in Japan 1992'," Lowry explained.

Jack turned it over, "Huh? I guess it does."

"You going back, aren't you?"

"I'm going to try."

"Then, Godspeed, my brother," Lowry embraced his friend patting him on the back, then offered to shake hands and attempted to place a wad of cash in Jack's.

Jack shook his head and pushed the money back at Lowry. "Keep it for your family."

Lowry frowned and slowly placed the cash back into his pocket. He started to go but stopped abruptly and turned to the tree, placing his orange next to Ella's. "Come on, Jack, maybe it'll help."

"What have I got to lose?" Jack said with a shrug as he placed his orange among the roots of the giant oak and wished for home.

"I hope I see you sometime," Lowry said with a smile and patted Jack's arm before heading off toward his family.

As Lowry turned out of sight, Jack felt alone. He looked around and spotted a small gathering of people across the square. A cheer rose, and the group parted, revealing a bride and a groom. A man with a painted skull face crossed the square before the wedding party, striking his sword near the ground.

"He's making way for the ancestors," explained a woman's deep voice from behind.

"Of the past, present, and future, I know. It's not my first Voodoo wedding, " Jack grumbled as he turned and found himself face-to-face with the Voodoo lady. "So, which one are you?"

"A bit of all of them. You're troubled, Jack Herman."

"The tether didn't snap back," Jack said with a sigh, "I've lost her."

"Patience," she said.

They watched silently as the wedding party moved to the center of the square and began the reception. Musicians began to play a lively tune while the rest of the party started to dance. Their bodies writhed. A mixture of bronze, tan, and umber shining in the fading light as the sun began to set. Jack found that he, too could not keep still as the percussion resonated through his weary body. The Voodoo lady left his side to join the throng.

Suddenly, he felt a tug at his shirt sleeve. "Dance with me," said a small insistent voice.

Jack looked down to see a little girl standing in front of him. Unlike the rest of the wedding party, she had an alabaster complexion. Her head was full of red curls. She was adorable. Without waiting for him to respond, the child took his hands and led him toward the celebration. She had an impressive sense of rhythm for such a small child. As they danced, she giggled with delight. For a moment, Jack felt the burden of his sorrow lift.

However, the brief respite ended when the dancers moved aside so the bride and groom could share their first dance. Though the music was very different, the rhythm matched the beat of his song "Come Home". The tempo was the beat of Beck's heart. Jack looked at the newlyweds, their eyes filled with love and hope. Beck used to look at him that way. His heart ached for her. Tears stung his eyes and then flowed freely down his cheeks.

The little girl took his hand again and squeezed it. "It's going to be okay. You'll see," she said as she placed a handkerchief in his hand.

He was moved by her kindness. *How could someone so young have such empathy?* He followed her gaze back to the couple. The song was winding down, and the bride and groom were sharing a kiss. In his mind, he saw Beck, her eyes closed, lips slightly parted. A highlight reel of their kisses played on a loop as his heartbeat synced with the tempo of the drums. Jack felt as though he was dissolving. Unable to steady himself, he dropped to his knees on the cobblestone. The little one hugged him tightly and then let go. Her sweet face was the last thing he saw.

CHAPTER 36

Beck and Victor sat side by side at the premiere of his play. He had allowed her to read through several scenes, but seeing his work played out on stage was exciting.

All at once, the hairs on the back of Beck's neck and arms stood on end, causing her to shiver as she sat in the darkened theater. Victor cut his eyes over to her, and she gave him a reassuring smile. He stroked her arm with his warm hand, gently caressing her with his long, slender fingers. Then he wrapped his arm around her as if to shield her from the cold.

After the performance, Victor was the guest of honor at the opening night reception. It was a blur of toasts and introductions. The two of them hardly had a moment alone. Victor squired Beck around, beaming with pride as he introduced her to the cast and crew. On the surface, it was a good night, but Beck felt an emptiness that she couldn't shake.

As the two exited the Le Petit Theater and stepped into the crisp night air Beck found herself searching the faces of the passersby. Victor helped her with her wrap and asked, "Where were you just now, Darling?"

Beck slid her arm in his and said, "Right here, with you." She saw an eager smile on his face. His eyebrows slightly raised. "I loved the play. Your dialogue is so witty."

Victor beamed. "You really think so?"

"I do. Your wit is one of my favorite things about you. But, I have to ask, Daphne, is she...?"

"I wondered if you'd catch that. I can't help but be inspired by you," Victor said as he pulled Beck close and planted a kiss on the top of her head.

"I'm flattered. I wish I was that vivacious."

"But you are, Becks. You're my bright spot. For me, the world is painted in shades of blues and grays, and then you come into view. You're a vibrant splash of color that elevates it all."

Beck felt her cheeks warm. She chuckled and said, "If you don't stop, my ego's not going to fit in through the front door."

"There's a lot more where that came from. We're simply going to have to find a place with a larger door," he said as he opened the door to the boarding house for her.

Beck walked through the door and began to climb the stairs. She was never the best at accepting a compliment, but the discomfort was compounded by the fact that it was coming from the wrong person. *Why couldn't Jack say things like that to me?* She wondered. *I would have given anything to have been his bright spot.*

Victor kissed her hand at the top of the stairs. "Tired, my love?"

"It's been quite a day," she sighed.

Victor took her key and unlocked her door. "Tomorrow will be even longer. I wish I didn't have to leave you so soon, but we need to pack. We'll have loads of time to chat on the voyage."

Beck nodded and entered her room. It was ice cold. "Oh no," she said.

"What's the matter?"

"Mrs. Brown forgot to light my fireplace. It's freezing in here," Beck said.

"Mrs. Brown doesn't light the fires. We all light our own," Victor said.

"I've never lit mine." Beck felt flustered. The only other night it hadn't been lit was her first; she'd planned to ask Mrs. Brown about it the next night, but it was already lit that evening and every night since. "I don't know how to build a fire," she mumbled. Her father and brothers had always been eager to do it when she was a kid. Jack always took care of it whenever it was chilly in the canyon. Jack. That was it. He must have come in and lit the fire. How did she miss that?

"Well, it's quite easy. I'll show you how," Victor offered as he removed his jacket and rolled up his sleeves.

Beck watched as Victor talked her through the steps. He made quick work of it, and soon the room was glowing amber. She stepped closer to enjoy the warmth that was beginning to spread through her room. As she did, Victor stood and took her in his arms.

"Is that better?" he asked.

"Yes, thank you."

Victor leaned down for a kiss that Beck didn't feel she could give. Instead of offering him her lips, Victor had to settle for her forehead instead. They bid each other an awkward adieu, leaving her alone with her thoughts.

Beck changed into her pajamas, turned off the lights, and sat in front of the fire watching the flames dance. If Jack had lit the fire every night, why was it dark tonight? Her mind flashed back to their confrontation at his cell. Remembering how angry they'd been with each other. *He's finally done with me*, she thought. It makes sense. *I did tell him I was leaving the country with another man.*

She stood up and stared into her large empty suitcase. Her fingers brushed the pillow where her lover had slept the night before, his red curls draped on the ivory pillowcase. She was, at last, able to identify the pain in her stomach -- grief.

Careful to shut the door quietly, she crept down the hall to Jack's room. Intending to knock, she noticed his door was ajar. She called softly as she opened it, "Jack?" His bed was made, and the fireplace was empty. Beck's pulse quickened as she searched the room for Jack's belongings. His instruments were missing. The closet and drawers had all been emptied out except for an undershirt discarded at the bottom of the closet. The only thing left behind save for a single piece of sheet music that she found on the floor between the bed and his nightstand.

Beck tucked the paper into the pocket of her robe, then picked up her husband's undershirt. Inhaling his scent of pine and ocean air mixed with sweat as she held it close. Her tears stained the fabric.

Back in her cold, dark room, she pictured Jack building the fire each night for her to come home to. He was good at it. It probably didn't take him that long, but Jack did it consistently. He did it for her.

He knew she was often cold and afraid of the dark. This simple act alleviated both issues. Another in a long list of thoughtless acts of kindness he performed for her. How often would he bring her tea while she was writing or slip fuzzy socks onto her feet on a cold night? He'd buy her purple trinkets because she loved the color, and he wanted to make her smile. Whenever there was an emotional scene in a movie, he would wordlessly grab the tissue, anticipating her tears.

That's what she'd missed. Jack wasn't often up for a night on the town, and it was easier for him to express his feelings with music instead of words. He'd been telegraphing his love for her in a hundred little ways. Beck's tears spilled down her cheeks. *How could I have missed it?*

She went through the contents of her room, setting aside her best gowns and costume jewelry. Then, she waited for the sunrise. Determined to get back what she'd given up.

CHAPTER 37

The pawn shop owner scrutinized the gowns Beck had received from Ginny and her mother. Then, he placed a jeweler's loupe to his eye and picked up a ruby ring.

"Oh, you don't have to do that. It's all costume jewelry," Beck said as she looked away and shuffled her feet.

Clarence sneered. "It's fake?" he asked in a thick French accent.

"Yes, Sir," Beck said softly.

"After that lovely opal you brought me, I assumed that these might actually be worth something," the man said with a sigh as he waved his hand over the baubles spread about the top of the display case.

"About the opal," Beck said, her eyes scanning the interior of the case, "that's why I'm here. I want to buy it back."

"You brought me a bunch of colored glass and used formals to exchange for an authentic opal and diamond ring?" he scoffed, "Ridiculous."

Beck felt her cheeks grow hot as she pleaded, "How much am I short? I'll make up the rest. Please, I need my ring back."

"You shouldn't have pawned something so precious. I've already sold it."

Beck gasped. She felt as though the floor had dropped out from under her. Her hands gripped the counter. Jack was gone, and now she'd lost her wedding ring. Somewhere in the distance,

Clarence was speaking.

"Mademoiselle, I'll pay you one hundred and fifty for the lot."

Her eyes scanned the shop in a fruitless attempt to locate her ring. Hanging on the wall next to the instruments were several records, including the one from The Cotton Club Revue. Her Red Devil smiled at her from the sleeve.

"Throw in the Cotton Club album and we've got a deal."

Clarence shook his head. "That album is signed. I'll have to deduct ten dollars for it."

Beck looked back at Jack's face on the cover. *I don't have any photos of him.* She thought of her grandparents, who were no longer living. Oh, how she'd treasured their photos as time made their faces fade and blur at the edges in her memory. She couldn't stand to think of Jack's face fading, too.

"I understand," she said.

The transaction complete, Beck ducked back out to the alley and cut over to Bourbon Street, grateful for the anonymity that its crowded sidewalks provided her. Wrapped up in their morning commute, the strangers passed her by, none of them noticing the redhead as she tried unsuccessfully to blink back the tears.

Out of the corner of her eye, Beck caught a warm green glow coming from the courtyard at The Court of Two Sisters. She entered, determined to locate the source. The place, which should have been full of employees setting up for brunch, was mysteriously empty.

Beck wandered past the tables and chairs into the middle of the dining area where a wishing well stood. It shone as if illuminated by a spotlight, but she couldn't locate one.

The ornate iron arch above the well featured a sign. "The Devil's Wishing Well," Beck read aloud and sighed.

She jumped as the Voodoo Lady's voice rang out from behind her "It's not named for an actual devil, my child. It's named for a misunderstood priestess and her equally misinterpreted religion. Marie Laveau conducted many rituals here."

"Oh, for a minute, I thought it had to do with Jean Lafitte and his duals."

"He was more of a handsome devil," the old woman chuckled, "Like yours."

"Jack's not mine anymore," Beck said softly as her tears spilled over.

"Are you sure?"

"He's gone. I think he's left 1948 altogether."

The Voodoo Lady raised an eyebrow. "How can you be certain?"

Beck began to pace, and exasperated, said, "I don't know how I know. Maybe it's that 'tethered' thing you keep saying. But I...I can't *feel* him anymore," Beck said as she sobbed.

The Voodoo Lady stared in silence. Finally, she produced a green doubloon from the small leather pouch around her waist. She flashed the tail end of the coin at Beck. "You have a choice to make, Rebecca Herman. Start over with Victor Shadley," she said, as she turned the coin to show the head end, "or find a way back to your husband." With that, she tossed the doubloon to Beck and started to walk away. "It's all up to you."

"But I don't know how to get back," Beck protested.

"The power is in your hands, Child," the old woman called back over her shoulders.

Beck turned the coin over and over in her hand, concluding that life couldn't be decided by a simple coin toss. Instead, she made a wish and lobbed the coin into the well, praying she'd made the right choice.

Back in her room, Beck packed the remainder of her belongings. She removed the album from its bag, and was disappointed to see that the old 78 record contained only two songs, Jack and Cab singing "St James Infirmary" on side A and "Demeter's Song" sung by Mama Esther on the B side. Cab had signed the album with a flourish. *No wonder it's worth so much.* Upon further inspection, she saw that his was one of only three signatures. Lowry and Jack had signed it as well.

She traced her husband's autograph with her finger. It reminded her of how star-struck she'd once been when they first met at the movie studio. She had been mortified when she ran into him and spilled a smoothie on his shoes. But now, it only made her laugh. If only she could look into his hazel eyes one more time, lace her fingers through his long slender fingers, and hear his voice.

Hear his voice!

A smile spread slowly across her face as she ran downstairs to the ballroom. The one room she was certain contained a turntable.

Beck opened the wooden lid and pulled the record out of its sleeve. It was shiny and delicate. Whatever it was made of, it certainly wasn't vinyl. She placed the fragile disc gingerly onto the turntable. Turning the album cover over, she considered what to listen to first. She loved Jack's cover of "St. James Infirmary", but "Demeter's Song" featured Mama Esther's commanding voice.

Jack would have to wait. Beck needed to hear Mama Esther sing.

The tinny old speaker crackled to life as the needle made contact with the record. Soon the ballroom was filled with Esther's sweet warbling. Beck wrapped her arms around herself and closed her eyes. She could picture Mama as big as life, enfolding her in a warm embrace.

So many memories flashed at once inside her head. It was Mama Esther who had comforted her in Harlem Hospital when she first arrived in 1938, after being struck by a car in 1992. She took Beck into her home, and gave Jack the third degree before their first date. Esther and Beck had shared the stage when Mama sang this very song.

Beck's relationship with her own mother was complicated. Their early lives were full of drama and chaos. Beck's distress from their ever-changing circumstances had predisposed her to vivid nightmares. A few times, she'd even woke up with dirty feet or minor injuries. Her mother claimed that Beck had been sleepwalking, but she always woke up in her bed. Her mother was terribly distraught by these episodes. Beck pushed the painful memories away, choosing to focus once more on her surrogate mother's song.

Esther's voice picked at the partially healed wound left by her absence. The grief that had gradually morphed into a tender spot in Beck's soul began to sting again. "Stop it," she admonished herself, "It was a miracle that I was able to know Mama Esther at all," she whispered as she wiped her eyes.

The music transformed the desolate ballroom into the Cotton Club of 1938. It reminded her of a quote from an artist Jack had introduced her to, Jean-Michel Basquiat. Who'd said, "Art is how we decorate space, music is how we decorate time."

How true, Beck thought.

Wait. Time. Music. Could it be?

Before Beck could come to a conclusion, she heard footsteps behind her.

"Morning, Darling," Victor said, "That singer was divine. Who is she?"

"She *was* Mama Esther from The Cotton Club," she said.

"Ah, yes. I remember her from your stories, but I didn't realize Ms. Esther had recorded an album."

"She sang in The Cotton Club Revue. I bought the album this morning."

His eyes landed on the bag from Clarence's next to her feet. Beck followed his gaze and made a half-hearted attempt to conceal it with her feet. Victor knitted his brow, "You've been to the pawn shop this morning? Whatever for?"

She continued to stare at the floor.

"To buy this?" he asked.

"No," Beck answered almost in a whisper as she fidgeted with the empty space on her ring finger.

"Then why did you -" His eyes landed on her left hand. "Oh."

A long silence passed between them until Beck worked up the courage to look up into his piercing blue eyes. Victor studied her face as she struggled to choose her words.

"My ring's gone," she said, her eyes stung with tears.

"I'm sorry, Becks. I'll get you a new one in London. Any ring you'd like, if you'd allow me." He sank to one knee.

Beck took his hands in hers, encouraging him to stand, "Please don't."

Victor stood, his shoulders slumped. She tried to meet his eyes, but his gaze never left his wing-tipped shoes. A lock of light blonde hair slid down and covered his face.

"I'm sorry. I-- I didn't mean to be so forward. There's plenty of time to discuss our life together," he said. Beck stood on her tiptoes and brushed the errant tress back from his face as he grinned sheepishly. "Come along. We have a boat to catch."

"I can't go, Victor. I'm sorry."

His smile faded, and he pleaded, "Please forgive me. I won't bring up marriage again. I'm just so happy we're a couple, and I didn't want to waste any more time. Not to mention, there's bound to be talk with us lodging and traveling together. I want to protect your reputation as a lady. But, now I've gone and made you change your mind. I'm really messing this up."

"There's nothing wrong with you. You're smart, caring, and handsome. Anyone would be lucky to have a life with you. It's just that…" her voice trailed off as Jack's voice sang out from the tinny speaker.

"It's just that I'm not *him*," Victor said as he gestured toward the turntable.

Beck nodded and said, "Jack has his flaws, but so do I."

"I don't understand."

Beck turned and walked closer to the turntable. "I'm going after him."

Following her, Victor asked, "Why would you do that? I'm right here, and I'm in love with you. Don't you understand? I want to marry you, Becks."

Beck wheeled around to face Victor. "I'm already married to Jack."

As she completed her confession, her hip knocked into the table, sending the record player crashing onto the floor.

Beck knelt down and surveyed the damage. The album and the player were in pieces. The air felt heavy, and her chest tightened. She attempted to gather a few pieces before the denial gave way to the realization that she'd broken the two most precious things in the room.

She stood and looked up at Victor. A tear fell onto his cheek, and he quickly wiped it away.

"Are you injured?" he asked tearfully. Beck shook her head. "So, this was all a charade? You lied to me. You were never free to be mine."

"I'm sorry. I do love you, Victor. You deserve better."

"I wish I deserved you."

Beck took a deep breath, "It never would have worked for a number of reasons. Some I can't even begin to explain, but most importantly, I made a promise to Jack. I have to try and fix things with him."

After a long silence Victor cleared his throat then said, "I've got a boat to catch. Best of luck, Rebecca *Herman*." Then he turned and slowly walked towards the double doors.

"Godspeed," Beck said, her voice trembling.

Alone again, she contemplated her theory. *Music decorates time.* She replayed what she remembered about being hit by the car years ago. It had caught her off guard because she was listening to Jack singing in her headphones. Then, she woke up in a hospital bed in Harlem in 1938.

She recalled her last moments in Harlem. After being attacked by Pipes, she had found herself in yet another hospital bed, temporarily blind. The darkness amplified the pain of her injuries until Jack placed his hand on hers. His singing was the last thing she'd heard as she was transported back from 1938 to 1992.

Even this slip into the 1940s had coincided with her exasperation and hurt over their fight while she had listened to her husband sing in her headphones. Fear, pain, and hurt, all strong emotions that had been coupled with music. Not just any music, but her husband's. Beck looked at the broken pieces of the record at her feet. Her only hope of going home lay scattered on the ballroom floor.

Unsure of what to do next, Beck headed out for a walk. She felt like a ghost, floating numbly through the quarter. As she reached Decatur Street, she saw the mighty ship that would carry Victor to London. The only friend she'd had left in New Orleans was bound for England, and no longer hers.

As Beck fidgeted with her bare ring finger, she noticed that her skin was purple. She'd left her coat and was now keenly aware of the bitterly cold February morning. She embraced herself for equal parts warmth and consolation.

Beck turned back toward Jackson Square. An icy mist began to settle on her skin. She lifted her gaze realizing that what she felt wasn't rain but snow. Flurries began swirling all around her, lifting her spirits.

I can't believe there's snow in New Orleans. Beck began to explore the quarter anew as the flurries drifted around the landmarks featuring them in a new light.

The scene brought to mind one of her favorite pieces of music. One that Jack had written for a movie before they had met. It played over a scene where an ice sculptor carved an image of his beloved, and she reveled as the flakes rained down upon her.

As she smiled at the memory, Beck's tears ran over the snowflakes that landed on her cheeks. "Ice Melts the Heart" was the perfect song, with a celeste and a choir singing softly. So, of course, she'd insisted they dance to it at their wedding.

"I don't get it," Jack had said as he handed her his dark purple handkerchief, "if it's your favorite, why does it make you cry?"

"It's the most hauntingly beautiful piece ever written, and now its brilliant composer is mine," she said as she'd beamed at him.

"Now and forever, *Mrs.* Herman," he had said as he grinned and pulled her closer.

Beck snapped back to reality. *That's it. I have to find a celeste or at least a piano.*

She marched back toward the quarter. Then, hid around the corner of the Broussard's house and waited for Ginny's parents to leave. Once she was certain Ginny was alone, she rang the bell.

"Rebecca? What's wrong?" Ginny asked.

"I need to use your celeste or your piano."

Ginny furrowed her brow then looked over Beck's outfit, and up at the snow. "Come on in, you must be freezing."

"Do you have one? Beck asked.

"I don't know what a celeste is but we have a piano."

Beck followed Ginny to the parlor where a stately grand piano stood. She sat immediately and pulled back the cover exposing the keys.

"I didn't know you played," Ginny said.

Beck hadn't played since high school, but she was determined to get home. She stared intently at the keys as Jack's melody played on a loop in her head.

"Um, why don't I make us some cocoa?" Ginny asked.

Beck nodded and began to plink the keys on the keyboard. *I only need the melody, if I find it I can go home,* she thought. Her finger struck the first key, one note below middle C, yes B sounded right. Next, she paired it with each note until she finally hit G. Yes, that was it, then one step down to F. However, as she searched for the fourth note, she heard footsteps. Two pairs of heels.

Ginny's cheeks were pink, her eyes red-rimmed. Evelyn Broussard, however, scowled. Her arms folded over her chest.

"Miss Taylor, you're not supposed to be here," she said.

"I know. I needed to stop in for just a moment. It's urgent," Beck said as she kept plinking at the keys desperately.

"Mama, please, I'm worried about her, " Ginny said as her mother pulled Beck off the piano bench.

"Look at how you've upset Ginny. You ought to be ashamed," Evelyn said.

Beck looked at the tears streaming down Ginny's flushed cheeks, "I'm so sorry, " Beck mumbled. She bolted out the door and through the courtyard.

Panicked, she ran through the quarter, certain Jack's song would leave her if she couldn't find the means to express it. Until she passed the open doors a cathedral. As Beck entered a couple passed her with ash in the form of crosses on their foreheads. Once they left, the place was empty. The warm glow was a welcome respite from the cold.

Beck stepped inside and found a small room to the right of the sanctuary. To her delight, an old upright sat against the far wall. Carefully, she lifted the cover, praying that her plan would work. She played the first note and was thrilled that the instrument was not a piano but a celeste. Using the same instrument her husband had played on the recording made it much easier to discover the notes for the melody.

Alone in the church she played the notes she knew over and over humming to help herself remember. As Beck grew more confident, her playing and humming grew louder. She felt fuzzy as the room's glow intensified.

No longer cold, Beck's heart overflowed with love and longing.

She stood to dance about the room, singing along to the tune that only she could hear, Beck could picture her groom and their first dance together. She could've danced and sang forever had she not collided, with a resounding thud, against her desk chair.

CHAPTER 38

Jack's cheek pressed into the plush rug on the floor of his Jazz room. He opened his eyes, taking in his vinyl collection that lined the wall. The stars shone brightly outside his window, which was cracked, allowing the slightest smell of an ocean breeze inside. He was home.

Relieved, he reached out and stroked Rufus' fur. The stillness of his beloved companion was agonizing. It had been easy to push the grief away in 1948, but not here. Not when they were in the same room. He sat up and pulled Rufus' body onto his lap. "Beck," he called out, hopefully. The silence confirmed that he was on his own.

The heavy body cradled in his lap reminded him of the time when as a pup, Rufus had weighed almost nothing at all.

When they moved from Jack's West Hollywood apartment to the vintage fixer-upper in Topanga, Jack had been able to carry the squirming puppy under his arm like a football.

In the years since, he had remodeled, landscaped, and filled the place with his macabre collection. Fashioning for himself, an Underworld where he and his floofy Hellhound could hide away. For two years, Beck had been their Persephone bringing light and laughter into the place with her presence. That's when it occurred to Jack that he was truly alone in his home for the first time.

Reluctantly, he attempted to move Rufus back onto the rug. His body was beginning to cool and had become quite heavy. Jack felt stiff from spending an extended amount of time on the floor. As he gave an extra nudge, the dog slid off his lap and onto the floor. A sudden *BRRRRP* pierced the silence as Rufus' body passed the loudest and most pungent fart the dog had ever released.

Jack's laughter was punctuated by coughs and gags. Still in his vintage suit, he stood up and was relieved to see that it had only been air that had left the dog's corpse. "I'd better go change," he said, "Don't worry, Buddy, I'll be right back." He stroked Rufus' head and left the room.

In his bedroom, Jack grabbed a faded T-shirt and ripped jeans. He'd just removed his suit when he heard a sudden bump down the hall. *Wonder what that fuzzy monster's gotten into*, he thought for a split second before remembering that Rufus could no longer get into anything.

Alarmed, he slipped on his jeans and grabbed a wooden baseball bat from his closet. He stepped lightly down the hall holding his breath when the wood floor released a slight creak as he shifted his weight.

In the silence, Jack heard a groan from Beck's office. Wielding the bat, ready to fight off the burglar, he approached. The desk lamp flipped on, and the shadow of a bouncing figure danced on the wall opposite the doorway.

"Ow, ow, ow! Aw, grits," cursed the all too familiar voice.

Jack hurried to the office. "Beck?" Her curls obscured her face as she hopped around, attempting to undo the buckle of her vintage shoe. She stopped at the sound of her name, one green eye peeking out from under her curls. "Do you need help?" Beck's visible eye was trained on the bat Jack forgot he was holding defensively in front of him. He put it down and helped her into her chair.

"Thanks," she mumbled, moving her hair away from her face. Then turned her attention back to her stubborn shoe buckle. "I stubbed my toe."

"Allow me," he said as he took her foot in his hands. "You almost had it."

"Is it bleeding?"

"No," he said, inspecting her big toe.

"I guess it's only painful on the inside," she mumbled.

"Yeah, there's a lot of that going around."

Assured that the toe wasn't as bad as it felt, Beck allowed herself to appreciate the sight of her husband as he stood in front of her, clad only in ripped jeans. She must have gazed a little too long at his physique because he cleared his throat and crossed his arms.

Freed from her other shoe Beck stood, "Jack, I -"

"You're supposed to be in England."

She winced at his words but said steadily, "No, I'm supposed to be here."

"You sound so sure."

"I am."

"What about all that other stuff you said?"

Beck smirked and said, "Listen, I'm not going to pretend that we don't have a lot to work on, but I'm here for it. Are you?"

Jack regarded her silently and then said, "I am. Change into your work clothes."

She knitted her brow and said, "You know I was speaking figuratively, right?"

"Uh huh, but we literally have to bury the dog right now."

How could I have forgotten? She thought as she nodded.

"Poor Rufus," she whispered as she moved past her husband. He was right. The relationship stuff could wait. Their baby deserved a proper burial.

CHAPTER 39

"Where to?" Beck asked as they stopped to allow their eyes to adjust to the moonlight.

Jack cocked his head to the side and said, "Under the magnolia, back right corner."

With a slight tremor in her voice, Beck said, "His napping spot."

Using Rufus' favorite blanket as a makeshift gurney, the two carried him into the deepest part of the backyard and set him carefully on the ground near his beloved tree. Jack had always known this would be the spot but had never had the heart to say it out loud. Fearful that Death would be listening and come for Rufus sooner.

Shovels in hand, they set about their grim work. After a while, Jack noticed that while he was making progress, Beck had barely turned the earth on her end. "I can do the rest myself," he offered.

"Why?"

"It looks like you're struggling."

"Your gloves are too big," she said as she held up her hand. Jack hated how adorable she looked with her delicate fingers ensconced in his work gloves. The urge to take her hand in his was almost irresistible. Almost.

She resumed digging with a renewed determination, "I don't want you to have to do this alone."

It was a kind sentiment, but Jack wasn't finished being angry with her. "Why not? There's a lot I've had to do alone."

"Same here."

"Don't start."

"You started it," she said. Suddenly neither of them was having trouble digging.

"No, you started it when you ran away. Typical Beck."

"I didn't run. I was pushed," she growled.

"By forces beyond your control?" he said with a smirk.

"Well, I certainly can't control you."

"Damn right. So stop trying."

"All I've ever tried to do was have a life with you," Beck said as she discreetly wiped her eyes on her jacket sleeve.

He felt a pang of guilt, but the memory of how she'd hurt him was too fresh. "Is that what you were doing this morning? Trying to have a life with me?"

Beck looked as if she'd been slapped. She took a breath and took in their surroundings. "I think we've dug deep enough, don't you?"

"I thought you wanted to 'do the work.'"

Beck stopped and glared at him. Then she said, "I meant the hole. Is it deep enough for Rufus?"

Jack looked away, his cheeks burning. He studied the edges of the hole, which came to just above her shoulder, right where a stray auburn curl rested on her exposed clavicle. *Keep it together.* He nodded and helped her climb out of the hole.

Beck sat beside Rufus and removed the gloves. She lovingly stroked his fur. "I'm so sorry I wasn't here for you, my sweet little hellhound. The Underworld won't be the same without you," she said, tears choking her words. She met Jack's gaze, "As hard as this is, there's no place I'd rather be. For tragedies and triumphs, remember? It's what we promised each other."

"I remember, but I don't believe it. You'd probably be on your way to England with Victor if you hadn't been yanked back here."

Beck stood up and walked toward him, "I wasn't *yanked* anywhere," she said as she reached for his hands, "I *chose* to be here."

He stepped back and scoffed, "There's no choice when we travel."

"I figured it out. Remember the Basquiat exhibit? He said that art decorates space like music decorates time or something like that. Anyway, every time I've traveled, I was listening to music -- Yours."

"That can't be right. I'm always playing music, and you're not constantly time traveling, are you?"

"Music is only one component. I have to be experiencing intense emotions for it to work," Beck explained.

Jack thought back to the times he'd time-traveled. The first time he was under extreme pressure when he sought refuge in his jazz collection. Later, in Harlem, Jack had just sang to Beck in the hospital and was terrified he'd lost her. This time he'd felt intense grief over the loss of Beck and Rufus as he lay once again in the jazz room while the music played. Finally, he recalled his despair as he sat under the Ancestry Tree listening to the Voodoo drums. Could it be?

"I don't understand. Everyone turns to music for comfort. Why us?" Jack asked.

"Why not?" Beck shrugged.

Jack didn't have a good answer. The two continued the sad work of interring their dog. He snatched a couple of blooms off the Magnolia tree and handed one to Beck. Then each solemnly placed their flowers on the fresh pile of earth.

"There has to be more to it," he said.

"Why do you say that?" Beck asked as they walked into the living room.

"Because we're the only ones who do it."

"As far as we know."

Jack sat down and pinched the bridge of his nose, "Did you ask the Voodoo Lady about it?"

Beck chuckled and said, "Sure, we discussed this very thing over brunch. When she wasn't going on and on about us being tethered together."

Jack looked at his wife and frowned. "You don't believe it anymore? The tethered thing."

Beck crossed to him. "We are tethered. That was never in question. When you left 1948, I felt it."

"You knew I'd traveled back?"

Beck nodded. Her chest ached as she recalled the lonely feeling of being left behind. As the morning's events replayed in her mind, she glanced at her empty ring finger. Then, she noticed Jack's wedding band was missing as well.

"Where's your ring?" she asked.

"On the dresser, I took it off to dig. Where's yours?" He retorted.

"I sold it," she mumbled as she looked away, "I'm sorry."

"Victor told me."

"That cop was going to keep hurting you. I had to do something," she said, glancing at the bruises on his face. Then, finally, daring to look him in the eyes.

Jack held her gaze and said, "I know."

"I tried to buy it back. But it was gone."

"I know," Jack said, "Hold on." He headed down the hall and returned a few minutes later with tissues.

As Beck wiped her eyes, she tried to comprehend what he'd said, "How do you know? You were already gone when I tried to get it back."

"I meant that I knew it was sold," Jack said, pulling her ring out of his pocket.

"You?"

"I was hoping you'd change your mind," Jack said with a shrug.

"I thought you were done with me," she said as she shook her head.

"Never," he said as he reached for her.

Relief washed over Beck as they embraced. The pair held each other for several minutes before she raised her head from his chest and asked, "May I have it back?"

Jack smiled and slid her ring gently onto her finger. It felt so good to have it back where it belonged.

Jack then pulled his wedding ring out of his pocket and handed it to her, "Would you?" Beck slid the ring onto his long dexterous finger. Jack gave her a small smile and said, "You're right. We have work to do."

Beck yawned, "Can we start tomorrow? I haven't slept in years."

CHAPTER 40

It was quiet upstairs. *Too quiet.* With all that had happened last month, Jack found himself comforted by the sound of his wife's footsteps above instead of disturbed.

He checked the time in the upper right corner of his monitor. It was just after four. He looked at the shared calendar they had started keeping. Beck was supposed to join his mom for dinner at five. Had she left without saying goodbye?

Jack frowned as he climbed the stairs. "Beck?" he called. "Beck, you still here, Doll?"

Not only was she still there, she was still in bed.

She regarded Jack with heavy-lidded eyes, "Umm?" she murmured.

"You okay? I thought you were headed to Mom's to work on your book."

Beck sat up quickly, "The ghost stories," she gasped.

"Yeah. I thought you two were having a working dinner at five."

Her eyes widened, "What time is it?"

"Four fifteen," Jack said as he looked at her paler-than-usual face.

Before he could ask if she was sick, Beck slid out of bed. "I feel blah, but I don't have a fever. Do I?" she asked as she ran her head over her forehead and hair.

Jack put his hands on either side of her head, and planted a lingering kiss on her forehead. She felt cool to the touch, as usual. "No. Are you achy?"

"Not really. It feels like I'm moving through wet cement," Beck yawned. "I gotta call Miriam, or she'll worry."

"I'll call Mom and tell her you're sick."

"I hate to cancel. Do you think I'm contagious?" she asked.

"No, but I don't want you schlepping down to Baldwin Hills in traffic if you're exhausted." Jack thought about the mountain of work he'd left downstairs. It would have to wait. "If you're still up for it, I'll drive."

"Really? Thanks, Maestro," Beck said as she beamed at him.

Miriam sounded thrilled when Jack called to say that he was able to join them. By the time they made if from Malibu to Baldwin Hills, she has prepared a feast. Stuffed from dinner, Jack relaxed in his dad's old recliner. As he dozed, he caught wisps of conversation from his two favorite ladies.

"So, he meant to shoot Chaplin, but Ince was in the wrong place at the wrong time? That's so sad," Beck said with a sigh.

"Chaplin was a real Tomcat. I'm surprised he *wasn't* shot by a jealous lover," Miriam said. "The case was swept under the rug because Hearst was so wealthy,"

"Ince's studio was in Culver City. That's not technically Hollywood. Can we still include it?" Beck asked.

"They say he still haunts the new studios over there. Hearst and Chaplin are still recognizable names. I say we put it in."

"Good point," Beck said, "Figments Films is on a part of that property. Wonder if we'll ever see him."

"I hope you do. That would sell some books," Miriam said as the ladies giggled.

Jack rested his eyes and reminisced about playing with his brother in front of the chair he now occupied. Both would try to entertain their father as he dozed in his favorite lounger. The task was excellent training for future entertainers.

Jack's parents had adored their wild redheaded boys, but they had always wanted a daughter. His dad would have loved Beck.

A hand ruffled his hair. Jack opened his eyes to see his mom standing over him. "Hey there, Sleepy Head."

"I wasn't asleep," he protested.

"Well, your bride is," Miriam said. He looked over to the loveseat where Beck was sleeping soundly wrapped in his grandmother's quilt.

"Did she nod off in the middle of writing?"

"She said she was cold, so I gave her the quilt and went to brew us some tea. When I came back, you were both snoozing."

"Sorry, Mom. It's been a hard month."

"No need to apologize. It's comforting to see you there," Miriam's eyes misted as she whispered. "I miss him every day."

"Me too," Jack said as he stood and hugged her. Then he crossed the room and kissed Beck's forehead. "Hey, Doll Face, time to go."

"Take care, you two," Miriam called after them.

Beck struggled to keep her eyes open as their car wound through the canyon. *This is stupid. I slept all day.* She sighed and tried to sit up straight.

"What's wrong?" Jack asked.

"I'm trying to stay awake. I don't get it. I'm usually such a night owl."

Jack guided the BMW into their driveway. "You're tired. Take the night off."

"Are you going to take the night off?"

"I gotta get back to it," Jack said.

"So do I," she said as they entered the house. "I haven't gotten a thing done today."

Beck walked into her office to check the calendar they had started keeping since returning to 1995. It was the beginning of December, and they had promised to take a two-week break from Hannukah to New Year's Day.

Jack had blocked off three solid weeks to wrap up his score. Saturday evenings were blocked off for their newly established date nights, but the other six days a week were full. Beck looked at her own section. It was pretty quiet since she wrapped up her screenplay for Warner Brothers. She was using the downtime to work on *Spirited Hollywood* with Miriam and taking meetings for next year's projects.

She located her dinner with Miriam on the calendar and gasped. "Aw, grits," she said.

"What's wrong?" Jack asked from the doorway.

"I have a meeting with a production team at Universal," she explained.

"Now?"

"In like two minutes. They're filming an epic romance, big budget, big names. I'm on the shortlist to direct," Beck said as she frantically rummaged through the piles of paper on her desk for her notes on the project.

Jack handed her a legal pad that had fallen between her desk and her PC tower, "But it's ten o'clock at night."

The phone rang, and Beck jumped to answer it. "Good afternoon, gentlemen. Yeah, it's late here...I don't mind. It's three in the afternoon there, right?"

Jack tilted his head and furrowed his brow. He looked as though he was attempting to listen in, but after a moment, he shrugged and left. Beck paced around her office to stay alert.

"We appreciate you agreeing to meet with us again, Rebecca. With a big budget picture, we have to be certain we have the perfect fit," explained the executive producer.

"I can appreciate that," Beck said as her pulse quickened.

The associate producer spoke up. Beck was comforted by her smooth voice, "It's crucial to have a woman at the helm for this film to succeed, and after careful consideration, we're certain you're the best fit."

The executive producer said, "As long as the schedule works."

It took everything she had not to accept immediately. *Ask your questions*, she reminded herself as she glanced at the legal pad. "My schedule for next year is filling up quickly, " she fibbed. "What's your timeline? Maybe we can work something out."

The associate producer said, "Well, we have a script doctor reworking the third act now. Principal photography will start in March, and we hope to wrap at the end of May before the weather gets chilly."

"Chilly? In May?" Beck wondered aloud.

"Yes, we're shooting on location," the executive producer explained.

"Oh, you're filming in Sydney," Beck said.

"On the outskirts. We'll film some exterior shots in the Outback in May. We want this to be as authentic as possible," the associate producer explained.

After the meeting, she was wide awake. Turning the conversation over and over in her brain. Jack came upstairs a little after midnight.

"You're still up? I thought you were exhausted."

"I got a second wind," Beck said as she scribbled notes on her legal pad.

"How was your meeting?" he asked as he attempted to catch her eye.

Beck stopped writing and met his gaze. She twisted her wedding ring as she answered him. "They offered me the job."

"That's great, Darlin.'" he beamed as he came over and wrapped her in his arms.

"It's in Australia."

"Where?"

"Around Sydney and in the Outback. I'd be there for three months. March to May." Jack let go of Beck and straightened up. He stared at the calendar. "Tell me what you're thinking," she said.

"That's a long time to be apart."

"I know."

"You asked me to schedule two weeks off after every score. Now you'll be on the other side of the world. You'll miss my birthday," Jack said as he crossed his arms in front of his chest.

"I've already thought of that. What if you came to see me for your birthday, and we'll fly home together? It will be an adventure."

Jack turned to May on the large wall calendar, "I have a movie premiere that week, and the day after my birthday, it's right back to work. Who's going to go with me?"

"Take your mom. This is a big deal, Jack. It's not an Indy operation like Figment. I'll finally have the chance to direct a big-budget movie for a major studio."

"You said we needed to make more time for one another?"

Beck pursed her lips, then said, "I'll make you a deal. This will be the only on-location film I'll do in 96."

"I guess we could celebrate my birthday in June," Jack sighed.

"Maestro, I promise you the biggest birthday bash ever."

Jack put his arms around her and said, "All I want is you,"

CHAPTER 41

Loud ringing woke Jack from a sound sleep. He smacked his alarm several times before Beck nuzzled his neck and mumbled, "It's mine, not yours."

She climbed out of bed and padded to the bathroom.

"Why are you up so early?" he called out, afraid he'd forgotten something.

"Universal requires a physical and Hepatitis A vaccine," she grumbled.

"Sounds like a good idea considering where you're going."

"I hate needles."

"Darlin', I almost died from Hepatitis A in Africa. Get the shot."

Beck stepped back into the bedroom and pouted. "It's actually *two* shots. I have to get another one right before I leave."

"I can move some things around and go with you," he offered with a yawn. Before she could answer, another object rang. Jack rolled over and slapped his alarm before he realized it was the phone, not the clock, that demanded his attention.

"Hello?" Jack said as he tried to sound like he hadn't just woken up.

A soft, raspy voice on the other end said, "Well, hello there, Africa."

Jack sat up bolt right in bed, "Lowry? Is that you?"

"The one and only."

"You're still...I mean, you're here. Of course, you are. Where are you?"

"California, same as you," Lowry said before he began to cough, "Sorry. I'm not as spry as I used to be."

"You're staying with Marvin?" Jack asked. He could hardly believe his ears.

"You know I am. Marvin told you I was. What I wanna know is why you haven't come to see me yet?"

Jack sighed, "I'm sorry. When is a good time?"

Lowry coughed again and cleared his throat. "Sooner rather than later, I'm afraid."

There was something in the way Lowry answered that Jack didn't like. "Are you okay?"

"I'm old, Jack," Lowry laughed at his own joke and cleared his throat, "and uh, I got this little thing going on with my heart."

"What little thing?' Jack asked. Lowry was silent except for a slight wheezing, "What little thing?" Jack pressed.

"I got a bum ticker," Lowry mumbled.

"A bum ticker? What does that mean?"

As casually as possible, Lowry said, "Congestive Heart Failure."

Jack's own heart hurt. "I'll be there later today."

"That's a good idea," Lowry said softly.

Beck studied his contorted face as he hung up the phone. Jack covered his eyes with his hands. "Was that...Lowry?" Jack nodded. "Is he alright?" Her husband shook his head.

"He's dying, Beck. He's old and dying. I don't think I can lose another friend this soon."

Beck began to dress. "Let's go."

"Nice try. You're going to the doctor, Doll Face."

"Fine, but please jot down directions to Marvin's for me. I'll head over right after."

The antiseptic smell of the clinic offended Beck's nose as she waited for the nurse to call her back. She was pale and tired. *Probably anemic*, she self-diagnosed. She had struggled with anemia a couple of times.

Once, in the exam room, a way too cheerful nurse asked her a barrage of questions. "I'm tired all the time, and I have the complexion of a vampire. I think. Vampires never really see how pale they are, do they?" Beck joked in an attempt to ease her own anxiety. "I still have a reflection, so it's not that," she said nervously, "My iron's probably low."

"Um, hm. I'll make a note for Dr.Bernard," the nurse said, jotting down Beck's vitals, "And when was your last period?" she asked without looking up.

Beck always hated this question. Her periods were like clockwork on the pill, but there had been no birth control pills in the 1940s. Not that she'd needed them. She had gone right back to taking them once she got home but hadn't had a period yet.

The nurse had stopped writing and was now staring at Beck, making her even more flustered. "Would it help to look at a calendar?" the nurse offered.

Beck almost laughed at the absurdity of the situation. She pictured herself trying to explain that she hadn't had a period in about 47 years. "I'm sorry. I can't remember," she mumbled as her cheeks burned with embarrassment.

"It's fine, Hon," the nurse reassured her.

Dr. Bernard was a tall thin blond woman with a kind face. The exam went fine until she said, "Everything looks good, but I would like to run some blood tests to figure out why you're so tired."

"A shot *and* a blood test," Beck said, her heart racing.

"We have an in-house phlebotomist. She's very gentle," the doctor attempted to reassure her.

As she approached the lab, Beck instinctively reached for her Walkman to ease her dread, then thought better of it. *Who knows where or when I'd end up.* The phlebotomist was waiting for her, dressed in blood-red scrubs. *Perfect color for a vampire,* Beck mused. As they entered the exam room, Beck said. "Do you have butterfly needles? My veins are tiny, and they roll."

"Let me take a look, and then I'll get what we need," the vampire said dismissively. "Hop into the chair for me."

The chair looked like a padded Medival torture device with a bar that came down for easy access to do the terrible deed while also restraining the victim. "I can't sit there. I have to lie down."

The vampire looked at a closed door across the hall and huffed. "The room with the table is in use."

Beck began to play with her wedding ring. She wished Jack was there. "I faint sometimes. I really need the table."

"You can return to the waiting room, and I'll call you when the room is available."

There would be no waiting. Beck knew that. If she left this room, she would continue out into the hall, downstairs to her car, never to return. "Alright," she said as she crossed her arms tightly against her body and sat in the chair.

"That's better. Which arm?"

Beck's right shoulder still ached from the insult of the vaccine's puncture. "Um, my left, I guess," she said barely above a whisper.

The vampire prepped her arm and began the dreaded procedure. Beck felt a pinch and a wave of nausea. The last thing she heard the evil creature say was, "Huh, your veins really do roll."

She opened her eyes to find herself lying on an exam table in a different room. Her arms hurt, and the back of her head ached. After a moment, Dr. Bernard's nurse poked her head in. "How are we doing?"

"*We* have a headache and two sore arms," Beck said as she rubbed the nape of her neck.

"Understandable. You bonked your head on the wall when you fainted. They had to try both your arms, but the good news is that they finally got enough for your labs."

She moaned as she sat up, feeling slightly violated. "Can I go now?"

The nurse looked at her chart. "Not yet. Dr. Bernard wants to talk to you about your test results."

"Wait. My results are back, already?"

The nurse shrugged, "When someone faints in the office, we suddenly become very interested in finding out why."

"I fainted because your phlebotomist didn't listen to me. She made me sit up, used a giant needle, and dug around inside my arm until I fainted," Beck snarled. She felt like a badass, but that lasted only for a second. She looked up to see Dr. Bernard and felt the sting of tears as she began to angry-cry.

Dr Bernard tilted her head, her eyebrows slightly raised. She took a deep breath and said, "I'm afraid that's only part of it."

CHAPTER 42

Marvin Ringold's home was one of the older bungalows in West Hollywood. The garden out front was meticulously groomed. With a symphony of roses, Beck's favorite flower.

When was the last time I bought her roses? Jack wondered, making a mental note to do so.

His horn player met him at the door with a bear hug. "You're gonna make Papa's week," he said as he showed Jack into the living room.

The drapes were drawn, and as Jack's eyes adjusted, they landed on a gallery wall full of old family photos. His heart ached as he saw the old black and whites of Ella and Lowry. Frame by frame, Jackie grew up before his eyes. He stopped at a photo of an older Ella holding a newborn. "Is that you?" he asked Marvin.

"Yeah, my parents were babies themselves. Ma and I always lived with Mawmaw and Papa." Marvin explained as he indicated a picture of a young black woman holding a wriggly toddler. Ella and Lowry looked on adoringly in the background.

"What about Jackie? I mean, your dad?" Jack asked.

"Daddy went to Vietnam right after my parents were married," Marvin indicated a tri-folded flag in a shadow box on his mantle and said, "he never came home."

Jack's heart sank. It was hard to reconcile that the baby he held weeks ago never got to hold his own. Then another thought took over. Poor Ella and Lowry, losing their son. "I'm so sorry, Jack said softly.

"Mar-mar, who you talkin' to?" Lowry called down the hall.

Marvin grinned and motioned for Jack to follow, "You got a visitor, Papa."

As they entered the cozy back bedroom room, Peeking out from under a handmade quilt, Jack saw a mass of grey curls and his old friend's big brown eyes smiling back at him. Lowry looked frail and wrinkled, but when he saw his friend, his smile was the same as when they met in Harlem decades ago.

"Call me if ya need anything," Marvin said as he left the room.

"Well, if it isn't the Red Devil. Come here, and let me look at you." Jack approached the antique brass bed and sat in the chair closest to it. Lowry extended his hand, and as Jack grasped it, Lowry said, "You're so young."

Jack chuckled. "I'm forty-two."

"Yeah, well, when *you're* seventy-eight, that will seem young to you, too," Lowry said as his laughter turned into a cough.

"You've still got it. I'm sure Ella still chases after you," Jack said as he patted his friend's shoulder.

Lowry slumped, and his face became clouded. "I wish. My sweet girl passed almost two years ago."

"Oh, Man, I don't know what to say. I'm so sorry."

Lowry squeezed his hand, "It's alright. We'll be together soon enough."

"Please don't talk like that."

"Death comes for all of us eventually. You know that. Besides, the best years of my life were spent with Ella and Jackie. When our boy went...well, if it wasn't for Mar Mar, they'd have had to dig a triple wide hole in the ground."

"You've got Marvin and your music. Wait, didn't you have another kid?" Jack asked as he looked for any reason for his friend to remain tethered to life.

"It never happened for us," Lowry said with a shrug, "But we practiced a lot. As for Mar Mar, he's engaged to a good woman, and his Ma lives right around the corner."

"What about your music? You have so much left to write."

Lowry pointed to a small bookcase across the room. "Grab that blue photo album on top, would you?" Jack picked it up and went to hand it to Lowry, "No, you look at it."

Jack opened the thick album. The heading on the first page was in Ella's handwriting. It read *California 1948-1982.* Under it was a poster for Lowry's first movie with Cab Calloway.

"That was so much fun," Lowry said with a sigh. "I wrote and performed for all three of his projects, and my baby danced her heart out."

Jack's heart swelled as he flipped through articles and small posters of each project Lowry was involved with. "Lowry, you're a film composer. Just like we always talked about. Wait, did we ever?"

"Work together? Yeah, but just once. You're a real pain in the ass when you're composing."

Jack looked up at Lowry, stunned. After a few moments, Lowry said, "I'm pulling your chain," he said with another combination of laughing and coughing, "I retired three years before you got your start. Man, your face sure looks funny. Imagine if we had worked together and *you* didn't remember."

Jack smiled and shook his head, his body was old and worn, but Lowry's spirit shone through. "Man, this is an impressive body of work. I look forward to seeing some of these."

"Some? You mean you ain't gonna have a Lowry Ringgold film festival?"

"I'll get around to listening to all of it, but some of these are new, and on others, you replaced another composer," Jack explained.

"I wondered how that worked," Lowry said as he rubbed his chin.

There was a knock at the door. The friends heard Marvin greeting someone.

"That must be Beck," Jack said as he checked his Casio.

"Hey. You still have the watch and your lady, " Lowry said with a grin.

"Yeah, she never went to England."

"Oh, I know," Lowry said matter of factly.

"You mean because you've seen us together in the present?" Jack asked.

"Well, yeah, but I know she didn't go with Shadley because…" Lowry stopped speaking as Beck entered the room.

"What kind of trouble are you two getting up to?" she asked radiantly.

"Well, hello, Ms. Rebecca. I didn't know you were coming to see me," Lowry said as he tried to sit up straighter.

"You look like you feel better," Jack added as he helped Lowry rearrange his pillows.

"Better?" Lowry asked.

Beck blushed and looked away. "I, uh, had a doctor's appointment this morning. It was nothing, just a check-up."

"What about the fatigue?" Jack asked as he turned to face her. The redness on Beck's cheeks deepened and spread to her neck.

He immediately regretted asking her in front of Lowry.

"My iron's low. The doctor prescribed some supplements," Beck said as she gently pushed past Jack to move closer to the bed, "It's so good to see you." she said as she hugged Lowry.

"You too. How's my favorite firetop?" Lowry asked as he smiled up at her.

"Hey, I thought I was your favorite," Jack said.

"She's prettier. Smells nicer, too," Lowry shrugged.

"Thanks, I -- we've been busy, " Beck said as Jack pulled up the chair for her.

The rest of the hour passed by as quickly as it does when friends are dear, and the prospect of goodbye forever is a distinct possibility. The conversation slowed as their friend yawned and rubbed his eyes.

"Feeling tired, Lowry?" Jack asked.

"I'd like to say no, but I don't like to lie."

"We understand," Beck said as she stood, "Life can be exhausting."

"Besides, we'll be back soon," Jack said as he took Lowry's hand.

"Don't bet on it, my friend," Lowry said as he slowly shook his head and squeezed Jack's hand. "In fact, y'all might wanna skip the funeral."

"Why?" the couple asked simultaneously.

"There are still some old timers around. You don't wanna risk being recognized."

"Don't worry about us," Jack said as he embraced his friend, "You just rest. Have Marvin call me if you need anything, anything at all."

"Your friendship is more than enough. Take care, Red Devil," Lowry said as Jack released him from the embrace. The old man wiped his eyes with his pajama sleeve.

"You too," Jack murmured, his own eyes glistening.

Beck gently hugged her friend, "It's been an honor knowing you and your family."

"Back at ya," Lowry said as he sniffled. Then, he clasped Beck's hand, "I hope you can forgive me for that trouble back in Harlem. I'm sorry I put you in danger."

"I forgave you ages ago," Beck said as her tears flowed freely.

"I wanna ensure all my loose ends are tied up before I go. Which reminds me, be patient with one another, okay?. Love is a journey, not a destination, you understand?"

The couple looked at each other and smiled. "We do." Jack said.

"Good, I love y'all. I want my favorite couple to stay together."

"We love you, too," they said as they reluctantly left the room. Jack felt a heaviness in his heart and a wish to stay, hoping against hope that his vigilance would somehow dissuade Death from coming.

He and Beck said goodbye to Marvin and got into their cars for the long ride back to the canyon. As he drove, Jack allowed his tears to flow freely. He sobbed for the impending loss of Lowry, his still raw grief from losing Rufus, and finally, tears of relief that his wife would be okay. As the BMW twisted and turned on the serpentine road, he fiddled with the on/off switch on his car stereo, half tempted for one last moment with his dear friend.

Relieved, Beck pulled her car up the drive. She'd only been out for the day, but it felt like she'd lived an entire week in twelve short hours. Her emotions were all over the place. The urge to listen to music had been overwhelming, but she didn't want to risk slipping out of time in light of her discovery. Another coping mechanism would be necessary.

As she approached Jack's car, she quickened her pace. A talk with her favorite person was exactly what she needed. Beck opened the driver-side door and was shocked to find him doubled over. Sobs racked his body. She dropped to her knees and wrapped her arms around him. "Jack? What's wrong?"

He wiped his eyes, but the tears kept coming. Beck stood, took his hands, and led him into their house. Her husband made his way to the couch, then reached out for her.

She sat next to him, holding his body close to hers. Jack was typically so stoic. In two years of marriage, she could count on one hand the number of times she had seen him this vulnerable and still have fingers left over. "Is this about Lowry?" she asked.

"It's Lowry, it's Rufus, it's everything all at once. All I want to do is hole up in the jazz room, but I don't want to go anywhere. How in the hell do I do this without music, Beck? How do I even work, for that matter?"

She laid his head on her chest and stroked his copper curls. "We'll figure it out."

"You sound so sure," he sniffed.

"We have to learn to control this instead of allowing it to control us."

Jack sat up to face her. "Well, when you figure it out, let me know."

"I can't do it without you. We're tethered together, remember?"

"I'm sorry. You're right. Oh, Darlin', I'm so glad you're okay. If anything ever happened to you, I don't think..." Jack sank back into her arms again and buried his face in her hair.

Beck tightened her grip on his broad shoulders and said, "You're not going to lose me. I'm not sick. I --" the phone rang, interrupting the moment.

Jack mumbled, "Could you?"

Beck extracted herself from the couch and picked up the receiver. "Hello?"

An unfamiliar female voice asked, "Hi, may I speak to Jack, please?"

Beck looked at her husband balled up on the couch, face puffy and red, "I'm sorry Jack is unavailable, but this is his wife, Rebecca. I can give him a message."

The lady was quiet momentarily, then said, "This Sandra, Marvin's fiancee'. He, uh, wanted me to let you know that his granddaddy 'went home' about an hour after you left."

"Oh Sandra, I'm sorry. Please give our love to Marvin. If there's anything we can do, please let me know."

"Okay. We'll be in touch with the details for Lowry's service," Sandra said as she hung up.

Beck's legs felt like rubber as she walked back to the couch. Jack had rested his forehead on his knees. Upon sensing the couch shift with her weight, he peeked up at her. "Lowry?" he asked. Beck could only nod.

CHAPTER 43

The days before Lowry's service, or 'Homegoing Celebration' as his family called it, were a buzz with activity. Marvin asked Jack to contact some of the musicians. He panicked at first, thinking that he would be asked to call up old men they'd played with in the forties. Fortunately for Jack, the list was primarily musicians from the film industry that they had each worked with previously. While calling people he had not spoken to in ages was typically a task he avoided at all costs, it felt good to be helpful. A much-needed diversion from the loss, yet an unintended distraction from his wife.

"Well, hello there," Beck said as Jack turned off his alarm on the morning of Lowry's celebration. "I don't think we've been awake and in the same room in days."

He took her in his arms and kissed her. "I'm sorry," he whispered.

"It's okay. Lowry deserves a fitting send-off. You're sweet to make sure he has one."

Jack smiled and took a deep breath inhaling the intoxicating smell of cooked apple and cinnamon. "Are you baking?"

"I made an apple pie for the service. We had a few good Fujis left on the tree. I needed to do something with all this sadness."

"You're so thoughtful," Jack said as he kissed her head and breathed in the smell of vanilla and cinnamon. It felt comforting to be close to her again.

"A good Southerner can't show up at a wake empty-handed. It's part of the unwritten code," Beck explained as they dressed for the ceremony, "I must say that I like the Ringgold's tradition of eating first. By the time we finished my grandmother's funeral, all the food was cold."

In the car, the two rode silently. Beck reached for the stereo's on/off switch. Jack covered it quickly with his hand. "Um, maybe we shouldn't."

"I've been worried too, but we're both calm right now. I thought it would be alright. It's a huge part of our lives, especially yours. It's not like we can avoid it altogether."

"I know. We were managing until Lowry passed, and then I just started, please don't be upset. I started wanting to go back and see him."

Beck raised her eyebrows slightly and smiled, "I'm not upset. That's perfectly normal," she said as she slipped her hand in his.

"We're going to have to listen to music at the funeral," he shrugged as he flipped on the radio. "May as well try it now."

Midway through the song "Minor Swing," Beck let go of his hand and rubbed the nape of her neck. Jack asked, "What's wrong, Doll Face?"

"Pull over," she said urgently.

"Why?"

"Pull over!" she shouted. Jack did as he was told. No sooner than they reached the side of the road, Beck bolted out of the car and retched all over the ground. He knew that she sometimes had trouble on the winding canyon roads, but they were on a straightway about a mile from the wake. It didn't make sense. He carefully exited the car. "You okay, Darlin?"

"Don't look at me," she gasped as she heaved again.

"I want to help," he said, but Beck violently waved him away. A few minutes later, she returned to the car and grabbed a napkin from the glove box. She daintily wiped her mouth, ensured her black dress was still clean, and casually reapplied her lipstick.

"We should get going. We're late," she said casually.

"I don't think you should go. You're obviously sick."

"I'm not sick," she said as he reluctantly pulled back onto the road and rounded the corner to the Banquet Hall.

"Then what was with the Exorcist routine? Did you eat something that didn't agree with you?"

Beck turned her body away from him and said, "No."

"You sure?"

"Yes, I'm sure. I haven't eaten anything," Beck snapped.

He pulled into the nearest space and shut off the car. "Then you probably have a virus. Let me take you home. Please? I'm worried about you," he pleaded with her as he stroked her cheek, which caused her to turn back toward him. "Listen, Darlin', I couldn't take it if I lost you, too."

"I'm not sick," Beck sighed, "I didn't want to do this right now. I, um, brought a little Lagniappe back with me from New Orleans." She smiled at him expectantly.

Jack tilted his head. "A what?"

"It's Cajun for 'a little something extra'," she explained.

Jack furrowed his brow while he searched his memory for where he'd heard the word before. Finally, he remembered that Nash at the 500 Club had once added a moonshine-soaked cherry to his cocktail, calling it a "lagniappe". But Beck had delivered her confession with such significance that Jack was confident she wasn't speaking of a cocktail garnish. "I don't understand," he admitted.

"I'm pregnant," Beck said as she twisted her wedding ring.

Jack's felt as if everything was spinning. He gripped the wheel to ground himself, "How?" was all he could say.

The color returned to Beck's cheeks, "You know *how*."

"No, I mean. You were on the pill."

Beck shook her head and said, "Not in 1948, Jack. There were no pills." Tears welled up in her eyes as she stepped out of the car. Jack retrieved the apple pie from the trunk and followed her. "I thought you'd be happy," she said, dabbing her eyes.

"I'm sorry, it's just a shock. We didn't plan this."

Beck balled up her fist and raised her voice, "Lots of stuff happens that we don't plan. I thought you'd roll with it like I have."

Jack decided to hold his tongue and let his brain catch up. His mind was a buzz with divergent thoughts. He loved his wife. He assumed they'd have a baby someday. Yet, he was swamped with work. They both were. They needed to wait for things to slow down. After all, Beck was only twenty-eight. There was plenty of time for children later.

On the other hand, the timing had been decided. He had to admit that his daydreams occasionally drifted to a little girl with flaming red hair and Beck's bewitching green eyes. Of course, it could always be a little boy with his hazel eyes and mischievous grin.

Jack felt himself getting excited about the prospect as he stared at Beck, who was fidgeting with her ring. The ring she sold when she decided to run away with that uptight British prick. "Wait a minute, are you sure it's mine?" He blurted out without thinking.

Beck reared back as though she'd been slapped. *A slap would've hurt less*, she thought. For days she'd tried to find the perfect way to tell him. Even rehearsed his potential reactions and her possible responses like movie scenes in her imagination. But, in all her calculations, this was one reaction she hadn'tt even counted upon.

"Of course, I'm sure. Why in the hell would you ask me that? You're my husband," Beck said

"But we weren't exactly together," Jack said quietly.

"We were together. We spent the night before Mardi Gras together."

"And then you left me for Victor," he said as he walked toward the entrance.

Beck stormed in after her husband. Her heart pounded in her chest, "Jack Herman, we are not finished. Get back here," she demanded, her anger exposing a bit of her Southern drawl. People were beginning to stare, so she lowered her voice as he stopped and allowed her to catch up. She turned him to face her, saying, "Look at me."

Jack glanced at her, his lips pursed. No sooner than their eyes met, he looked away again. "Jack, please, I need you to look me in the eyes," Beck pleaded. She took his chin gently in her hand. As soon as he met her gaze, she said, "This is your baby. I never slept with Victor. We never even came close."

Jack took a step back and regarded his wife. For once, she was still. No fidgeting. "But you were running off to England with him."

"I understand why that would make you wonder. Why didn't you just ask me? You know I'd tell you the truth," she said.

"That's what I was afraid of, that you'd tell me you'd been with him, and I wouldn't be able to get past it. I didn't want to know. But --"

"With the baby, it matters," Beck said. Her shoulders drooped as she turned and entered the hall.

As they sat and had lunch with Lowry's relatives and the other musicians, Jack observed the families around the room with fresh eyes. The loving glances and touches shared between spouses. Fathers lifting their babies into the air, one of them showing their wiggly son how to tap out a beat on the table, and another carefully wiping sauce off his little girl's face to keep her from wiping it with her dress sleeve. Jack wanted all of it, the entire experience, with Beck.

He looked across the table. She was moving her untouched lunch around her plate as she frowned. Jack took her empty hand in his. "You need to eat, Darlin'."

"I'm not hungry," she said as she looked at her plate.

Jack grabbed a piece of cornbread from the basket in the middle of the table, "Come on, just a couple of bites. Our baby needs you to eat."

Beck looked at him and tilted her head. "Our baby?"

"I'm sorry I doubted you," Jack said.

Beck nodded, then took a couple of bites from the cornbread.

More mourners arrived for the graveside service. People from the film industry mingled with the musicians and Lowry's family. Jack put on his fedora to keep a low profile. "We could just stand on the hill in trench coats with umbrellas," Beck joked.

"I don't want people to draw parallels between Jack Hermann and Jack Herman," he said as he pointed to himself.

"That's ridiculous. One's German, and the other's Jewish," she said with a wink, "But we can sit in the back if you'd like." Beck chose a pair of seats in the second to last row.

Musician after musician played tribute to Lowry. Jack sat back and enjoyed the sound, but as the pastor walked to the pulpit and led the mourners in prayer, Jack's mind began to dissect and blend the notes and chords he'd heard. A melody unlike any he'd ever heard began to play in his head.

As he began tapping the rhythm on his knee, Beck took his hand and whispered, "Do you need to go use your tape recorder?"

He smirked at her and whispered, "How did you know?"

"I always know. It's who you are," Beck said with a small smile as she released his hand.

He quickly appraised his surroundings. It would be relatively easy to slip into the vestibule. However, as he looked from the portrait of his fallen friend to the glowing profile of his beloved, Jack decided to stay in his seat. There would always be more melodies. He eased his recorder back into his pocket and gently placed his hand on Beck's belly.

"It's not all I am, Doll Face," he said as he softly kissed her cheek.

For the first time in a week, Beck relaxed, placing her hand on Jack's. No sooner than they'd settled, a latecomer came up to the aisle and quietly pointed to the empty seat on the other side of Beck. The couple moved their legs to allow the white-haired man to pass.

As he sat down, the man glanced at the pair. Beck turned and met a pair of all too familiar blue eyes, which widened as the British man whispered, "Becks? Is it really you?"

ABOUT THE AUTHOR

 Angela M. Herrick is a writer, drama teacher, actor, and director with a passion for storytelling. A teacher at heart, she believes that stories not only entertain but offer a way to explore other points of view. Her published novels include Devil's Chord, Devil's Dissonance, and Project Mulligan. She is also an accomplished playwright. Angela lives in Central Florida and loves hanging out with her husband, five children, cats Gatsby, Chaplin, and Keaton, and Griffin the dog.

To find additional books by Angela M Herrick, visit AngelaMHerrick.com or follow her at Angela M. Herrick: books, biography, latest update - Amazon.com

You may also find Angela on Facebook, Instagram, and LinkedIn.

ACKNOWLEDGEMENT

When I released Devil's Chord in 2021, I thought it would be my only novel. Before the project, I had only ever written plays and short stories. So, my initial thanks must go to the readers who said, "This is great! When's the next one coming out?"

I write in so many different spaces, but the most frequent has been the Oviedo Mall, particularly at Imagine Performing Arts Center, which changed hands while I was working on this book. Thanks to James Brendlinger and Sarah Troxel Fanok for recognizing writers as artists and allowing us a creative home away from home.

Thanks to my friends, who took the time to read the first book. Makena, Jennifer, Linda, Ashely, Amytra, Tommy, Karla, and Sam (even though he's only halfway through).

This book is so much better because of my beta readers. Thanks, Nancy, Jennifer, and Thomas.

My mom also beta read this book, but she thinks everything I do is excellent because she's my mom. Thanks for your encouragement, love, and for giving birth - I know it was difficult -you keep telling me!

To my best girlfriend, Emily Zaas, thank you for your honest and thorough editorial notes. You didn't just make this novel better. You made me a better writer.

Thank you to my children Devin, Cagney, Elijah, Meah, and Natalie for believing in me and being proud to tell others your mom's an author. You're the best cheerleaders and hype people.

Last but never least, thank you to Jay for your love, encouragement, and inspiration. Jack wouldn't be who he is without the love you've shown me. I also appreciate the hours you spend as my eager alpha reader. I appreciate your ability to see the gold nuggets in the garbage!